ONCE UPON A LIST

ONCE UPON
A LIST

ROBIN GOLD

AVONIMPULSE
An Imprint of HarperCollinsPublishers

ONCE UPON A LIST. Copyright © 2012 by Robin B. Gold. All rights reserved under International and Pan-American Copyright Conventions. By payment of the required fees, you have been granted the nonexclusive, nontransferable right to access and read the text of this e-book on screen. No part of this text may be reproduced, transmitted, downloaded, decompiled, reverse-engineered, or stored in or introduced into any information storage and retrieval system, in any form or by any means, whether electronic or mechanical, now known or hereinafter invented, without the express written permission of HarperCollins e-books.

EPub Edition MAY 2012 ISBN: 9780062193711

Print Edition ISBN: 9780062193728

10 9 8 7 6 5 4 3 2 1

For my Grandma Edie, better known as "Edie The Great."
And great she certainly was.

"Grief turns out to be a place none of us know until we reach it."
—Joan Didion

"You might not always win, but you never, ever give up."
—Patrick Swayze

PROLOGUE

Clara stared at the rectangular, gift-wrapped box in her hands, smiling from ear to ear. "A present?" she asked her fiancé. "For me? But why? I don't understand." It wasn't her birthday or Christmas. Heck, it wasn't even Flag Day.

"What do you mean, *But why?*" Sebastian, just home from a long day at work and still wearing his winter coat, leaned in toward her for a kiss, which she happily accepted.

"Why do I get a gift?" Clara recognized the shiny silver bow as part of the signature wrapping from Ivy, her favorite boutique in Boston.

Sebastian shrugged, his brown eyes twinkling as he gazed at her. "Just because."

Shaking her head, Clara let out a little laugh. "Of course. *Just because.* I should have known." *Just because* was one of his preferred reasons for doing things. Sebastian didn't need a designated holiday or special event to extend a kind gesture or express how much he cared about her. Every day with him was special, not to mention unpredictable, which Clara never took for granted. Forget Saturday night dinner—he would surprise Clara by taking her out for a romantic date on a random Tuesday evening. He didn't rely on Valentine's Day as a reason to give her a heartfelt love note, or Mother's Day to lavish her with a gorgeous bouquet of flowers, despite the fact that she was not yet a mother (although they had already decided to name their first daughter Edith, their first son Julian, and their first dog—whenever they finally found proper time to devote to one, that is—Milk Dud). His strikingly thoughtful nature was just one of the many reasons Clara had fallen head over heels in love with Sebastian over a decade ago.

Still standing near the front door of their recently purchased "starter home," where Clara had run to greet him as soon as she heard his car pull in the driveway, Sebastian sniffed the air in an exaggerated fashion. "Is that brownies I smell?"

"Sure is." Clara grinned, aware of how much he adored her homemade goodies. Since she was a child, she had always loved baking. But nothing beat baking for Sebastian, who, with a raging sweet tooth the size of Asia, typically made her feel as if she could put both Betty Crocker and the Keebler Elves to absolute shame.

He inhaled the heavenly chocolate aroma and planted another kiss on her lips, this one longer and steamier than the last. "I knew there was a good reason why I decided to marry you."

She laughed. "Yeah, how about because you love me beyond words and I'm the woman of your dreams?"

"*Well* . . . I suppose there's that too."

Clara cocked her head to the side, narrowing her eyes. "Need I remind you that I still have eight weeks, three days"— she glanced at her watch—"and one hour to change my mind about saying *I do?*" she teased. Like a child counting down the days until Christmas, Clara was tallying the minutes until she would officially become Mrs. Sebastian McKinley at the end of March. If she'd been any more excited, it was likely that horse tranquilizers would have been required to get her to sleep at night.

Sebastian chuckled.

"Can I open my present now?" She gave it a curious little shake.

"Be my guest."

Clara tore open the box to discover a bright red pair of flannel pajamas covered with whimsical white stars. Several weeks earlier, she and Sebastian had been taking a twilight stroll around Bean Town when the pajamas displayed in the window at Ivy caught her attention. She'd casually mentioned she liked them, but hardly paid them any mind and forgot all about them within minutes. But not Sebastian. He secretly returned to the store the next day in between appointments with patients to buy them. The busy podiatrist knew they would make Clara happy. And seeing her happy made him happy. Just because.

"*Honey . . .*" Her jaw hung open. "These are the PJs from our walk. I can't believe you remembered!"

"Come on, I remember everything you say," Sebastian replied sheepishly. And it was true. When Clara spoke, he really listened, not just with his ears, but also with his heart. Early in their relationship, when they were first getting to know each other, Clara had shared that her favorite poet was Walt Whitman. Several months later, Sebastian returned from a reflexology conference in New York with a surprise for her: a first edition of Whitman's *Leaves of Grass*, one of only eight hundred copies reportedly published. Upon receiving the rare treasure, Clara had been too stunned to respond verbally, but the tears in her eyes reflected how much it meant to her. The binding was damaged, a few pages were missing, and it smelled like old cabbage soup, but the fact that the book came from Sebastian only increased its precious value to her. Indeed, his genuine attentiveness was something that Clara never took for granted. She knew damn well how special her fiancé was. And she knew, without a question of a doubt, that she was the luckiest girl in the world.

"These PJs are so soft!" Clara traced her finger across the flannel. "I love them. Thank you, baby."

"You're welcome. I hope I got the right size."

Clara flashed him her most seductive smile. "Hmm . . . why don't I go try them on and see?" Then, taking hold of his hand, she slowly began leading him toward the staircase, adding in a raspy, provocative tone, "That way you can take them off me."

"Twist my arm." Sebastian gave her bottom a playful pat before chasing her up the stairs.

"Mourners? Excuse me, may I have your attention?" Leo, the funeral director, raised his arm in the humid afternoon air, commanding the attention of the quietly chattering crowd dressed mostly in black. He cleared his throat, waiting for silence to prevail. "On behalf of my little sister, Clara, I'd like to thank everybody for coming today, and invite you all to please gather around the grave. The ceremony is about to begin," he announced in a controlled, solemn tone, which he'd practiced using earlier that day, speaking into a hairbrush in front of the bathroom mirror. Then, as if an imaginary light bulb suddenly illuminated in his mind, he quickly added, "*Oh!* And please be careful not to step on any lettuce or tomatoes! Mind the veggies." He glanced at Libby, his mother, who had reminded him several times that morning to please urge guests not to traipse all over her treasured garden.

Winking, she gave Leo an encouraging thumbs-up gesture with her free hand. Her other hand was clasped tightly around Clara's.

The previous afternoon, Clara had arrived home from ballet class to discover Leo standing at the open front door with his arms folded across his chest and his eyebrows furrowed. He appeared to be waiting for her. And he did not look happy.

"Come on, butt-face, let's go sit down," Leo suggested in an odd tone.

Clara trailed her brother into the den and plopped herself down on the sofa. Though there was plenty of space on it, Leo sat directly beside her.

"Listen, Clara"—he cleared his throat, swallowing hard—"um, something very bad happened while you were at kindergarten." He looked away, but Clara witnessed the flash of sadness in his emerald eyes. Then, inhaling a deep breath and facing her once again, Leo softly explained, "It's Porkchop . . . he died."

For Clara, time stopped.

All she remembered was her brother's hand on top of hers.

Clara could not speak.

She could barely breathe.

"I know he was yours, and I know how much you loved him. *We all did*," Leo assured her with the sensitivity of a wise adult, rather than an eight-year-old boy who glued his hand to the wall earlier that week in order "to test how strong" super glue really is. "But, Porkchop was a very, very old cat, Clara, and he just—" Leo's voice cracked. "He just . . . never woke up from his nap today."

Great big tears spilled down Clara's cheeks, and she felt a searing pain worse than anything she'd yet to suffer in all her six years—even worse than the time she gave Natalie Marissa, her most favorite Cabbage Patch Kid doll, a ghastly, lopsided haircut, only to discover that orange yarn never grows back.

"I'm sorry." Leo quickly wiped his wet eyes.

As Clara sat there in her pink leotard and tutu, sobbing uncontrollably, she thought she saw Libby peek her head in the room, but if she did, she chose not to intrude, and instantly disappeared.

Clara and her brother remained on the couch while she cried for what felt to her like a very long time. Leo put his arm tightly around her shoulders and didn't say another word.

No words were needed.

"I told you before we got here, it's impolite to poop at funerals! *Bad dog!*" Clara's friend, Hazel, scolded Motley Crue, her Great Dane.

"Don't worry, Hazel," comforted Leo. "Considering today's guests, I doubt old Motley'll be the only one who goes on the grass."

Earlier that Saturday morning, before Clara woke (and

without his mother's permission), Leo had dug a fresh hole near Libby's tomato plants in their backyard and organized a memorial service for later that afternoon. Most of their neighborhood friends had pets, and as Leo knocked on local door after door, sharing the news about Porkchop, he made sure to stress that both human beings and animals were welcome at the ceremony.

Leo insisted on wearing his best (and only) suit to Porkchop's burial. Due to a juice spill on her navy dress earlier that week, Clara's dark apparel options were limited to either a black bathing suit or a Grim Reaper costume (complete with scythe) from last Halloween—which, considering the circumstance, didn't feel quite right. Thus, she opted for the swimsuit. She panicked upon realizing that Natalie Marissa also lacked proper attire, but Libby saved the day, as usual, by fashioning her a simple, toga-style dress out of a black plastic garbage bag. Libby also explained, "Often at these events, people like to cover their heads," and offered to create a handy Hefty hat for Clara's doll. But in the face of real tragedy, Clara no longer cared about a bad haircut.

Porkchop's funeral was attended by five boys, six girls, two adults, four dogs, three cats, and one and a half bunnies ("Ernestine" was pregnant), among others. The first mourners to arrive were Hazel and Motley Crue, whom Leo welcomed, placing the tray of ants-on-a-log that Hazel had made all by herself between the funeral sign-in book and the platter of cupcakes that Libby had baked on the picnic table nearby. "I made 'em with extra ants, just how you like," Hazel said, grinning at Clara. Giving her hand a tight squeeze, she softly added, "I like your bathing suit."

Makiko from down the block—accompanied by her gerbil, Barnabus—wore an ornate turquoise kimono. Feeling a familiar lump forming in her throat, Clara gently stroked Barnabus's tan coat. "You know, it is okay if you are sad or needing to cry," said Makiko. "Dying is awful. Here . . ." She offered Clara one of her breezy kimono sleeves.

"Oh, no you don't!" interrupted old Mrs. Stewart, the kind, gray-haired lady from across the street who didn't have any grandchildren of her own and had more or less adopted all of the neighborhood kids. "Use this instead," she said, handing Clara a tissue and then enveloping her in an enormous hug, whispering, "I am so very sorry, Clara Black."

Libby was careful not to get in the way of things, but every time Clara glanced in her direction, she found her mother's eyes on her, and Libby's warm smile was a comfort.

Once the guests had formed a circle around the grave, Leo shared his favorite memory about Clara's beloved cat and invited the group to tell theirs. When it was Clara's turn, she slowly stepped forward, fishing her swimsuit out of her fanny crack with one hand and clutching Natalie Marissa to her chest with the other. Shaking, she recited from memory the following haiku, which she'd composed earlier that day while hiding in her tree house, Maple Manor:

> I miss you Porkchop
> my dead furry pet and friend
> I'll always love you

After a simple R.I.P. marker had been laid at Porkchop's grave, everyone—including Motley Crue—bowed their heads for a moment of silence. To conclude the service, Clara's next-door neighbor, Cotton, played "Silent Night" on his new flute. He'd been taking lessons for just a few weeks, and that was the only song he knew how to play. About halfway through, right around "all is calm," he hit a wrong note and snapped, "Fuck!" (Cotton had a devious older brother with a habit of cussing.) The children immediately turned to Libby and Mrs. Stewart to gage the adults' reaction. Clara noticed her mother fighting to suppress her amusement, and then Mrs. Stewart shrugged and said, "Phooey! If you can't say *fuck* on a day like today, what's the word good for?"

All of the children's jaws dropped open, and Hazel clasped both hands over her mouth in disbelief.

Libby burst out laughing. "She's right! But we really ought *not* to make a habit of using that *terrib*—" She was chortling too hard to complete her sentence.

And a nanosecond later, the entire group was doubled over cackling.

While Clara was sitting on Libby's lap during the reception, licking the frosting off a chocolate cupcake and pondering the universe, she asked if Porkchop was in heaven with Daddy. Her father, James Black, hadn't been sick a day in his life when he dropped dead of a sudden heart attack at age thirty-five, leaving Libby with two kids under age three to raise on her own. Leo claimed to remember him, but he also claimed to have night vision and the ability to levitate. Clara had no memory of her father, but one of her prized possessions was a small, framed photograph of the two of them taking a nap together in a hammock when she was just a tiny baby. Libby had always kept it on top of her piano in the music room—the space most commonly referred to as the "living" room in a majority of homes—among a collection of her favorite family photos, but one night when Clara was feeling rather blue, she brought the picture up to her bedroom to keep her company. At Libby's insistence, it had been hers ever since. "To answer your question"—Libby took a bite out of Clara's cupcake—"I believe Porkchop *is* with Daddy, and that they're having a wonderful time together in heaven."

"Me too," Clara concurred.

"Well, I don't think we could have given Porkchop a nicer sendoff."

"Nope," said Clara, grinning.

Indeed, it was such a lovely funeral that it became the funeral to which all others that followed would be compared. And twenty-seven years later, it was one of the very first thoughts that crossed Clara's mind when she was informed by a solemn-looking police officer that Sebastian was dead.

November

I

"This is ridiculous. We've been sitting out here for ten minutes. You're going to have to leave the car eventually," Leo told Clara. He glanced at her slumped in the passenger seat of his Jeep, staring off into space. "You didn't fly all the way from Boston to wait in Libby's snowy driveway."

"I know. I know . . ." Clara shivered as she pulled her wool scarf over her mouth. "Please," she closed her eyes, exhaling a weighty sigh. "Just give me two more minutes to mentally prepare and then I'll be ready to go inside."

"That's what you said two minutes ago." Leo tapped his thumbs against the steering wheel, not bothering to hide his worried expression. "You're stalling."

Clara didn't respond.

"Look"—he paused for a moment, choosing his words carefully as he studied his younger sister—"I know you haven't been home in a long time, and I know you're anxious about this weekend, but it's not gonna be *that* bad. Really. Thanksgiving is supposed to be a time of joy, not torture."

"True. But you're not the one under a microscope," Clara mumbled in a meek voice, shrinking in her seat like a child.

Leo shook his head. "Neither are you." Smiling, he gave Clara's shoulder a reassuring squeeze before turning off the ignition. He threw open the car door, letting in a frosty blast of November night air. "And if Libby catches us sitting out here in the dark cold like this, she'll only worry about you more."

Clara rolled her eyes. "Like that's possible?"

"Sorry. You know I love you." And with that, Leo slammed his hand on the horn, alerting their anxiously awaiting mother that they were home.

"Hallelujah! You're here!" Libby squealed from upstairs when she heard her children enter the front door, to which a colorful WELCOME HOME CLARA! banner had been affixed. She'd planned to join Leo in retrieving Clara from the airport, but ended up stuck at home with Todd, the perpetually tardy but drop-dead gorgeous part-time piano technician, who had arrived three hours late to service her Steinway due to a last-minute gig he'd booked modeling menswear for the Sears catalogue. It was an annual holiday tradition for Libby Black, an internationally renowned winner of five Clio awards (the equivalent to an Oscar in advertising), to entertain her Thanksgiving party guests with a medley of her most famous commercial jingles, and she had no intention of performing with an instrument that didn't share her perfect pitch. "*Finally!* I love you I love you I love you!" She bounded down the mahogany staircase at lightning speed with her untied bathrobe flying behind her like a superhero's cape. When she reached the bottom, she wrapped Clara in a powerful embrace. "Clara-pie! It is so wonderful to finally have you home." Libby squeezed her even tighter, cradling Clara's head in the back of her hand. "Oh, thank God you're here," she whispered. *"Thank God . . ."*

Clara had not returned to her childhood home in River Pointe, a suburb located north of Chicago and filled mostly with successful lawyers, doctors, and other "highfalutin types"—as Leo called them—since before the fatal automobile accident that claimed her fiancé's life the previous March, less than two weeks before they were to be married. Prior to this tragedy, Clara had made it a regular habit of visiting her mother and brother at least once every few months, if not more often. The hardest part about living in Boston was not being near Leo and Libby; however, planning frequent trips to the Windy City helped dull the pain of the distance and made it at least a little bit more tolerable. Sebastian often teased Clara that if they had a dollar for every time she said, "I wish we lived closer to my family," they would have been millionaires. Clara agreed. This was the longest period of time she had ever stayed away—a point Libby highlighted during a recent, tense telephone conversation when Clara mentioned there was a chance she might remain in Boston this year for Thanksgiving.

"No way. Not happening, sweetheart," Libby had threatened, worried more than ever about her depressed daughter's increasingly withdrawn behavior. "If you believe for one second that you're spending the holidays alone, I'm telling you right now that you're mistaken. I am not going to let you wallow in misery doing God knows what. You may be thirty-four, but you are still my baby, and I will drive to goddamn

Bean Town, throw you in the goddamn backseat, and drag you back to River goddamn Pointe myself if I have to. Do you understand me? I am *not* messing around," promised Libby.

"Yeah. I got that," Clara had snapped.

Libby inhaled a slow, deep breath. When she spoke again, it was with a softer, milder tone. "*Believe me*, Clara-pie . . . I've been where you are now. I lost a husband. I know how difficult the holidays are. And I know how much it hurts not to have Sebastian here. I honestly do. But, I've got news for you. Like it or not, you *are* going to have to get back in the swing of things and get on with your life. Take it from one who knows. And trust me, it will be a hell of a lot easier if you stop isolating yourself and let the people who love you *in*, rather than insisting on going it alone."

"That's not what I'm doing," countered Clara, growing short on patience.

"Oh, that's *exactly* what you're doing," Libby assured her.

Sebastian had been gone for eight months now, though to Clara it felt more like an eternity, each gloomy day blending into the next. And the last thing she had wanted to do was discuss it with her mother. "Fine," she muttered, trying her best not to dwell on the tragedy that had taken her soul mate—her anchor—away from her, leaving her drifting and unglued.

"There's been an accident near Logan Airport," the solemn-sounding Boston police officer had told Clara during the haunting telephone phone call that forever altered her world. "*An accident . . .*"

"Just *please* stop this annoying soap opera speech, Libby. I can't take any more talk about Sebastian, okay?" Clara's chest ached with excruciating emptiness even to conjure her fiancé's name. "You made your point, and I will see you at Thanksgiving. Happy? Gotta run! There's someone at the door." Clara hung up the phone abruptly.

There wasn't really someone at the door.

Now, in the warmly lit foyer of the home Clara grew up in, she remained locked in her mother's tight, organ-crushing embrace.

"It's such a relief to see you," Libby said, beaming.

"Nice to see you too," Clara responded halfheartedly.

About thirty seconds later, when Libby still hadn't let her go, she silently mouthed *"Help!"* to Leo, who stood nearby beside her suitcase.

Obviously amused, he warned their mother, "Careful, now. You break her, you buy her. House rules."

Libby loosened her grip on Clara, but did not release her. Instead, her hands explored the length of Clara's spine, vertebra by vertebra. Then, suddenly, they moved to both sides of Clara's protruding ribcage, patting it up and down before she gasped, "You're a *bone*! Let me look at you . . ." Finally letting her daughter go, Libby stepped backward, an alarmed expression spreading across her face. "Jesus Christ. And you're pale as a ghost. When was the last time you ate?" She paused, gawking. *"August?* Honey, I have never seen you this small before."

"I can assure you, I'm the same size I've always been," Clara muttered. "You just haven't seen me in a while, that's all."

"I can assure *you*, that ain't it, kiddo. Try again. You're practically emaciated." Turning to Leo with one hand planted on her hip, Libby demanded, "Doesn't your sister look emaciated?"

"Uh . . . I—I don't know." He shrugged, clearly not appreciating being thrust into the spotlight. "I . . . reckon she might be a *little* on the skinny side."

"*A little?*" Libby parroted at the same exact time that Clara, equally surprised by her brother's choice of words, repeated, "You *reckon?*" Leo had a puzzling habit of only "reckoning" things when tangled in the process of whipping up a big, fat lie. Curiously, he never seemed to "reckon" diddly-squat when telling the truth.

"Huh." Clara blinked at his choice of words. "You really . . . *reckon?*" She wondered if perhaps it might be true. Clara glanced in the bathroom mirror on most mornings after she got out of the shower when she was combing her wet hair, but she rarely, if ever, bothered to really look at her reflection. It made no difference to her anymore.

Exasperated, Leo sighed. "What do I know?"

Tilting her head to the side, Libby raised an index finger to her chin, examining Clara. "A buck fifteen. A buck twenty, *tops*," she announced after several contemplative seconds. "You don't weigh a pound over. Believe me." Libby Black had always considered herself to have two special, God-given gifts in life: one was perfect pitch, and the other was the ability to accurately assess an object's weight without the aid of an outside instrument. The latter had earned her the nickname "The Human Scale" at the Libertyville County Fair, where she had worked for three consecutive summers during her teenage years as the Guess-Your-Weight-or-What-Month-You-Were-Born Girl. This unique skill also came in handy at the supermarket. Libby knew exactly what a pound of cherries looked and felt like, and when her children were younger, she often turned grocery shopping into a fun game, challenging them to try to stump her. If they succeeded, for their prize they could each choose any box of sugar cereal that they fancied (a stellar reward in the mind of a freeze-dried-marshmallow-obsessed girl whose personal heroes at the time included Cap'n Crunch and the monstrously dreamy Count Chocula). Clara and Leo would hand Libby what they estimated to be a one-pound bag of snap peas, she'd raise it in the air, pause, add or remove however many snap peas were necessary—one-by-one, making a theatrical show of it—and then let them race to the scale in the center of the citrus section to weigh the bag and see if she was right. She was always right. On Clara's ninth birthday she had a sleepover party, and though Merv the Magician had been hired to enchant her guests, The Human Scale was a much bigger hit with the kids, who giggled with glee when Libby lifted them up and correctly guessed each and every one of their weights.

Clara recognized that old, focused gleam in her mother's big, chocolate brown eyes and, knowing exactly what was coming next, slowly started inching away from her. "No . . ." she warned, staving Libby off with both hands. "I just got home. I'm in no mood for games."

Tucking her chin-length, black-and-white-streaked hair behind her ear, Libby took a small step toward her daughter.

"Seriously . . . I'm not joking," pleaded Clara.

Libby took another determined step forward.

"I said *don't!*"

Suddenly, Clara darted off toward Leo.

She had intended to use her brother's sturdy, six-foot-two-inch frame as a shield, but her agile mother, having broken into a full gallop, was too close on her heels for her to reach her destination, forcing her to twirl around and hurry in the opposite direction.

"Stop running! The floor was just waxed! You'll fall, dammit!" Libby chased Clara around the elegant foyer.

"And you wonder why I had to build up the energy to come inside?!" Clara huffed to Leo.

"I said stop it this instant! Do you hear me?!" Libby's arms were extended straight out in front of her.

"*Help!*" Clara beseeched her brother, nearly tripping over a pair of Libby's snow boots.

As Clara bent forward, with arms flailing, to catch her balance, The Human Scale seized the moment with a quick lunge, grabbing her around the waist and swooping her up off the ground, such that they were facing each other with their stomachs touching. There were several inches of air between Clara's dangling toes and the hardwood floor, which, now that it had been pointed out to her, did look particularly shiny.

"Yep. Just like I thought." Libby panted, trying to catch her breath. "One hundred and fifteen pounds."

Leo shook his head back and forth, amazed. "You truly belong inside a big orange tent beside a Bearded Lady or Frog-Boy," he marveled. "*Un*believable . . ."

Gently returning Clara to the ground, Libby looked deep into her daughter's vacant eyes with an almost palpable intensity and smiled sadly. Though Leo was standing within arm's reach, in that brief, blink-and-you'll-miss-it moment, Clara felt as if no one, or nothing else, in this whole wide world existed other than the two of them, and somehow her mother was able to see right through her and feel her agony.

Then, without breaking her powerful gaze, Libby placed her hand on Clara's cheek in the same, tender manner that she used to when Clara was a little girl with a boo-boo and needed to be comforted.

"You have no idea how much I love you," Libby whispered, quickly wiping away a single tear.

2.

Entering her Barbie-pink childhood bedroom with a reluctant sigh, Clara dropped her suitcase on the ground, observing that aside from Libby's fancy new stationary bicycle set up in the corner, the space still did not appear to have been altered since she left for Boston University. Her complete collection of *Sweet Valley High* books remained in a neat stack beside her baton-twirling trophies on the bookshelf, the crystal tissue box was right where it had always been on the nightstand, and there was good ol' Natalie Marissa, her beloved Cabbage Patch Kid doll, propped against some frilly eyelet pillows in the center of Clara's bed. Natalie Marissa looked as if life hadn't been kind to her either—weary and beaten—similar to the way Clara felt and imagined herself to appear (though, thankfully, Clara's head wasn't loose and droopy as a result of having once been accidentally popped off by an overzealous boy scout).

Prompted by natural instinct, Clara picked up Natalie Marissa and gave her an affectionate squeeze. "Hi, old girl. Long time no see. How've ya been?" she inquired. Then it dawned on her that she'd just asked an inanimate object with a disastrous orange yarn "Mohawk" (compliments of "Clara's Hair Salon" and yet another "healthy trim" gone awry), a sincere question. "Holy crap," Clara mumbled, quickly returning Natalie Marissa to the bed, wondering if perhaps she was a touch closer to the proverbial edge than she'd imagined. "No offense," she added apologetically to her doll. *"Oh God!* I'm still doing it!"

Stepping inside this vestige of a room was like boarding a direct portal to her past. Nothing had changed. Except for Clara herself.

Clara haphazardly hung a few items from her suitcase in the closet, including the dress she planned on wearing to the big Thanksgiving party, and tossed some clothes inside an empty dresser drawer. Next, she moseyed into the bathroom, which connected her bedroom to Leo's. After splashing a handful of cold water on her face, Clara spotted the digital scale and decided to step on for the hell of it. She watched the bright red numbers do their frantic little dance until at last they stopped at 115 pounds, exactly as The Human Scale had predicted. Clara was shocked.

At just over five-foot-eight inches tall, and blessed with a metabolism that most people wouldn't think twice to kill for, her body had always been lithe and lean, typically fluctuating between 135 and 138 pounds—not that Clara was the type of person to attach a particular value to this genetic factor, which she had apparently inherited from her late father. Clara used to joke that she could eat like a huge, beefy bar bouncer named Biff, who drank raw eggs for breakfast and shopped at the Big & Tall Warehouse, and not gain an ounce. Come to think of it, lately her pants did seem to hang a bit looser than usual around her waist, but Clara had simply tightened her belt a few notches. Never did it dawn on her that she'd actually dropped a good twenty pounds. Maybe Tabitha—whom she had chosen to serve as maid of honor at her wedding and whom she'd recently been drifting away from—was correct, Clara worried. Maybe she really had stopped taking care of herself since "the loss," as Tabitha had suggested. Maybe during their last, heated confrontation she shouldn't have snorted at Tabitha's stinging accusation of "being stuck in a devastating downward spiral" and then called her a "judgmental, meddling witch," a particularly low blow on Clara's part since she knew her best friend—or perhaps *former* best friend was more accurate—loathed sharing her name with that bratty, nose-wiggling child sorceress from television's *Bewitched*.

Clara was trudging her way out of her bedroom to go meet Libby and Leo downstairs for a nightcap when a brown, mangled, square box sitting atop her dresser—next to the framed photograph of Patrick Swayze in a rather dreamy pose from *Dirty Dancing*—caught her eye. It was hard for her to believe that there had actually been a time in her life when she'd fantasized about becoming Mrs. Clara Swayze. Or fantasized about anything, really . . .

She picked up the mysterious package, addressed to *Ms. Clara James Black* in fancy, cursive penmanship, gave it a gentle little shake, and searched it all over for a return address. But there wasn't one. How odd, she thought.

"What's this?" Clara asked Libby, carrying the box into

the music room, which, adorned with polished oak panel-ing, jewel-toned fabrics, and overstuffed leather furniture, possessed a rich, club-like atmosphere. Clara discovered her mother and brother sitting in front of the fireplace, where a crackling fire blazed. She took a seat on the couch beside Leo.

"Got me. Why don't you open it and see?" said Libby, rising to retrieve a wine goblet for Clara from the fully stocked, built-in bar in the corner of the room.

"You're a poet and you don't even know it." Leo pointed at her accusingly.

"I do too, darling." Libby smirked, asking Clara, "What did you think of the floral arrangement in your room?" She waited for a response.

And waited.

And waited.

Clara felt Leo give her foot a light kick. Quickly straight-ening her spine, she opened her eyes wider. "Pardon?"

Libby and Leo exchanged a glance of concern.

"Uh . . . Libby asked you a question," he prompted help-fully.

"Oh, I—I'm sorry." Clara tried her best to look alert. "I was"—she used the first excuse that popped into her mind—"just thinking about this box."

"Well, you were clearly lost in thought about *something*. I wanted to know if you like the flowers in your bedroom." Libby examined Clara closely, filling her glass with a fragrant Merlot.

"The . . . flowers?" Clara repeated, dazed. She automati-cally launched into fib-mode, a well-intentioned tactic she had recently mastered in her ongoing effort to discourage people from worrying about her. "Oh, yes! That's right. I meant to thank you for them. They're beautiful."

Sitting down in a club chair, Libby narrowed her eyes. "Oh yeah? What color are they?"

Busted. Clara had no idea what she could have been thinking. Her mother's keen sense of awareness had never worked in her favor. Sighing, she cringed, lacking the energy to pretend she hadn't just been caught red-handed with her dirty paw in the cookie jar. "Crap. I'm sorry, Libby. I didn't notice. But, I'm sure they really are beautiful. *All* of your arrangements are." She attempted to save face, though this was no lie. Her mother's glorious floral displays were worthy of the cover of *House & Garden* magazine, and while Clara's bouquets paled in comparison, Libby had passed her botanical passion down to her.

"I don't get it. I thought chrysanthemums were your favorite," exhaled Libby, deflated.

"They *are*," Clara assured her. Because the chrysanthemum blooms in November, it represents the light of hope in dark times, which is why she had always loved it most, despite its ordinary appearance.

"I can't believe you didn't see the arrangement. It's huge! What are you, a zombie?"

Clara knew her mother's words were teasing, but only on the surface. This was not the first time since Sebastian's untimely passing that Libby had compared her to the so-called walking dead. Nor was it the second, or tenth time. Come to think of it, "zombie" was a pretty accurate description,

Clara—feeling numb like usual—admitted to herself, offering her mother a forced, unconvincing half-smile.

She had tried her damnedest to bounce back after Sebastian's "accident," as she referred to it. Even the word "death" was too painful and final for Clara to accept, much less say out loud. In the blink of an eye, her entire universe had shattered, instantly becoming an inconceivable memory. BAM! In one second. Just like that . . . *gone*. It struck Clara on a daily basis how one moment—one little, tiny, itty-bitty moment—could change *everything*. And it never ceased to leave her trembling.

Still, though it felt like something had been brutally ripped from the inside of her chest, Clara had no intention of going down without a fight. At least, not at first. The last remaining sparkle of eternal optimism in her wouldn't allow it. Thus, she had tried every known solution under the sun to help her cope with her unbearable grief and get her deteriorating life back on track, including, but not limited to: private counseling, group counseling, acupuncture, denial, kick-boxing, cupping, meditation, music/sound therapy, bonsai (*"Clip clip, hooray!"*), prescription drugs (antidepressants and anxiety medication), illegal drugs (marijuana and ecstasy, which ironically made Clara feel sad), aromatherapy, writing (she lit her "grief journal" on fire), spiritual cleansing, self-help books, knitting therapy (*"Knit one, purl two, everyone can heal, so can you!"*), dolphin therapy (don't ask), long contemplative walks, short violent runs, Camp Good Grief for bereft adults, needlepoint, and deep tissue massage (ouch!).

Finally, when all else had failed, and Clara continued to sink deeper and deeper into melancholy, she decided to attempt suicide by leaving her car running in her closed garage. Only that didn't work either, thanks to her busted garage door, which had an aggravating mind of its own and refused to remain shut—prompting Clara to recall the film *Poltergeist* and wonder if perhaps the home she and Sebastian loved so much was built atop an ancient Indian burial ground.

After eight excruciating months, Clara had officially suffered her fill of torture attempting to pick herself up, dust herself off, and start all over again. Ultimately, she'd gained nothing but command of the dolphin alphabet, a couple clay pinch-pots, and a pathetic-looking handmade sweater with two neck holes. And so, with her grief sitting on her soul like a ten-ton brick, Clara—the same peppy girl voted "Most Likely to Brighten Your Day" in her High School senior yearbook—finally yielded to the escalating despair she'd battled so desperately to overcome, and allowed herself to descend into a thick, black fog of nothingness. At last, accepting that no other viable alternative existed, Clara ran out of steam and gave up on life. Simple as that. She just couldn't fight anymore. She was too depleted and broken to try, or even care. She was done—like her *Frisky Kittens in a Fruit Bowl* needlepoint that she'd completed a tenth of and knew would never see another stitch.

"Well, zombie or not, it's a treat to have you home." Libby winked at Clara.

"So when did this box arrive?" Clara steered the conversation in a new direction, hoping to avoid further discussion about her disappointing absentmindedness. "Why didn't you mention anything about it to me?"

"I called you in Boston when it was delivered back in July

and you specifically told me to put it in your bedroom. So I did." Libby sipped her wine. "Remember?"

Clara drew a complete blank, which was reflected in her vacant expression.

"You said it probably wasn't anything important, or it would have been sent to you directly, and you'd just open it when you came home next." Libby continued to attempt to jog her memory, but Clara's confused appearance revealed that she might as well have been speaking Klingon. "*Hello?* Is any of this ringing a bell?" Libby's voice was now laced with unequivocal concern. "Christ on the cross," she exclaimed, snapping her fingers a few times when Clara didn't respond. "*Come on.* Get with the program, Clara-pie. Wake up!"

Right then, Leo, bless his little buffer heart, cleared his throat, interrupting, "I would like to propose a toast." He raised his glass. "To Clara! Welcome home. It is wonderful to have you back." He smiled at his sister.

Setting her concerns aside for now, Libby lifted her goblet and grinned as well. "Hear, hear! I will happily drink to that."

The reunited Black family clinked their glasses together.

"Me too," Clara felt obliged to say, wondering how she was going to make it through the weekend with her remaining sanity intact. Gazing out the music room window at the gently falling snow, she longed to be one of those snowflakes, swirling in the evening wind so peaceful and carefree, that come dawn would dissolve with the rising sun.

"Well, what are you waiting for? Open the package," Libby coaxed, nodding at it as she sipped her wine, knocking Clara out of her dismal reverie.

Leo leaned over to get a better look. "There's no return address?"

"Nope." Clara peeled off the brown paper wrapping. "But maybe there's a note or something inside."

"That's strange," he remarked.

When Clara finally managed to rip the cardboard box open and first glimpsed the astonishing object that lay inside, her jaw all but hit the Oriental area rug. "No . . . way . . ." she stammered in disbelief.

"What is it?" asked Libby. "Let's see."

Flabbergasted, Clara slowly, and ever so carefully, removed the clear, foot-long, cylinder-shaped tube from the protective bed of Styrofoam peanuts it had been cushioned in, making sure not to damage it. She stared at the startling item with silent, genuine amazement.

"What the heck is *that*?" Leo asked.

"Yes, what is it?" echoed Libby, bending down with a grunt to pick up a couple of rogue peanuts that had fallen on the floor. "It looks futuristic."

"Just the opposite," Clara murmured, transfixed.

Suddenly, Libby gasped. "*Wait a minute . . .*" Giving the mysterious object a closer gander, her eyes expanded like saucers with a look of both shock and recognition. "I think I remember that thing. Yes . . . I *do*! I know what it is!"

Unable to tear her eyes from it, Clara softly stated, "It's my fifth-grade time capsule."

3

Upon completing their history class unit on legendary ancient and lost civilizations, Miss Jordain, Clara's fifth-grade teacher, assigned each student to create a personal time capsule. Referencing a worn Oxford English Dictionary, she read aloud to the class, "A time capsule is defined as *a container used to store for posterity a selection of objects thought to be representative of life at a particular time*." After listing some specific guidelines to follow when filling the capsule, Miss Jordain distributed to each student an empty glass tube and announced that she would collect their finished creations the following week. "I want you all to think very hard and very carefully about the personal artifacts and information that you choose to include in your time capsule," she cautioned. "Do not lose sight of the fact that it will be used as an important method of communication with people in the future. For other generations it will serve as a valuable reminder of your story so that it is not forgotten or lost, like our dear Atlantis and Lemuria."

Never in Clara's wildest dreams did she imagine she'd

see her time capsule again. In fact, she'd completely forgotten about it. Which was why to be sitting here now, in her mother's music room, decades later, balancing the "ancient" relic in the palms of her hands sent shivers down her spine.

Her fifth-grade time capsule contained an interesting collection of gems: a photograph taken after a January blizzard of Clara, Libby, and Leo poking their heads out the icicle-laced window of Maple Manor; a crinkled admissions ticket stub to Disney World; an individual packet of McDonald's "fancy" ketchup; a "Finding Your Way" Brownies patch, which Clara had earned with her troop by mastering command of the compass; and a small, brittle molar tooth. A horrified expression crossed Libby's face when Clara displayed the tooth. "Where did you get that?" she harrumphed. "Does the Tooth Fairy owe you money?"

At the bottom of the time capsule, tucked neatly inside of its original pink envelope, Clara also discovered Natalie Marissa's official Cabbage Patch Kid birth certificate.

"My God. Remember what you went through to get one of those dolls?" Libby smiled. "I had never seen you so hell-bent on attaining something in all my life. The unwavering determination you had . . ." Shaking her head, she chuckled at the memory. "There was no stopping you."

Clara recalled her quest to have a Cabbage Patch Kid, searching toy store after toy store, adding her name to waiting list after waiting list—she'd even once contemplated Cabbage Patch–napping a doll from her friend Stella. Finally, after trying for over a year, Clara's prayers were answered in the form of Natalie Marissa. The moment she held Natalie Marissa in her arms and inhaled her sweet, fresh plastic and artificial baby powder scent, the pain and frustration of her struggle to adopt a Cabbage Patch Kid instantly vanished. At the time, Clara viewed Natalie Marissa's birth certificate as an unequivocal symbol of hope: tangible proof that good things *do* indeed come to those who are patient and believe. And so into her time capsule it went.

Clara stared at the birth certificate, a million miles away. She wished she could have but a tiny fraction of that youthful hope back again. If only it were possible . . .

The final remaining relic inside the glass tube had been a specific requirement by Miss Jordain. Slowly, Clara removed it as a surprising flood of memories washed over her. She gawked at the tightly folded sheet of white paper before carefully unfolding it. On it was a detailed list of things ranging significantly in importance that Clara hoped to accomplish before age thirty-five, when she figured her time would probably be up, just as it had been for her father. Miss Jordain's original assignment had been to create a list of everything you hoped to accomplish before the end of your lifetime, which implied when you were wrinkled and gray with grandchildren and hair growing in places it shouldn't. But when Clara asked Miss Jordain for special permission to modify the term of her list, explaining the reason for her request, Miss Jordain gave Clara's shoulder a gentle squeeze and nodded, "Of course that's all right, dear."

Miss Jordain did attempt to convince her that there was absolutely no correlation between when her father passed and when her time would eventually come, but Clara was steadfast in her conviction, and when the wheels in her head began spinning, she suddenly feared the worst for her teacher, gulping, "Why? Are *you* thirty-five yet?"

"*Okay then*," Miss Jordain, forty-seven, replied, smiling at Clara, "I look forward to receiving your time capsule next week," and continued strolling down the narrow aisle of desks.

"That's terrible!" Leo almost spit out his wine when his sister recounted this tale. "Why haven't I heard about this before? I would've straightened you right out. I had no idea you were really convinced that life ends at age thirty-five. Jesus, that's awful."

"Not as awful as when Miss Jordain called me after school that day to suggest it might be beneficial to have a friendly little *For Whom the Bell Tolls* chat with my daughter *with the vivid imagination*." Libby extended an open hand to Clara. "Okay, Wednesday Addams. Let's see your list."

But Clara was too absorbed in reading it to hear her mother's request. Created at age ten, before reality encroached upon that magical sense of childhood power that allowed her to believe anything was possible—something she had continued to believe up until Sebastian's "accident"—it felt to Clara as if her list belonged to a complete and utter stranger.

And in a way, it did.

4.

Clara tossed and turned in bed. She'd been struggling to fall asleep for almost two hours (typical since Sebastian's death) with Patrick Swayze staring at her (not typical) when the intoxicating aroma of grilled cheese sandwiches wafted up the staircase, down the hall, and underneath her bedroom door. This was one of the perks of having her brother around. Clara was happy that Leo had decided to pack a suitcase and lodge at Libby's, rather than at his own bachelor pad in the city, while she was in town. Lord knows their mother couldn't have been more elated to have both of her children home for the holiday. Throwing off her covers, Clara grabbed her favorite Harvard sweatshirt, which had once belonged to Sebastian, and proceeded directly to the kitchen.

"Hey. What are you doing up?" Leo, standing by the stove, waved his spatula at her.

Clara shrugged, inhaling the heavenly scent. "I haven't been sleeping well lately. But, I *have* been craving one of your sandwiches for months."

"Say no more. You want it with or without?"

"With, please." Clara yawned, taking her usual seat at the kitchen table.

"Order in! One midnight grilled cheese *with* avocado coming right up."

Once again, Clara forced a semi-smile that sort of made it look as if she had to use the bathroom. She had no idea what Leo's secret touch was—it could have been the precise ratio of Muenster to American cheese—but his grilled cheese was honestly the best she had ever tasted, and seemingly impossible to replicate. She'd long since given up on trying.

When their late-night snack was ready, Leo joined Clara at the table. She was grateful to have this time alone with her brother. It reminded her of the good old days. Throughout the years, they had probably spent hundreds of hours bonding at this kitchen table during the midnight hour while the rest of the sane world slumbered, discussing anything and everything—or sometimes, just sitting there together in silence, not uttering a single word, with their noses buried in some book or magazine, warmed by the comfort of each other's company. These were the sacred hours that Clara missed most when she was in Boston, the hours when their masks came off that reminded her no matter how low or lonesome she felt, she was never really alone. Nor was her brother.

While they ate, Leo picked up Clara's time capsule, which had been left on the table when everyone retired to their bedrooms for the evening. "I wish I'd made one of these when I was in elementary school." He eyed it enviously. "How incredible is it that your teacher took the time and energy to send these back to her students twenty odd years later?"

"I know," Clara nodded while chewing. "I thought about

that before. It couldn't have been easy for her to locate everybody." It was difficult for Clara to imagine that Miss Jordain, the same woman who was rumored to enjoy topping her RITZ crackers with children's bone marrow, had extended the impressive effort to return the time capsules to their rightful owners. Perhaps she wasn't so wicked after all. "I wonder why she chose to send them back to us now? You know? Why exactly at this particular point in time?"

"You mean *in July?*" Leo corrected her.

"Whatever. Think she had a reason?"

"I don't know." He shrugged. "Could be." Leo unfolded Clara's list of things she had hoped to accomplish before age thirty-five. "Let's see what we have here, shall we?" Grinning mischievously, he began reading aloud:

- Have a pet dog (who cares if it sheds! BESIDES LIBBY!)
- Replace Lincoln's mom's beautiful vase I broke
- Serve on a real live court jury (awesome!!!)
- Visit the Wisconsin Dells
- Dig up Leo's recorder from the backyard & apologize for burying it (& letting him stay punished for losing it!)

"I still can't believe you did that, by the way," he interjected. "Nor can I believe you managed to keep it a secret from me for all these years. That was low. *Very impressive . . .* but low."

"I'm sorry. But if you'd been forced to listen to you play that darn thing night after night you would have buried it too."

Leo shot her a deadpan look. "A), That recorder wasn't even mine. It belonged to River Pointe Elementary School and was on loan to me for our class performance in the Spring Concert. B), That recorder was awesome. And C), I wasn't *that* bad."

"Uh, I love you dearly, but I'm gonna have to beg to differ with you on that one." Clara finished off the last of her sandwich, muttering, "Delicious."

"Moving on!" Leo grinned and continued reading:

- Become a teacher
- Become the President of the United States
- Attend the Ice Capades
- Learn Morse code
- Eat at America's largest buffet
- Ride in a hot air balloon
- Run a race (10K like Dad used to run? Find out what a K is!)
- Donate blood
- Swim with dolphins
- Build a gingerbread house from scratch (no dumb farty kits allowed!) (and who cares if it's messy! BESIDES LIBBY!)
- Sleep in a real tent
- Eat sugar cereal & McDonald's during the week (not just on weekends!)
- Apologize to Stella for stealing her Twirly Curls Barbie & give it back to her
- Grow my own garden with an avocado tree

- Apologize to Stella for stealing her Chia Pet (and accidentally killing it)
- Beat Leo at Memory
- Help others through charity like Libby (donate time if I'm poor when I'm old)
- Find a cure for heart attacks
- Kiss Billy Warrington (Clara + Billy = TRUE LOVE FOREVER!)

"Billy Warrington. Oh my God . . ." Cracking a tiny smile, Clara shook her head, amazed, letting out a faint but fleeting giggle. She hadn't heard the name of her first schoolgirl crush in decades, and Leo noted that he felt as if he hadn't heard the sound of his sister's laughter in just as long.

After they'd returned Clara's list to her time capsule, Leo leaned back in his chair, stretching his arms. His expression turned more serious. "You haven't mentioned work since you've been home."

"Neither have you," Clara quickly countered.

"Touché." Leo smiled. "Same old, same old really. Though I did just start an interesting new case translating for a deaf plaintiff in a personal injury lawsuit. Poor man had his knee shattered in a terrible escalator accident at a movie theater downtown." At the fresh age of thirty-seven, Leo was not only considered one of Chicago's "sexiest most eligible bachelors" (as per a recent issue of *Chicago* magazine), he had already earned a highly regarded reputation as one of the city's premiere certified court sign language interpreters, a challenging profession he not just liked, but genuinely loved. "And that's really all I got," he said. "How are things going with The Beer King of Boston?"

Clara exhaled a forlorn sigh. She had feared this subject would come up. "Well . . . to be honest"—she focused on picking at her nails—"they've definitely been better."

Leo's eyebrows pulled together. "Why? What's going on?"

"Do you promise you won't tell Libby?"

"Promise," he said, nodding.

"Swear on our siblinghood?" Clara double-checked, her face tensing. Never mind God or that little book called "The Holy Bible," swearing on their siblinghood was as sacred as it got between Leo and Clara. It was their hallowed code of honor and neither would ever dare consider breaking it.

"I swear on our siblinghood," Leo vowed with a growing look of concern. "You're making me nervous."

About a month earlier, Clara's boss, Mr. Franklin, the president of Scuppernong Beer, also known as "The Beer King of Boston," had urged Clara to take a sabbatical after she accidentally came to work one Saturday morning thinking that it was Friday. When she arrived at the microbrewery's corporate headquarters, the office was completely empty aside from the janitorial staff and Mr. Franklin, who was there catching up on some business. Clara wasn't aware that she'd done anything wrong until he inquired with a look of surprise, "To what do I owe this unusual pleasure?" Confused, she tried to act casual and told him that she figured she'd come to work today just like she did every other day, at which point The Beer King of Boston crinkled his gray, bushy eyebrows and asked if Clara was aware that it was the weekend. Then he suggested that he and Clara step inside his office for a little talk.

Explaining that he and other "concerned colleagues" at Scuppernong had "all" observed that Clara had not been acting like herself "since the awful tragedy," Mr. Franklin stressed how "very, very concerned" he was about her. "It's as if you're in a perpetual daze. Yes, you're physically here, Clara, but your mind is obviously elsewhere. And it's causing your work to suffer. Your sales numbers have been slipping for months now and you lost the Parker House hotel account. It's no secret what a blow that was for the company. I've let this continue for far too long. It's not good for Scuppernong, but more importantly, it's not good for *you*. Something has to change." Encouraging Clara to take as little or as much time as she needed to get herself straightened out, Mr. Franklin assured her that she would always have a place at the company.

After a fair amount of groveling, Clara had somehow managed to convince him that a sabbatical was the *last* thing she needed. She promised to be more alert and improve her performance, assuring The Beer King that he would not have to speak with her about this matter again.

Since then, the Scuppernong ice Clara had been skating on was so dangerously thin she was frightened it might crack at any point.

The week before Sebastian's accident, The Beer King had delighted in letting her know that he viewed her as an asset with tremendous potential at the company and he was personally nominating her for a promotion. Although Clara had worked as an accounts manager for only two years, he

was highly impressed with her excellent sales numbers and
the lucrative relationships she'd cultivated with a majority
of the Scuppernong vendors. Confident Clara would make
an outstanding director of sales (and probably a powerful
vice-president "someday in the not-too-far-off future," as
he'd phrased it), he'd already arranged for her to meet with
Human Resources the following week to discuss details.
Clara had been elated about her promotion. In fact, it was
a struggle for her to keep from jumping for joy right there in
his office. While she majored in English in college, she mi-
nored in business, mostly because her father had been a great
businessman and she wanted to follow in his footsteps. Well,
what she *really* desired was to be a professional poet. But as
she enjoyed reading poetry far more than she enjoyed writing
it—and she also wanted to be able to pay her bills and eat
food other than Ramen noodles—she knew she would need
a more realistic backup plan. Little did Clara know when she
joined Scuppernong that, like her father, she was actually
an exceptionally skilled businessperson. As a beer drinker,
she had always been genuinely fond of Scuppernong's delicious brew, so it was easy for her to use her enthusiasm for
the product—combined with her apparently innate business
savvy—to sell large volumes of it to vendors. The laid-back
atmosphere at the popular microbrewery's headquarters
complimented Clara's easygoing style, and she got along well
with associates at all levels. Happy and thriving in her position, it didn't take long for her to realize that she had met her
corporate calling. Nor did it take long for her to decide that
someday she would be the company's president. Her promotion would advance her one step closer to that ambitious goal.

The meeting with HR that The Beer King had scheduled on her behalf was cancelled, however, when Sebastian passed away. And the distinguished promotion eventually went to someone else, which Clara failed to notice until Mr. Franklin brought it to her attention.

Exhaling slowly, Leo ran his fingers through his thick, brown hair, which was just beginning to show the faintest hint of gray at the temples. "Well, it definitely sounds like you're on shaky ground at work," he said, frowning. "And it also sounds like The Beer King is genuinely worried about you." He paused for a moment, chewing his bottom lip, seeming to debate whether or not he should continue. "To be honest . . . and I *hate* to have to bring this up"—he sighed, clearly distressed—"but, after hearing that story, and knowing how depressed you've been lately . . . he's not the only one."

Clara pointed at the remaining corner of grilled cheese sandwich on his plate. "You gonna eat that?" she asked in a low monotone, avoiding eye contact.

"All yours." Leo pushed his plate across the table toward her. He studied Clara closely. There was a long, heavy moment of silence before he finally spoke. "I think we should talk about this."

"Talk about what?" She pretended to be dense.

Leo cocked his head to the side. "Oh, come on. You *know* what"—he insisted, not playing games—"the way things have been going for the past eight months. The way you've completely withdrawn from everything and everyone—from . . . *life*."

"Please. I'm fine." Clara tried to sound convincing.

"You are far from fine and we both know it," Leo argued. "I hardly even recognize you."

"Don't be dramatic."

"I'm not," protested Leo. "Look, the truth is, I'm not just worried about you, Clara," he swallowed hard, wincing. "I'm *scared*."

"Scared?" she echoed in a detached tone.

"Your voice doesn't even sound like yourself anymore. And you sure aren't acting like yourself. You aren't acting like, well . . . *anything*." Leo's fist came down on the table. "Are you even listening to me?"

Actually, Clara, staring at her lap, was so used to tuning everything out, it had become an unconscious gesture, as natural as blinking. "What? Yes. Of course."

Leo's mouth turned down in an uncharacteristic scowl. "You know what? The Beer King's right. It's like you're the walking dead."

Clara grimaced. She may have been existing in a numbing fog, but she wasn't *that* bad. *Was she?*

"I—I'm sorry." Leo reached across the table to touch her arm. "But if I can't say these things to you, who can?" He waited for Clara to respond. But she said nothing. "I've bitten my tongue for as long as I could. I was praying things would get better, but they're only getting worse. There's no way I can continue to watch you sink further into darkness. I can't do it, Clara. I love you too much." Leo inhaled deeply, hesitating for a moment. "The kind of trauma you've suffered . . . you—you *have* to get help."

"I've tried every form of help that exists," Clara, slumped in her seat, said flatly. "And then some."

"I know." He nodded. "I know you have. But you've got to try again."

"Yeah. Easy for you to say."

Leo stared at her. "No. It's not. Believe me." His voice was thick with emotion. "You're in real trouble, butt-face," he whispered. "Can you honestly tell me this is how you want your life to be?"

Clara didn't have the heart to tell him that Sebastian's life wasn't the only one that ended back in March. Nor did she have the guts to ask, *How do I hold on when there doesn't seem to be any end in sight?* Finally, she lifted her chin and looked her brother in the eye, fully exposed and knowing that she could not lie. Not to Leo. Not while sitting across from him at that old marble table, inside those trusty, familiar four walls that held their secrets and deserved to be honored. All she could do was hope to repress the prickly knot that had started to form in her throat. "Listen," she said softly, "I love you too. And I know your heart's in the right place, but I really don't want to talk about this right now. Besides, Libby gave me this same exact speech before bed. She also sang 'Turn That Frown Upside-Down' in an octave that was totally out of her range." Clara rolled her eyes, trying her best to appear animated. "I think I've had just about as much as I can take for my first day back." She stared at her brother. "Please," she begged in a whisper.

Standing up, Leo began clearing the table. "That song's the worst." He collected her plate.

Clara smiled gratefully at him.

And he smiled back.

What a gift it was to be understood.

5.

The following afternoon, Libby, in her usual frenzy preparing for the annual Black family Thanksgiving party, sent Clara, against her will, to Foodthings, the local gourmet shop, to retrieve enough preordered side dishes to feed an army.

Foodthings reeked of holiday cheer, with chattering shoppers zooming about in all directions. In years past, the store's merry decorations and well-known festive atmosphere during holiday time always delighted Clara, signaling to her that her favorite time of year was finally here, which was why she typically made it a specific point of volunteering to go there on Libby's behalf. But not this year. After waiting in line for almost half an hour, Clara was finally on deck. She couldn't help but notice a young couple holding hands by the fresh seafood counter. When the obviously love-struck man fed the woman a free sample shrimp, tenderly plopping it into her open, waiting mouth, Clara immediately looked away. How she wished Sebastian could be there with her! This was supposed to be *their* first Thanksgiving together as a married couple. They were supposed to be the seafood couple making innocent shoppers nauseous. Clara's eyes quickly settled at the deli counter, but once again her stomach turned when she spotted an elaborate hanging array of salamis. Salami was Sebastian's all-time favorite food. He put it in everything from scrambled eggs to macaroni and cheese, and included it as the "secret ingredient" in his "famous" spicy chili. When he and Clara vacationed together in Italy, he even sampled it dipped in dark chocolate, declaring *salame al cioccolato* was the best thing he'd ever eaten. Sometimes the mere sight of an aged Genoa brought Clara to tears. Other times, it made her laugh out loud, summoning fond memories of her salami-loving soul mate. Such was the unpredictable, tempestuous roller-coaster ride of grief that had come to define her. The sea of shiny, happy faces that Clara felt like she was drowning in appeared to her to have so much to be thankful for. And though it shamed her, she was envious of every last one of them.

"Thanks again, William." The female checkout clerk smiled at the man in line in front of Clara when he finished paying his bill. "Have a happy holiday. And tell Hans I say hello!"

"I will. And happy Thanksgiving to you too," replied William, grabbing his grocery bag and turning around to leave. Coming face to face with Clara, he stopped in his tracks and did a double take. "Clara?"

Peering up from the *National Enquirer*, which she'd grabbed off a nearby shelf to help keep her distracted while she waited, Clara's jaw nearly fell open.

"I thought that was you," William said.

Could it really be? She silently wondered. *No. . .*

"My goodness, it's been *ages*!" He extended his hand.

There, before Clara's eyes, stood none other than her childhood crush. Or at least she thought it was her childhood crush. It was hard to tell for sure. The last time she saw him had been decades ago, when he still had metal braces on his teeth, far more hair on his head, and far less meat on his bones. "Billy . . . *Warrington?*" Shocked, Clara shook his hand.

"I go by William these days," he said, smiling at her. "Wow. Nobody's called me Billy in years."

"Well, I'm still Clara," she replied sheepishly, unable to believe that she was actually standing next to Billy fucking Warrington in the flesh. He smelled good and manly, like a combination of spearmint and musty cologne.

"It's terrific to see you," he said. "Do you live around here?"

"No, I'm just visiting for the weekend from Boston. And you?"

William glanced at his Rolex. "Shoot! I apologize for having to rush off like this. Someone's waiting for me in the parking lot and we're already running ten minutes late to an appointment. Please forgive me." Hurrying toward the exit, he stopped, looked over his shoulder, and grinned at Clara. "Maybe I'll see you around town over the weekend."

She hadn't so much as even considered Billy/William Warrington in decades, and now, in the span of a day, his name had come up not once, but twice. And here they were actually standing in the same room together! What were the odds? Clara did not believe in coincidences. And though she had stopped believing in God, she speculated that this random encounter surely had to hold some level of significance. If everything in life happened for a reason, which seemed to be a popular—not to mention annoying—theory applicable to her fiancé's untimely passing, then certainly this too had to be some sort of sign. Why, it just *had* to be.

Suddenly, before Clara had time to even think about it, or realize what she was doing, she dropped the *Enquirer* on the floor, gave up her place in line, and raced after William. *"Wait! William! HOLD ON!"* she shouted. Operating on autopilot, she navigated her way through a slalom course of uniformed bag-boys, caught up to William just as he was about to step inside the revolving glass door, spun his body around, grabbed him by his trench coat lapel, yanked him toward her, and planted a big, wet, passionate kiss right smack dab on his lips.

Several amused shoppers witnessing the spectacle clapped their hands, as if it were the climactic scene in a romance film, and a little wrinkled old lady wearing a shawl around her shoulders made a triumphant fist, grinning. "Go get him, honey!"

When she finally ended their impromptu smooch, Clara pulled away from William, beaming.

In an obvious state of confused astonishment, he pointed at the parking lot, stuttering, "Hans . . . Hans . . . Hans is out there waiting for me."

Equally surprised, Clara felt lightning bolts of adrenaline coursing through her veins.

"He's—He's my husband," said William, frozen in place with his startled eyes opened unnaturally wide.

6.

Clara raced through Libby's front door to discover her family decorating the foyer with jewel-hued floral arrangements, candles, and gourds. "Hello!" she greeted them, grinning exuberantly and removing her coat to hang it up in the closet. "It looks wonderful in here. Very festive!"

Libby and Leo shared a curious look.

"You'll never believe what happened to me at Foodthings. I mean, *never!*" Clara rushed on. "To be honest, I still can't quite believe it myself."

"What happened?" asked Leo.

"You didn't accidentally forget to pick anything up, did you?" Libby cringed, adding some autumn leaves to the cornucopia on the table in the center of the foyer.

"Of course not." Clara practically bounced in her shoes. "But I *did* accidentally make out with a gay man!"

"*Excuse me?*" Leo's eyes bulged. "What are you talking about?"

"I'm talking about Billy Warrington!" Just saying his name

made Clara smile. "Oops! I mean, *William* Warrington. He goes by William these days."

"Are you serious? You saw Billy Warrington?" Leo confirmed, slack jawed. "And he's gay?"

"Quite! He's married to Hans."

"Oookay." Libby attempted to follow along. "And, just to be clear . . . you *kissed* this *gay William* who's married to *Hans?*"

"Yes! Can you believe it? I really did it!"

"And . . . this is a *good* thing?" Libby rubbed her brow, squinting.

Clara paused to consider it for a moment. She was unable to comprehend the strange phenomenon herself. "Yeah. I suppose, somehow, it is."

"I'm not sure I understand"—Libby shrugged—"but you seem happy about it. Remind me to send you to Foodthings more often."

Suddenly, Leo's eyes lit up with understanding. "*I know what this is about,*" he declared, shocked. "Holy cow. I—I can't believe you really did it!"

"*I know!*" Clara agreed.

"Kissing Billy Warrington was the very last thing on Clara's time capsule list of things to accomplish by age thirty-five," Leo explained in a matter-of-fact tone to their puzzled mother. "Billy was her fifth-grade crush. He had an awesome mullet that drove girls wild."

"*William,*" Clara corrected.

"I see." Libby placed a candle inside of a freshly polished silver votive.

"Out of nowhere, there he was . . . standing directly in

front of me in the check-out line. I didn't even know it was him! One minute I was reading the tabloids about the poor little *unicorn-girl* who sawed off her own horn, the next minute I was chasing William down for a kiss," Clara slowly recalled, as if the words she was choosing to describe the baffling sequence of events were stuck in molasses. "It all happened so fast. I—I didn't *mean* to do it. It's not like it was premeditated . . . I don't even know what came over me! Honestly! I've never done anything like this before in my entire life! I guess I just figured *why not?* I mean, it was on my list. And I'll probably never have the chance to do it again," she rationalized. "Somehow, it just *happened*."

"Well, it looks like you can officially cross *Kiss Billy Warrington* off your list." Leo handed Libby some more candles.

"I can, can't I?" Clara twinkled. She picked up two small pumpkins from the ground. "Need an extra hand decorating?"

A look of pleasant surprise crossed Libby's face. "You *want* to help?"

- ~~Kiss Billy Warrington (Clara + Billy = TRUE LOVE FOREVER!)~~

7

Laughter wafted throughout the convivial dining room, where two long tables of dear family and friends carried on spirited conversations while partaking of the bountiful Thanksgiving buffet and endlessly flowing wine. Guests punctuated the leisurely meal with toasts to their hostess and one another, though all of these sentiments were lost on Clara, whose exhilaration from yesterday's gay kiss had long since worn off. Staring down at her watch, her focus remained on the second-hand crawling at a frustrating turtle's pace ever so slowly around the dial.

"Excuse me everyone." Aunt Billie, Libby's inebriated older sister, stood up. She tapped her knife against her almost empty wine glass. "If I may add just one more thing." She hiccupped, tilting slightly to the side. *"All hail the mighty Turducken! We're not worthy!"*

An enthusiastic round of "Hear hear!" followed.

Leo, seated beside Clara, shot her a look. *"Oh boy,* here we go," he muttered under his breath in her ear. "Think we better cut Aunt Billie off?"

Clara just shrugged, grateful to no longer be the focus of attention.

Earlier, a stir regarding her diminutive appearance had ensued among the murmuring party attendees. It had been over a year since Clara last donned her navy cocktail dress, which she'd haphazardly tossed in her suitcase. When she slipped it on shortly before guests were due to arrive, she discovered, to her dismay, the elegant garb that once did all the right things for her body—highlighting her long, muscular legs, shapely waist, and rounded bosom—now appeared to be several sizes too large, as if it belonged to a stranger. And for all intents and purposes, it did.

Clara frowned at her reflection in her bedroom's full-length mirror. It looked to her as if she was draped in an ugly tent, rather than the beautiful, designer-label frock that had cost her an arm and a leg. Though, it *had* been well worth the price to see the dazzled expression on Sebastian's face the first time she wore it to the opera. "Have mercy," he'd uttered, awestruck and attempting to hide his growing erection. From that point on, it was known between them simply as "the boner dress." Banishing such agonizing memories from her mind, Clara clutched her arms around her chest, as if to cover the gaping hole in it. Then, she did the only sensible thing she could think of: call for Libby.

Frightened by the piercing shriek, Libby, dressed in diamonds and a stylish gray suit, literally came running. "What is it? What's wrong?"

Slowly pivoting around from the mirror to face her mother, no words were required for Clara to explain her obvious dilemma.

"Oh. I see." Libby exhaled, absorbing the image of her daughter standing before her, lost in excess fabric, fragile and ghostly white, like a delicate porcelain doll with cracks.

"It's the only nice thing I packed." Clara cast her brown eyes downward, their once fiery glow now extinguished.

Libby dashed away and returned several moments later holding a basic black dress. "I shrunk this in the wash. It's nothing fancy, but it should hopefully do the trick for to-night."

Smiling weakly, Clara allowed her navy gown to crumple to the carpet as she reached for the impromptu alternative.

Libby stifled a gasp, observing her daughter's bony, exposed form. "Here"—she swallowed, trying not to stare—"let . . . let me zip that in the back for you. Careful now, lift up your hair for me."

Clara didn't move.

"Sweetheart? Can you lift up your hair for me, please?"

"Oh, sorry." Clara did as her mother asked.

"*'Atta girl.*" It was as if Libby was speaking to a lost child, rather than a grown woman. After adjusting the dress while Clara stood there like a limp puppet, she finally grinned. "Okay! *There* we go. What do you think?"

Clara sighed. "That I'd like for this night to be over," she mumbled, daunted by the idea of having to interact with forty party guests—of having to remember to look interested, to nod or smile at appropriate intervals. She knew it was not going to be easy.

Libby examined her with a growing expression of concern. After a minute, she took a deep breath. "You know, I always miss your father more on Thanksgiving. Every year. Without fail. It's just how it goes," she confessed in a soft tone. "Are you thinking about Sebastian?"

Clara's chest ached with crushing emptiness at the sound of his name, at the idea of spending her first Thanksgiving in ten years without him, at the impossible realization that she would not hear his infectious laughter around the holiday table that night. Or ever again. Her thoughts turned to last year's jovial Thanksgiving meal during which, fancying herself a stand-up comedian, she had told a dirty and absolutely hilarious lawyer joke, captivating the attention of everybody in the room and bringing the house down. For the life of her, she couldn't remember what specifically the joke was about. But she recalled with shocking clarity Sebastian's facial expression—the way his dimple in his left cheek creased, how he closed his eyes—as he threw his head back in laughter and slapped his hand against his thigh, struggling not to spit out the cranberry sauce that was in his mouth as the room erupted. The joke had been such a hit, in fact, that Clara, shamelessly hamming it up, took a bow and teased, "Thank you very much, ladies and gentlemen! I'll be performing here all week. Don't forget to tip your waiter!"

Later that night in bed at Libby's, while discussing their favorite parts of the evening, as they often did, she and Sebastian had laughed about it all over again. What a truly fantastic holiday it had been . . . To answer her mother's current question, when was she *not* thinking of Sebastian? Looking away from Libby, Clara nodded, fighting back the tears that had been threatening to flow since she woke up that morning. "This dress is nice." She forced herself to focus on it in an effort to avoid spiraling deeper into depression. "Thanks for letting me borrow it."

When the last bite of pumpkin pie had been swallowed, and a round of potent aperitifs had been poured for those who weren't full enough to burst, the guests retreated to the music room for the evening's main attraction: Libby's annual medley of her most notorious jingles.

"Ladies and gentlemen." Leo stood before the clattering group, his cheeks rosy from wine. "The tryptophan will soon take effect, so, without any further ado, it is my pleasure to introduce, *for one night only*, the incomparable *Libby Black!*"

The room erupted with merry, boozy applause, and somebody lounging in a club chair whistled.

"All right, everyone, you're familiar with the old drill by now." Libby handed her glass of cognac to Leo, taking a seat at her beloved Steinway. "You all know the words, so everybody's invited to sing along. And don't be shy! Dignity be damned!"

"You're a star!" bellowed Aunt Billie, petting her sweater's puffy cornucopia appliqué, which suddenly lit up and began blinking.

"*You* might want to be a little shy." Libby winked like an experienced lounge singer. At last, her fingers landed where they most belong, and began tickling the ivories, starting off the show with a slow and romantic, "*With a cheeseburger in my hand . . . I'll show you the promised land . . . At Burger-In-Your-Car . . . Everywhere that you are . . .*"

Normally, this whimsical tradition pleased Clara to no end, for the comforting sound of the piano and the sound of her mother's voice were one in the same in her mind, and never failed to lift her spirit or make her heart swell. However, haunted by Sebastian's ghost, it would have taken a miracle to accomplish this feat.

After an especially peppy polka for Pepto-Bismol, Libby took her performance down a notch, playing the poignant and tender salt-free seasoning jingle for which she was awarded her first Clio. Swaying dramatically on her piano bench with her eyes closed, she crooned, *"So I'm cooking with So-Not-Salt, because I love you, yes I dooooo"*—some of the guests chimed in—*"my life would mean nothing if I didn't have youuuuuu . . ."*

Tears slid down Clara's cheeks.

When Aunt Billie, seated beside her on the Oriental rug, glanced Clara's way, her bloodshot eyes filled with fear. "What's wrong?" she whispered, leaning toward her.

"Nothing," Clara whispered back, her limbs splayed in the extremity of her grief. "Why?"

"You're crying," answered Aunt Billie, gently placing her hand on top of Clara's.

"Me?"

"Yes, *you*. What's the matter?" Aunt Billie hiccupped again.

Confused, lost in the numbing haze, Clara slowly touched her cheek with her free hand. Her fingertips felt the warm, wet tears that she was unaware were falling.

Bowing her head, Clara allowed a single teardrop to land on Aunt Billie's hand, which she held on to a little bit tighter.

"It's okay, love. Shhhh . . ." Aunt Billie soothed. *"Look!"* she whispered a bit too loud. She tapped her puffy cornucopia appliqué. "Pretty lights! Like Broadway!"

8.

The early morning sun beamed its gleaming brightness through the kitchen window, prompting Clara, immersed in the Saturday *Chicago Tribune*, to switch seats at the kitchen table to avoid a bothersome glare.

"What is this, musical chairs?" Leo inquired.

"Is it always so damn sunny in here at this hour?"

"Only when you're present." He buried his nose in the entertainment section. "What's that pasty chef's name who you love so much?"

"Who? Alfred Guillaume?"

"Bingo. Check it out." He flipped the paper around so that it was facing Clara and pointed to a large black-and-white photograph of the popular French chef, appearing under the headline, "*Move Over, Santa. Celebrity Chef Storms Into the Windy City!*"

"Let me see." Clara snatched the paper away from Leo and began reading. She gasped. "Wow. He's teaching a one-day-only intensive class on advanced gingerbread architecture at the Cooking and Hospitality Institute of Chicago."

"Advanced gingerbread *architecture*? Sounds like it requires an engineering degree. What is that? Like a Frank Lloyd Wright cookie?"

"It means constructing houses and other edible edifices out of tasty spiced dough," Clara replied, as if it were the most obvious answer in the world. It dawned on her just then that she hadn't baked a single item since Sebastian's accident. Although she used to wear it all the time, she didn't even know where her apron was.

"Ah, like on your time capsule list of things to accomplish," Leo said. "How did you phrase it again? *Build a gingerbread house without using a stupid farty kit?*"

"Something like that." She soaked up the article.

"You don't hear *farty* enough these days."

"Listen to this." Clara read out loud: "*Receiving rare, one-on-one guidance from Chef Guillaume—world-renowned pastry master and Oprah-endorsed author of the bestselling how-to book* C Is for Cookie, Bitch!—*each student will create their own unique, delicious, and 100 percent edible holiday gingerbread house guaranteed to wow even the grumpiest Scrooge. A scrumptious, once-in-a-lifetime opportunity not to be missed! Register now!*" She put down the newspaper. "Wow. How great . . ."

"Do it," Leo suggested nonchalantly, leafing through the sports section.

"Do what?"

"Register for the class. You're obviously gaga for Chef Guillaume. You're a terrific baker. And the subject clearly interests you. You just said it sounds *great*." He gestured quotation marks.

"I'm not gaga."

"Seriously." Leo selected a muffin from the breadbasket on the table. "It sounds like you would really enjoy this class."

"Yes," agreed Clara. "But it's two weeks from today. I have to be in Boston the Friday before for work. Even if I *wanted* to register, it's not feasible."

"So take a couple days off. Hell, take more than a couple days off. It's not as if you're exactly invested in your career at Scuppernong at the moment. You said so yourself the other night," Leo reminded Clara. "Besides, Mr. Franklin urged you to take a sabbatical. This could be just what the doctor, or, in this case, *The Beer King* ordered."

"Yeah. I don't think so."

"Think about it," he persuaded. "You don't have anything else concrete or pressing keeping you in Boston right now. What if you were to take him up on his offer and spend some time back home?"

"*Oh please*. Right. Why? So I can make a silly gingerbread house from scratch and then cross that off my time capsule list too?"

"Why not?"

"Perfect." Clara sipped her coffee. "While I'm at it, why don't I just go ahead and do everything else on my list until it's *all* crossed off?"

"I think that's an excellent idea."

Clara shot her brother a look implying he might be stark-raving mad. "I was kidding. Only *kidding . . .*"

Slowly, and with emphasis, Leo met Clara's bemused gaze with an expression void of humor. "I wasn't. You need a plan of action—something to help get you out of this horrible rut you're in. Sure, it might sound a tad unconventional, but it's no more farfetched than some of the other methods you've tried to overcome your grief. This could actually be worth consideration."

Clara stared at Leo, dumbfounded. "My God . . . you're—you're really serious, aren't you?"

"Completely."

"Oh, come on, Leo. I'm not in fifth grade anymore. I'm not *ten*."

"No, but I'll tell you something. I just saw your eyes light up as if you were when you were reading that article. For a brief minute there, you weren't"—he searched for the correct word—"*lifeless*."

Clara winced.

"I'm—I'm sorry." His face flushed with guilt. "I'm not trying to be cruel."

"I know." Clara sighed, closing her eyes, neither asleep nor really awake. She was just so damn tired of it all. She forced a quivery, unnatural chuckle. "Hell . . . Might as well call a spade a spade . . ." She looked down at her lap, as if saddled with some bleak, terrible shame, quietly confessing, "I feel lifeless. Actually? *Dead* is more like it. And apparently there's nothing I can do about it."

"Jesus, Clara." Leo's face tensed at her resignation. "What would Sebastian do if he heard you say that?"

She gave a weak, dismissive shrug. "Doesn't matter . . . He's gone."

"It does matter!" Leo, visibly shaken, pounded his fist on the table. "I know for a fact he'd tell you that you're *not* dead—not at all. So you have to do whatever it takes for you to stop feeling that way. Even if it means building a fancy cookie house!" Leo inhaled a deep breath. When he spoke again his tone was softer, yet even more intense. He looked Clara directly in the eye. "You know as well as I do it would have destroyed Sebastian to see you like this."

Clara straightened her spine, shaking her head as if trying to clear away a thick cobweb of dust. *"UGH!"* She released a huge, pent-up sigh. "I don't know . . . Maybe you're right," she conceded, considering it further. "Insane—and I do mean *insane*—as it sounds, maybe Sebastian would tell me to at least give that silly old time capsule list a try."

"Maybe he would," Leo mused, returning his attention to the newspaper, for he knew his sister did her most productive thinking in silence.

Later that afternoon, Clara lay in bed trying to focus on a mystery novel, which, desperate for distraction, she'd randomly picked up at the airport on her way to Chicago. But, after turning page after page and not processing a single word, she finally surrendered, closing the book—and then her eyelids—with a weighty sigh. A former bookworm, there was a time not too long ago when Clara read at least one novel per week. Sebastian would curl up in bed with the latest issue of *Podiatry Today* or *Journal of the American Podiatric Medical Association* (his favorite!), she'd snuggle up with something on the *New York Times* bestseller list or an old classic she hadn't read yet, and their shared reading bonanza—also known as "Literary Nerd Fest"—would begin. It wasn't necessarily the "coolest" way to spend a Sunday afternoon, but for them, lounging around for hours together in bed was not only an indulgence, it was perfect. Besides, it usually led to pretty great sex. Or a pretty great nap. Or, if they were lucky? Both.

Clara couldn't stop her breakfast conversation with Leo from turning over and over (and over) in her mind. Sure, when she'd first mentioned accomplishing everything on her time capsule list she was only teasing. But now, the more Clara considered it, the more sense it somehow made. After all, she was at the bottom of the proverbial barrel, about as desperate as they come, she figured. And she couldn't deny that kissing Billy/William Warrington had jolted her with a gratifying, hair-raising rush, which she hadn't felt in far too long, ultimately reminding her that she was alive. It was as if, but for a brief, super gay, magical moment, she'd awoken from a deep and powerful slumber, only to fall right back under its cruel spell.

Leo had been correct about so many things. She'd lost her ambition, and there used to be so much. Becoming president of Scuppernong . . . Taking the company global . . . Seeing the Northern Lights in Alaska with Sebastian before becoming mom to Julian and Edith, the children they'd have . . . Corny annual holiday photos where they'd all wear matching hand-made sweaters, as would Milk Dud, their dog . . . Summer vacations back home in Chicago with Libby and Leo . . . Visiting all fifty states together . . . A bigger house in a great area of Boston—nothing fancy, just someplace nice where Julian and Edith (and the identical twin girls they'd have later in life named Marsha and Barbra, although she hadn't yet broached this subject with Sebastian) would have lots of space to run around and ride their bikes and build a tree house like Maple Manor . . . Saving every last art project the kids made in school, and cherishing their childhood poetry more than that of the "Masters" . . . Supporting Sebastian as he opened his own successful practice, growing wrinkled and old with him by her side, never taking for granted just how very, very lucky they were . . .

Contrary to the way Clara currently felt, she knew that she was not dead. And something in her life did need to change in order for her to stop feeling and behaving as such. Indeed, action was required. Considering the myriad solutions she'd already tried to no avail, she was officially lost enough to wonder if maybe, *just maybe*, her time capsule might possibly be the answer.

When Clara's eyelids fluttered open once again, she peered at the flashing clock on her bedside table. She was stunned to discover this idea had been somersaulting in her mind for over an hour! And that's when she knew there was something to it. Surely there must be, Clara told herself. How sick she was of being trapped in a prison invisible to others because the walls were inside her. Perhaps her time capsule could help unlock the penitentiary door, and remind her of who she was once upon a time, before tragedy darkened her life and the numbing evil slumber spell had been cast.

Or perhaps she was nuts.

In her mind, both were real possibilities. Either way, as far as Clara was concerned, she had nothing to lose, and everything to gain, by trying.

On September 2 she would turn thirty-five, which gave her approximately nine months to accomplish her list before her deadline.

With no time to waste, Clara jumped out of bed and hurried to her dresser to retrieve her time capsule.

December

9.

Clara returned to Boston, registered for the Advanced Gingerbread Architecture course, cancelled her daily delivery of the *Boston Globe*, and forwarded her mail to Libby's address, since she wasn't yet certain where she'd be lodging during her temporary stay in Chicago. Then she informed The Beer King of Boston that she was going to take him up on his generous offer of an extended sabbatical after all, packed a few suitcases, and by the first of December was back in River Pointe. Back on a mission that even she herself thought was crazy. She just hoped it might be crazy enough to work. So far, nothing else had, and now Clara feared that her future, *if* she had one, hinged on it: her time capsule from the past.

On her first day in town, Clara woke groggy and discombobulated after the long drive from Boston. She hadn't a clue where she was. Sitting up in bed, glancing around, Patrick Swayze soon set the record straight.

Well, this is it, Clara thought to herself, stretching as she considered her time capsule list. According to Leo's hypothesis, having a distinct purpose would help her heal, and her list provided her with just that: a purpose. Clara peered at the alarm clock on her bedside table, which read 9:30 a.m., reminding her that time was ticking and she best get started straight away. After all, she had a lot to accomplish in a matter of just nine months. She had a sneaking suspicion September would be here before she knew it.

Yawning, Clara slid out of bed. She removed a copy of her time capsule list from her pocketbook (the original, along with several extra copies, remained safely tucked away inside the capsule in her suitcase), unfolded it, and gave it a quick review:

Things to Do before I'm 35

- Have a pet dog (who cares if it sheds! BESIDES LIBBY!)
- Replace Lincoln's mom's beautiful vase I broke
- Serve on a real live court jury (awesome!!!)
- Visit the Wisconsin Dells
- Dig up Leo's recorder from the backyard & apologize for burying it (& letting him stay punished for losing it!)
- Become a teacher
- Become the President of the United States
- Attend the Ice Capades
- Learn Morse code
- Eat at America's largest buffet
- Ride in a hot air balloon
- Run a race (!0K like Dad used to run? Find out what a K is!)
- Donate blood
- Swim with dolphins

- Build a gingerbread house from scratch (no dumb farty kits allowed!) (and who cares if it's messy! BESIDES LIBBY!)
- Sleep in a real tent
- Eat sugar cereal & McDonald's during the week (not just on weekends!)
- Apologize to Stella for stealing her Twirly Curls Barbie & give it back to her
- Grow my own garden with an avocado tree
- Apologize to Stella for stealing her Chia Pet (and accidentally killing it)
- Beat Leo at Memory
- Help others through charity like Libby (donate time if I'm poor when I'm old)
- Find a cure for heart attacks
- ~~Kiss Billy Warrington (Clara + Billy = TRUE LOVE FOREVER!)~~

Then, ready to get to work, she made her way downstairs in search of Libby.

A pleasant melody floated from the music room, leading her straight to her target. Before entering the space, she paused in the polished oak, domed archway. Debussy's "Clair de Lune" had always been one of Libby's favorite tunes, and Clara could recall being soothed by it as a young child while drifting off to sleep at night. Watching her mother's balletic hand gestures from behind, she considered how comfortable, how inexplicably right Libby appeared sitting on that red velvet piano bench, swaying ever so gently, her head tilted to the side. Somehow, her mother had found her purpose. She'd identified precisely where she belonged, like a cat that fit perfectly in a windowsill. Wondering if she too might someday discover her "inexplicably right" place in this world, Clara exhaled a dreamy sigh.

"HOLY CHRIST!" shrieked Libby, glancing over her shoulder and jumping. "I had no idea you were there! How—How long have you been listening?"

"Just a minute or two." Clara remained leaning in the doorway. "I'm sorry. Sounds beautiful."

"Well, come in," Libby beckoned. Regaining her composure, she gestured to the sheet music before her. "Want to turn pages for me? Like old times?"

"Oh gosh, it's been so long I don't think I even remember how to read music anymore. But thanks . . ." Clara, a former flute student who was forced to quit playing after suffering continual fainting spells from forgetting to breathe (a minor problem), took a seat on the sofa. "Would it be all right if I interrupt you for a minute though?"

"Of course." Libby zipped over and joined her on the couch. "What's up? Would you like me to make you some breakfast? I have fifty boxes of frozen blueberry waffles out in the garage freezer."

"*Fifty* boxes?" Clara's eyebrows arched upward.

"I did a jingle for Wanda's Waffles."

"Ah . . ." Clara chewed her bottom lip, hesitating. "Wow. No, thank you. I wanted to ask you something though. And *please* feel free to say no. Really. I promise you I'll understand if you're opposed to this. I know how you feel about disorder and mess and crumbs and little pieces of string and dust and hair and—"

"I'm going to interrupt you before you add wire hangers to that list." Libby smirked. "What is it you're trying to ask, Clara-pie? Name it. Anything."

Had Clara been presented with this dream offer as a child, she'd have asked for either a Pegasus or her own hot dog stand. Instead, she reluctantly handed Libby her time capsule list. "See *number one*." She couldn't believe she was actually doing this.

Springing up to retrieve her reading glasses from the piano, Libby returned to the couch with an expression of curiosity. "Okay, let's see what we've got here—" She squinted her eyes a bit, reading aloud, **"Have a pet dog (who cares if it sheds! BESIDES LIBBY!)."**

Clara grimaced in anticipation of what was to come next.

Slowly refolding the piece of paper, Libby's eyes grew large. She crossed her long, willowy arms. "You want me to buy you a *dog?*"

"No, no, no," Clara said, shaking her head. Her mother had this all wrong. "Of course not. I'll pay for it myself. You know I'm only staying here temporarily until I find a more long-term—albeit *short-term* while I'm in town—solution. The thing is, I'd kind of hoped to get started with my list right away. As in, *today*. Which is why I wanted to know if it might *possibly* be okay if I were to *maybe* get a dog while I'm still staying here? With *you*." She felt the need to clarify. "The person who views shedding animals as proof of the devil and never allowed us to have a dog in the past."

Libby removed her reading glasses. Her lips curled into a smile as she shook her head in what appeared to be amazement.

Confused, Clara fidgeted with a limp strand of chestnut-colored hair that used to receive a healthy trim every six to eight weeks in order to help maintain its lustrous shine, but had long been neglected. "What? Why are you grinning at me like that? You're not gonna offer me fifty boxes of waffles again, are you?"

"Well, I can't say I'm surprised you want to hit the ground running with your list. You've always been a bound and determined, feast-or-famine type of person."

Clara assumed her mother was referring to the fact that when her interest in a subject was piqued, or she committed herself to something, she tended to dive in headfirst—immersing herself in it, devoting herself wholeheartedly—as she'd done with Boston, opera, and all of her favorite poets. Upon falling madly in love with Keats when introduced to his poetry during her sophomore year of high school, Clara, moved openly to tears right in the middle of English class, not only dedicated herself to reading all of his poems, she mastered the complete works of Blake, Byron, Shelley, and Wordsworth until at last she'd consumed the entire canon of British Romantic poetry. And then she read it all again. Similarly, once Clara determined she didn't care for something or lacked interest in a topic, it was often difficult, if not impossible, to change her stubborn mind. Hence her disdain for exercise, religious zealots, and tofu. "I can't help it," Clara said to Libby, shrugging. "I guess I'm just an all-or-nothing kind of girl."

"I love that about you," said Libby. "So then I suppose you'd like to get a dog this week?"

"Well, not exactly."

"*Good!*" Libby clasped her hand over her heart, exhaling a sigh of relief. "Good . . ."

"I was thinking more along the lines of today."

Libby's alleviation vanished. "Today? *Today?*"

"Based on your clenched teeth and need to repeat everything twice, I'm gonna assume that's a *no*."

"No, honey, not—not at all." Libby took Clara's frail hand in her own, offering her best stab at a reaffirming grin. "Listen to me. I think what you're doing with your list is wonderful. I want this to work so badly." She paused, a more serious expression crossing her face. "It *has* to. And Lord knows I'll help you any way I can." She shrugged her shoulders in a gesture of acceptance. "If it's a filthy canine that you want, how can I deny you? I'm just thankful you didn't want a hippo when you were ten."

"Honestly?" Clara couldn't help but wonder if it was "Backwards Day."

"I'll stock up on lint rollers."

Clara cracked a half-smile. "My treat. Wow. Leo bet me twenty dollars that hell would freeze over before you'd allow this."

"Well, I'm delighted I inspire my children to gamble."

Filled with appreciation of her mother's surprising support, Clara impulsively hugged her. "Thank you. Really." Then she had an idea. "Would you like to come with me to the animal shelter to pick out a puppy?"

Though Clara suspected Libby would have rather placed a cold beverage directly on the English antique mahogany coffee table without a coaster, she accepted the invitation, adding, "But first, how about we stop by the mall to check out one of those nifty Japanese robot dogs? I hear they're *much* better than the real thing. And no pooper-scooper required!"

"Nice try," Clara replied, already on her way upstairs to get dressed.

Still sluggish from her journey, Clara entered For Pets' Sake, River Pointe's local animal shelter, with zero preconceived notions about what type of dog she wished to adopt. Size, breed, age, and sex weren't of the slightest concern to her. She didn't care about the animal's personality, or how well it got along with other pets or people. It made no difference to her if it was cute or ugly, hairy or bald, neutered or pregnant with triplets. Considering such basic factors hadn't even occurred to Clara. As far as she was concerned, the only thing that mattered was accomplishing the first task on her time capsule list and crossing it off with the new red pen she'd purchased solely for this purpose. That is, until she spotted the scraggy, white-and-caramel-colored beagle. "There," she said, pointing. "At the end of the row over in the corner"—she indicated the puppy's cramped cage, telling Jane, the overzealous shelter employee wearing a sweater with a howling wolf on the front and back—"how about that sad little Snoopy spawn with only one ear?"

"You mean *Dumbo*?" Jane double-checked, surprised. Unlocking the metal cage, she removed the lethargic puppy. "You're the first person who's wanted to meet this fella. He was found in an alley about two months ago after being attacked by a bigger dog. The poor pup had most of his right ear bitten off and some other serious wounds. We weren't sure he was gonna make it. But, as you can see, he persevered. *Yes he did!*" She cooed in a silly voice, tickling the dog's belly. "He diddy widdy *did!*"

Dumbo didn't bat a lash.

"Can he hear?" Clara inquired.

"He sure can. He's just a quiet guy. *Aren't you?*" Jane scratched his head, but the dog remained motionless. "Aren't you waren't you?"

Libby rolled her eyes.

"Is he playing dead?" asked Clara.

"He sometimes looks that way at first," Jane explained.

"Charming. And he's healthy?" Libby probed. "He seems rather thin."

"Fit as a fiddle!" Jane nodded. "He's had all his shots and there's no sign of fleas or heartworm. He's been through a lot of misfortune, which is why he can seem a bit aloof, but he's very gentle and sweet."

Dumbo growled at Jane.

"His teeth were just cleaned. Would you like to hold him?" she asked Clara.

The moment the puppy landed in her extended arms, he began to bark, quietly at first, then louder. With his tail wagging back and forth like a high-speed windshield wiper, he covered Clara's thin face with wet, spastic kisses. "Well, hello there," she said and smiled. "Pleased to make your acquaintance." Then, turning to Jane, she declared in an emotionless tone, as if she were ordering a ham and cheese on rye at a deli counter, "I'll take him."

"Uh . . . Isn't this a bit hasty?" Libby cautioned, stepping forward. "You're certain he's the one? Don't you want to look at any others? A dog with two ears perhaps?"

"Nonsense." Clara nuzzled the wiggling puppy's head. "That's what makes him special."

Dumbo howled and licked her nose.

"Well, I'd say he likes you! *Yes he does!*" beamed Jane. "I'm delighted. We were concerned that because of his trauma, people might view him as damaged goods and disregard him."

Clara understood this theory all too well.

Libby narrowed her eyes. "Suffering a trauma does not render one *damaged goods*," she stated emphatically, accessing her inner Bette Davis and placing an authoritative hand on her hip.

Jane gulped.

And Clara, crouching down to pet Dumbo, managed to tear her focus away from her new pet long enough to smile up at her mother.

Libby shot her a quick wink. "Pack him up," she instructed the guilty-looking employee with a sweeping arm gesture. "He's coming with us."

When Clara asked if it would be all right to change his name, Jane stroked the dog's back and said, "Of coursey wourse."

"You hear that, Milk Dud?" Clara kissed her new puppy's paw. "Let's go home."

- ~~Have a pet dog (who cares if it sheds! BESIDES LIBBY!)~~

10.

Clara collected her coat and purse from the front hall closet. "I hate leaving you!" she said to Milk Dud. "Mommy just needs to take care of some very important business. I promise I'll be right back."

Milk Dud barked, jumping at her heels.

"Shhhh! Quiet now; Libby's trying to work." Clara nuzzled his head. "We don't want to get in trouble for disturbing her."

"Not to worry." Libby entered the foyer. "The Kleenex jingle I'm working on isn't due until after Christmas. My granddog can make all the noise he wants."

Clara was sure her ears were betraying her. "*Granddog?*"

"Got a problem with it?" Libby's eyebrows arched skyward. For someone who claimed not to care for dogs, she certainly took a natural and instant liking to Milk Dud, spoiling the scruffy beagle with expensive gourmet kibble and a boatload of new toys that squeaked, rattled, and bounced, creating a symphony of racket that Clara tried her best to stifle. "Now scram. If you don't get going soon, the stores will all be closed before you get there." Libby scooped Milk Dud up into her arms. "Don't worry. He'll be fine."

To Clara's surprise, earlier that day Libby had offered to dog-sit while Clara tended to the second point on her time capsule list: **Replace Lincoln's mom's beautiful vase I broke.** Leaving Boston with a ruthless singleness of purpose, she'd set a goal of accomplishing at least three list items during her first week back in Chicago in order to start her mission off on the correct foot. It was as if she needed to prove to herself that this wacky, unconventional plan of hers wasn't just hogwash, that it might actually work, and she possessed inside the necessary heart and resolve to see it through. Having been faithless for so long, an initial speck of belief was required to fuel her internal fire and propel her forward. Thus, Clara was determined to find the perfect vase and cross a big, fat line through said task on her list before Chef Guillaume's gingerbread class tomorrow. "You're positive you don't mind keeping an eye on Milk Dud?"

"Don't be silly," insisted Libby, stroking his remaining ear. "He'll keep me company while I wait for Todd to come fix the piano. The damn middle C key's sticking. I hope it's not serious."

"Todd the Tuner to the rescue again. I swear you should put that man on retainer. All right, I'm out of here." Clara kissed her mother and Milk Dud goodbye. "Wish me luck. I'm crossing my fingers I can find something that resembles Mrs. Foster's vase."

Once upon a time, Lincoln Foster and his family lived down the block from the Blacks on Broadview Lane. They moved to Sarasota when Lincoln and Clara were both fifteen, at which point they lost touch with each other, despite the fact that they'd always shared a close friendship growing up, even during their awkward teenage years, when hormones set in and relations between blossoming young men and women tend to become complicated.

Oh, did those two have a knack for getting into trouble together! They were nine years old and playing "Olympics" in Lincoln's living room, when Clara, "a two-time, gold-medal-winning gymnast from Yemen," accidentally double-cartwheeled into an antique, hand-blown glass vase that had belonged to Lincoln's great-great-grandmother. His mother came running when she heard the commotion, and upon discovering the broken shards of pearly, iridescent glass scattered about the carpet, she began to sob.

Although Clara, frightened, had known Mrs. Foster for years, she recalled looking at her more or less for the first time. She'd seen Libby shed tears on rare occasion—usually something involving her father, like on what would have been his birthday, or their wedding anniversary. But never had she witnessed an adult other than her own mother cry before. And it gutted her. Prior to this, it hadn't yet sunk in that grownups had real feelings too—that they were fragile, and human, just like herself. Who knew? Seeping with guilt, she instantly recognized this experience would leave an indelible mark in her memory. And she was correct.

Mrs. Foster forgave her right away, acknowledging, "Like it or not, accidents happen, and all we can do is move on." But Clara's remorse thrived. For a long time, she considered destroying the vase one of her biggest regrets. Even bigger than the summer Sun-In scandal that turned her hair green, or "Garbonzogate," when Leo dared her to snort a chickpea, resulting in a panicked trip to the emergency room to have it surgically removed from her nasal passage before it entered her brain.

"You don't sell any others? Possibly something about twelve inches tall, five inches wide, and pear-shaped with a delicate pearl or opal-type finish?" Clara asked Greg, the pint-sized Pottery Bin employee who smelled like Chanel No. 5. Clara recognized the fragrance because she used to wear it when Sebastian was alive and she actually bothered to spray on perfume. It always made her feel glamorous. It also didn't hurt to know that her fiancé adored the way it smelled on her. Clara recalled the time he attended a week-long podiatry conference in San Francisco. Neither of them had been happy about having to spend seven whole days apart (translation: an eternity). Late one evening while he was gone, Sebastian called Clara from his hotel room to wish her good night, which was something he always did when he was out of town, no matter how late it might have been. Clara could tell immediately by the sound of his voice that something had him down. "I just rode the elevator up to the twenty-third floor, where my room is, and there was a woman going to the penthouse who was wearing Chanel No. 5." Sebastian sighed. "I don't know. It sounds silly, but it's been a long couple days. I was already missing you to begin with. Smelling that scent just made it even worse."

Though Clara didn't like hearing the sad longing in his tone, she couldn't help but feel touched by the sweet sincerity of his response to her signature fragrance. "Oh, love," she replied sympathetically, "I'm sorry. I wish it would have been me on that elevator."

"So do I," said Sebastian, adding, "I wish you were here with me in my room right now."

"Well, that definitely makes two of us," Clara confessed. And an hour and a half of nonstop conversation later, they finally hung up the telephone.

"Well, why don't you be more specific about the vase you're looking for?" Greg teased Clara as he patted his stylish, side-swept bangs, ensuring they were in place. "I'm sorry, but this represents our entire inventory of vases. Unfortunately, what you see on this shelf here is what you get."

"I was afraid you'd say that." Clara sighed, trying her best to tune out the Christmas carols playing merrily in the background. *Hark go the bells, damn fucking bells . . .* She'd already heard that song twice that day. Ignoring the holiday was becoming harder and harder.

Leaning in toward her, Greg lowered his voice to a whisper. "This is *so* deviant of me, but have you tried looking at Crate & Basket yet? We're not supposed to say the *C-and-B* word here. Shhh! Don't tell!" He raised an index finger to his glossy lips, kicking his right leg up behind him.

"I was there earlier today. They didn't have what I'm looking for either," Clara said, moderately amused. "Thanks anyway, though. It looks like this ridiculous wild goose chase of mine is officially over."

Jutting out his bottom lip, Greg pouted.

Clara trudged out the door empty-handed yet full of frustration. After searching five different stores, she was starting to think it would be easier to locate a new kidney than a vase that even came close to resembling Mrs. Foster's. What a pain in the rear this stupid search was turning out to be.

Considering it was probably the thought behind the gesture that counted most, she pondered plodding back inside the *C-and-B word's* competition and purchasing any old vase, when suddenly she heard a high-pitched voice shouting at her.

"Hold up, buttercup!" Greg, wearing an oversized, lilac cashmere scarf, galloped toward her, his hair-sprayed bangs not blowing in the breeze. "You looked so blue when you left, I just couldn't take it! Two words: *Frank's Antiques.* It's on Ridge Road next to the diner. Tell the old dear Greg sent you. Toodles!" And with a flip of his hair, he spun around and sashayed back into the store.

Clara had never heard of Frank's Antiques, but she was familiar with the only diner in River Pointe and drove directly there.

The cluttered, musty-smelling shop was the size of a matchbox, and covered from floor to ceiling with what appeared to be mostly old junk. When Clara mentioned the name "Greg" to Frank, the portly Native American proprietor with waist-length gray hair, he kissed the top of her hand and assured her that he had exactly what she was looking for. "That would be lovely, but I must tell you, sir, at this point, I don't have much hope."

Examining her, Frank touched the long, turquoise amulet hanging from a weathered suede rope around his neck. "Well, then you've come to the right place." His smile was wide and sincere as he disappeared behind a crimson curtain into a back room.

Not likely, Clara thought to herself, staring at an old banjo with a bright-colored donkey painted on it. She couldn't imagine what type of person would own such a monstrosity.

Undoubtedly, someone with an unusual affinity for mules or with a mental illness.

Frank returned a few minutes later, huffing and puffing, holding a pearly white vase. "Here you go. From Switzerland. One of a kind." He handed it to Clara, eyeing her closely.

She inspected it, judging its weight in her hands.

"Well? What do you think?"

"I—I think it's perfect," she answered, amazed. The vase was smaller and more square-shaped than Mrs. Foster's had been, but it was gorgeous and would certainly suffice. Clara stared at Frank, shocked. "I can't believe it! How much does it cost?"

"Seventy-five dollars. But for you?" The Native American man grinned, forming deeply indented dimples in both cheeks. "The *Greg Special*: fifty dollars. Make it sixty and I'll throw in the beautiful banjo."

"That's very nice of you," Clara replied, tickled by his generosity. "And much appreciated. I'll take it. Uh, *just* the vase, that is." She returned it to him.

Frank nodded and began wrapping it in old newspaper.

Feeling the need to make polite small talk, Clara leaned against the dingy glass countertop covered in fingerprints. "With all due respect, I was positive I was wasting my time. *Positive*. I had no hope when I walked through your door."

Frank stopped wrapping to scrutinize her.

Clara wasn't sure why he was staring at her so intensely, but it was impossible for her to dismiss his penetrating gaze. "What?" she finally asked, shifting positions on her feet, self-conscious. "Is something wrong?"

"It's like I tell my other customers like you. Hopeless is *all* up here." He raised an index finger to his head and tapped it a couple of times.

Then he resumed packaging the vase. "Nobody wants that banjo."

Clara rummaged through her purse for her time capsule list, placed it on the countertop, and used her red pen to cross off **Replace Lincoln's mom's beautiful vase I broke.** "Well, I'll tell *you* something. You just made my day."

"Oh." Frank smiled again. "You did that all by yourself."

Clara glanced at her watch.

"In a hurry?"

Libby had given her Mrs. Foster's Florida address earlier that day, and Clara couldn't wait to get home, write her a letter to accompany the vase, and bring the package to the post office before it closed. She was also eager to return to Milk Dud, whom she already missed. "I'm a bit pressed for time," Clara confessed.

"Then I won't keep you." Frank placed the vase in a used shopping bag and handed it to her. "I can tell you're on an important mission."

"Actually?" She looked at Frank, surprised by his insight. "I am."

"Come back soon when you have more time," he said, grinning. And then, maintaining eye contact with her, he slowly lifted his finger to his head and tapped it again.

Clara couldn't quite identify what it was exactly, but there was something different and curious about him. Perhaps it was the simple kindness of a stranger, or maybe it was something deeper, but she left the antique shop feeling a little bit lighter.

Rushing through the front door of the house, Clara trumpeted to Libby, "Mission accomplished!" and crashed right into Todd, literally bouncing off the hunky piano tuner's chiseled chest and against the heavy oak door. "Oh my God! I didn't—I didn't see you there," she shrieked, grabbing her head with both hands, thankful she left the vase in the car. "I'm sorry!"

"No, *I'm* sorry! Are you okay? That wasn't just your *head* that made that awful thwack. *Was it?*" Todd looked terribly concerned. He also looked like Prince Charming from Walt Disney's animated version of *Snow White*, minus the tights.

"I'm fine. *Fine.*" Clara could feel the back of her stinging scalp beginning to throb. "Don't worry, my head's like metal." She had no idea why she just said that.

"Todd, I'm not sure if you remember my daughter, Clara." Libby closed her arm around Clara's waist. "She just moved back from Boston."

"*Temporarily,*" Clara added, seeing stars. "I'm in town on business."

"It's nice to bump into you again," Todd replied, grinning at his pun, which Clara failed to catch. "Uh"—he cleared his throat—"are you positive your head is okay?" He touched the side of Clara's arm.

Clara forced an artificial smile, assuring him she was fine.

Todd, however, did not appear convinced. "I know your head is like metal, but I think I might feel better if I could check up on you to make sure you're not just trying to set me at ease by *claiming* to be all right." Raising his chin and grinning at Clara, he eyed her skeptically. "By any chance would you happen to be free for dinner tomorrow night?"

"No, I'm taking a class in the city on gingerbread architecture that lasts until early evening. It's advanced." Distracted, Clara scanned the foyer for Milk Dud. "And I'm meeting my brother afterward."

Libby gave her an inconspicuous nudge.

"Fair enough," Todd said, nodding. "That sounds like fun. How about next Friday then?"

"Is Milk Dud asleep? Where's he hiding?" Clara asked her mother, calling, "Here boy! *Milk Dud!*"

Suddenly, she froze.

It dawned on her, better late than never, that Todd had just asked her out. On a date. *A date!* Clara hadn't gone out with another man since before Sebastian, and she wasn't about to set her sights on her mother's Sears catalogue-modeling piano tuner. Sorry, no way. Think again.

But then something most peculiar happened. Out of nowhere, her favorite Walt Whitman poem, "The Untold Want," invaded her brain. *The untold want, by life and land ne'er granted, Now, Voyager, sail thou forth, to seek and find* . . . It had been a long, long time since Clara last pondered these familiar verses, which she'd studied as an English major during college. And she'd all but forgotten that when she was starting out in the "real world" after graduation, and then embarking on her new life with Sebastian, they had served as a powerful source of inspiration, reminding her that she was responsible for her own fate. If ever there was a time to re-embrace this theory, it was now, Clara realized, wondering if it was her imagination, or if Todd's front tooth really did just sparkle. Alas, it couldn't hurt to give the man a few hours for one meal, she decided. It's not as if she was agreeing to pick out china patterns. Plus, she could always cancel if she changed her mind. Though it scared her, Clara knew what she had to do.

"Actually?" She tucked her hair behind her ear, taking a deep breath. "I . . . think I am available next Friday."

"Great," said a smiling Todd. "How about I pick you up around seven o'clock?"

"Sure," she muttered, still considering "The Untold Want."

- ~~Replace Lincoln's mom's beautiful vase I broke~~

II.

"The power of gingerbread should never be underestimated. Gingerbread is *more* than a cookie," Alfred Guillaume, standing behind a long, stainless steel countertop in the Cooking and Hospitality Institute of Chicago's test kitchen, dramatically declared in his thick French accent. "It is more than a lavish ornament. Gingerbread is *art*! It is a feeling inside here," he said, touching his heart, bowing his head. "Do you understand what I am saying? Do you *feel* what I say?"

Chef Guillaume's students, transfixed, with eyes open wide and pencils furiously jotting down notes, nodded at the *Time* magazine-dubbed "culinary God" as if he were preaching the gospel and they, his loyal disciples, could not get enough.

"It takes skill and the ability to follow instruction to bake a cookie. It takes *talent, passion,* and *soul* to *create* gingerbread architecture. I'm pleased to see you all brought your aprons today, because we will be getting messy on our journey to gingerbread land!" Bursting with enthusiasm, he plunged both hands into a giant mound of flour before him and then wiped them on his traditional chef uniform, laughing like a loon as tiny specks of white sprinkled his mustache. "We must not be afraid to get dirty on our delicious voyage together! And now, everybody up, *s'il vous plaît!* Up, up, up! *Un, deux, trois!*" He clapped his hands, signaling for the class to rise. "Let the gingerbread guide us!"

"*Let the gingerbread guide us?*" echoed Leo when Clara finished recounting the eccentric celebrity chef's wild introduction to the class. "I don't believe you. You're making this up," he said with a chuckle, turning the glass of Scuppernong Winter Ale in his hand.

"I couldn't make this stuff up if I tried," Clara assured him. "Chef Guillaume's more than a few buns short of a baker's dozen, but the man's a genius. In my life I have never seen gingerbread structures this intricate before. I still can't believe I actually built one myself. Of course, it's far from perfect. But it's not as bad as I thought it might be."

"I know it's become a challenge lately for you to enjoy anything positive or give yourself credit, but you *do* realize it's not a sin to have expectations, don't you?"

Clara picked up her glass of Merlot. "I'll show it to you after dinner. It's in my car."

"I'm sure it's outstanding." Leo grinned. "I'm glad you had fun. I had a feeling you would."

"*I'm* glad you were able to take a night off from prepping for your court case. Nice call to meet here. Despite all of these damn Christmas decorations everywhere." Clara rolled her eyes. It had been over a year since she and Leo last dined at a restaurant together, and she was especially pleased to be at one of their old favorites, Willie's, a classic Italian steakhouse near the famous Chicago Water Tower, which she'd always fancied due to its unique history. No matter how many times she strolled past the distinguished, Gothic Revival–style landmark, she couldn't resist giving its yellowing limestone a quick pat hello, and it never ceased to amaze her that although all of the city's other public buildings had perished in the Great Chicago Fire of 1871, this one, lone structure had managed to persevere. Somehow, through unfathomable devastation, it survived. The rare monument, now aglow with twinkling white holiday lights, had come to symbolize Chicago's fierce drive to continue. And in Clara's mind, it was the picture of beauty.

"Well, Ebenezer, I know how much you love this part of town," Leo replied.

Picking at her baked rigatoni and meatballs, Clara described the other students in the class, including a large woman named Svetlana who accidentally dropped her gingerbread "jailhouse" on the floor and cried like a baby, and how Chef Guillaume not only autographed Clara's copy of C Is for Cookie, Bitch!, but also wrote a thoughtful note in which he referred to her as "My darling Claire." People had mistakenly been calling her "Claire" her entire life. It used to drive her bananas, but such trivialities no longer even registered on her radar. Clara, Sara, Tara, Tyrone . . . Did it really matter?

When the subject of gingerbread had at last been exhausted, Clara briefed Leo on her time capsule list progress. Showing him several photographs of Milk Dud, she mentioned that she'd stopped at the post office on her way downtown to mail Mrs. Foster's vase, and then oh-so-casually spilled the beans about her upcoming date with Todd, quickly adding, "I'm debating if I should order another glass of wine or switch to Scuppernong."

Leo put down his steak knife, a look of amusement covering his face. "*Todd* Todd? You mean, piano tuner *I'm-a-suave-Sears-model* Todd?"

Clara nodded.

"That's great news," he said without a trace of insincerity. He resumed eating. "Todd seems like a good guy."

Clara was surprised when Leo left the teasing at that and didn't bombard her with questions. She suspected her brother was making a careful effort not to cross the line on such a sensitive subject as dating. His internal moral barometer had always been properly calibrated when it came to pushing her too far, especially lately. Still, for some reason Clara felt the need to spell out her stand on the issue, as if Sebastian was sitting right there with them. And for all intents and purposes, he was. "Trust me, I have no interest in dating Todd, or anyone for that matter. It's just too soon. *Way* too soon . . ." She picked at something on the table with her finger. Then she stopped picking. "But when he asked me to dinner, all—and I mean *all*—I could think about was 'The Untold Want'—"

"You mean that poem you used to be obsessed with?"

"Exactly." Clara held her fork in midair and looked at him. "I could not get it out of my head, Leo. It was the strangest thing. And then it made me realize, maybe now is not the best time to be rejecting new opportunities and experiences."

"I couldn't agree more. I'll have you know you're impressing me here."

"So, I was thinking that as long as I really am doing this time capsule thing, then *perhaps* it might not hurt to adopt a '*Now, Voyager*' type of attitude in tandem. Know what I mean? 'Sail thou forth, to seek and find'?" She took a small bite of meatball. "It's not like I have anything to lose."

"I think it's a brilliant idea." Obviously pleased, Leo extended his bottle of Scuppernong and clinked it against Clara's glass. "Feliz navi-*Todd*!"

"Oh, I knew you had more in you!"

After Leo stopped chuckling and the waitress had cleared their empty plates, he put his hands behind his neck and leaned on the back legs of his chair. "I have an idea I've been meaning to run by you."

"Shoot . . ."

"A judge I know, terrific man—Judge Bennett's his name—he's relocating to San Diego for work after the first of the year. His condo's been on the market for the last six months, and so far there have been no takers. Now he's in a real jam because irrespective of whether the place sells, he has to be in California sitting behind that bench come the first week of January."

Clara twirled the ice in her water glass. "I think I see where this is going . . ."

"It's a one-bedroom unit in a luxury high-rise overlooking Lake Michigan. You couldn't ask for a better neighborhood." Leo watched his sister's expression closely. "If you're interested in checking it out, it could be a nice, short-term living situation. And it would be helping the judge out, so I presume he'd offer you a good deal. The only thing is, it still won't be cheap, and in the event that the place sells, you'll have to vacate immediately. Oh! And it comes unfurnished, so you'd probably need to buy a few things."

"Does the building allow dogs?"

"Affirmative. The judge has a Maltese."

Pondering it, Clara stared behind the restaurant's tinsel-adorned bar at the automated Santa Claus waving from his flying sleigh. Rocking his head back and forth as he laughed and waved . . . laughed and waved . . . laughed and waved . . . he seemed to be egging her on in an almost sinister fashion. Clara shifted her focus to her lap. Her sabbatical was not paid, which was fine with her. Still, money wasn't an issue, thanks to Sebastian's sizable life insurance policy. So far, she'd refused to touch a penny of it, for in her mind there was a direct correlation between accepting the money and moving on, farther and farther away from him. Not only did she want nothing to do with the money, the thought of it actually sickened her. However, the concept of continuing to lodge with Libby in her time warp bedroom brimming with the spirit of Swayze was also unappealing. After spending too long together, Clara and her mother had a tendency to clash like mayonnaise and sunshine, and she viewed finding her own Chicago digs as a necessary preemptive strike. Plus, she'd been in town less than a week and already yearned for the privacy and independence she'd long been accustomed to. Alas, sooner or later, she was going to have to dip into those forbidden funds. It was inevitable. And she knew it.

"Okay." Clara nodded solemnly at Leo, still staring down at her lap. "I guess I'll take a look at it, if possible."

"Done. I'll make arrangements with the judge."

Clara hugged her thin arms and began running her hands up and down them. She sighed. Her voice was quiet and low. "Thanks for keeping your eye out for me."

Aware of her stand on the insurance money, Leo crumpled

his napkin into a ball and tossed it at her face, softly adding as it bounced of her nose, "It's all gonna be okay."

Somehow, when it was her brother saying these words, Clara almost believed it. *Almost.*

After paying the bill, Leo walked her to her car. She commanded him to close his eyes while she carefully removed her gingerbread creation from its protective box and positioned it on the backseat. "Hold on two more seconds. I just want to get it angled right for you."

When she was finally ready for the big reveal, she invited him to take a gander. "Okay. You can open your eyes now."

"*Whoa . . .*" Leo stared at it for a minute, awestruck, while Clara held her breath. "Are you serious? You made that?"

Sticking her hands in her coat pockets, Clara nodded, the frosty night air blowing her hair back. "Guilty as charged."

"Wow, Clara. I don't know what to say. It's . . . it's amazing! It's the *WATER TOWER!*" Leo glanced behind him at the actual landmark down the block. "It looks *exactly* like the real thing! Only much tastier," he gushed, gently touching the green gumdrop wreath hanging from a red licorice ribbon on the nougat door as if he were feeling the tender spot on a newborn's head. "Jesus. I'm blown away."

"Thank you." Clara's cheeks grew pink. It had been ages since she'd blushed with any emotion. For the first time in as long as she could remember, she actually felt proud of herself. And it made her smile.

- ~~Build a gingerbread house from scratch (no dumb farty kits allowed!) (and who cares if it's messy! BESIDES LIBBY!)~~

12

Clara closed her closet door with more force than she'd intended. "Why did I agree to this? This is a terrible idea. The last thing I want to do right now is have dinner with *Todd*." She said his name as if it were laced with poison. "I don't even know the man. He probably has herpes. And I left my brown boots in Boston!"

"I have a pair of tan, high-heel boots that you're welcome to borrow," Libby offered in a calm tone, keeping a safe distance from Clara in the hallway outside her bedroom. "And Todd does not have herpes. Why would you say such a thing?"

"I don't know." Clara moped across her room. "Why would I tell a complete stranger that I'd have dinner with him? If you haven't noticed, I'm not exactly in top form." She slumped into the chair at her mirrored vanity. "I hope Todd likes ponytails because I'm not doing my hair for him."

"You haven't done your hair in close to a year. And you're acting ridiculous. Todd is not a *stranger*. He's a perfectly lovely, herpes-free gentleman and you're going to have a wonderful time if you'll just change your attitude and relax."

"Know what would be *perfectly lovely?*" Clara snorted. She didn't wait for Libby to answer. "Staying home and watching a *Golden Girls* rerun on TV with Milk Dud."

Reclining on Clara's bed with his new friend, Natalie Marissa, Milk Dud raised his head as if on cue, listened a minute with his remaining ear up, and then put his head back down between his paws.

"And why are you lurking in the doorway like a perp?" Clara demanded.

"Because I'm afraid to get any closer." Libby had never been one to lie. "And I'm sorry to have to point it out, but you are using Betty White as a form of escape."

"*What?*"

Exhaling, Libby entered the room with caution, walking on eggshells toward her daughter. Standing behind her, she placed a hand on Clara's tense, bony shoulder, locking eyes with her reflection in the mirror. "I can vividly remember how it felt going on my first date after your father died. His name was Warren Noble. He took me to Chung's Chinese Palace." Libby smiled, recalling the event. "I was sure it would be a disaster. It felt like I was doing something deceitful and wrong. Like I was violating a sacred code . . ." She scrutinized Clara's reaction to what she was saying. Then she shrugged. "In my mind, I was cheating on your dad. I was nervous and conflicted—"

"*And?*" Clara impatiently pressed, fingering a bobby pin. "Did your date with Warren turn out as badly as you expected?"

"Yes," her mother said, nodding. "It did."

Clara got up and began pacing. "Great! Thank you for sharing."

"*At first,*" Libby stressed, "thanks to a rancid sweet and sour shrimp. I tossed my fortune cookies right there at the table. I even got some on poor Warren's bolo." She shook her head at the memory. "But you know what happened after that?"

"Warren required therapy for the rest of his life?"

"Hey. Watch your tone. *It broke the ice,*" Libby said slowly. She paused to make sure Clara was paying attention. "I was so humiliated that I stopped worrying and feeling guilty about your father, and I started to actually enjoy myself. The next thing I knew, Warren and I were getting on like wildfire. We even went out again."

"Really?" Standing still, Clara wondered why she had never heard this story before.

"Really." Libby smiled. "I only wish I'd figured it all out sooner. The point is, eventually, Clara-pie, I realized it was not a crime to spend time with another man. It wasn't even a crime to care about another man. But it *was* a crime to hole myself up in a room with my piano and deny myself the chance at companionship or love. Your father wouldn't have wanted that for me. Not in a million years." Tenderly cupping Clara's chin in the palm of her hand, she looked her deep in the eyes. Her next words were spoken in the gentlest of tones. "Sebastian wouldn't have wanted that for you either."

Although it made her heart sink, Clara knew her mother was right.

Libby ambled back toward the doorway. "I also realized one should never order shrimp on a date. *Never.* On that note, can I interest you in a glass of wine to take the edge off? *I* could certainly use one."

Clara nodded. "Yes, please. I think that's probably a good idea."

Clara stared at her reflection in the mirror. She couldn't remember the innocence and excitement that once coursed through her veins when she sat in this very same spot as a teenager preparing for a big date, wondering if perhaps that evening she might get a hickey or go to second base—or, if she was lucky, *both*. She couldn't really feel life before Sebastian as something she'd once lived. It seemed light-years away, almost like a dream. It reminded Clara of a line spoken by Satan, the miserable fallen angel, in John Milton's epic poem, "Paradise Lost": *We know no time when we were not as now.*

Still staring in the mirror, deep in thought, Clara sighed. Considering Libby's anecdote, she removed her ponytail holder, gave her limp hair a good shake, and picked up her brush. Then, feeling badly for behaving like a herpes-hating handful, she thanked her mother before she disappeared down the hallway. And it wasn't the wine for which Clara was grateful.

"*Look!*" Clara squealed. "It's a mariachi band!" She pointed at the three musicians dressed in traditional, silver-studded charro outfits with wide-brimmed hats weaving their way toward Todd's and her table. "I love mariachi music!" She clapped her hands with delight.

Clara wasn't sure how Todd had managed to score a table on a Friday night with such short notice at Mantequilla, the hottest Mexican restaurant in town. The last she had heard, it took months to secure a reservation at the renowned, vibrantly colored cantina with a private telephone number and secret celebrity entrance in the back. When Todd first mentioned that's where they'd be dining, Clara had immediately wished she was on better terms with Tabitha, a true Mexican food aficionado and celebrity gossip fan, so that she could call her up and tell her all about it. She hadn't spoken to her estranged best friend since she left for Chicago, but she knew Tabitha would have been chomping at the bit for details. Clara might not have been certain how Todd was able to breeze through the exclusive door at Mantequilla, but she was certain that the fresh pomegranate margaritas they were drinking were *muy, muy deliciosa.* "Let's order another round," she suggested. "These puppies are fantastic!" She slapped her palm against the table, causing their shared basket of tortilla chips to jump. "Hey! Did I tell you I just got a new puppy?"

Amused, Todd ran his fingers through his thick, brown hair. "You did mention 'The One-Ear Wonder' a couple of times. I'm looking forward to meeting this Milk Dud . . ."

"That's my favorite candy." Clara drained the last sip of her margarita. "What's yours?"

"Are you sure you're up for another round?" Todd peered at her from across the table as if he wasn't quite positive this was a wise idea. "I'm wondering if perhaps we should get some dessert instead. My old college buddy Luke is the executive chef here and sweets are one of his secret strengths. He makes a vicious vanilla flan. Any interest in splitting one?"

Tilting her head to the side, Clara mulled it over. "Mmmmm . . . no thank you. I'm stuffed from the carne asada. Oh, and *that guacamole!* Guacamooooole," she repeated. "That's a fun word to say. Talk about green ecstasy in a bowl." She let out a soft little satisfied moan. "I vote for another margarita."

"Well, I suppose if you *insist*," Todd conceded. "Who am I to argue with Milk Dud's mom? Not to mention Libby Black's daughter."

Todd certainly was a charmer, Clara thought to herself. He was also an excellent conversationalist. She appreciated that he really seemed to listen when she spoke about Scuppernong and Boston and rare gingerbread decorations. He knew when to crack a joke, yet he also knew when to be serious and sincere. And Clara had no idea how it had taken her this long to notice Todd's strong, chiseled jaw, or those perfectly shaped lips, or those big, sexy, capable hands. There was no denying the man was blessed with incredibly attractive physical features.

Bouncing to her feet, Clara excused herself to visit the *señoritas'* room.

Before Todd had a chance to rise, Clara was already slipping in and out and sideways between groups of animated people waiting to be seated at the crowded bar. Shaking his head with a chuckle, he waved their waiter over and ordered a final round of drinks.

Clara hadn't quite realized how strong the beverages were until she took a few steps and noticed that her head felt pleasantly light, and the chaotic, Technicolor room appeared to be slightly off kilter, like a carnival fun-house attraction. "Hi!" she said to a primitive-looking mask hanging on the wall when she almost bumped into it on her way to the bathroom. "Wow . . ." She opened her eyes wide, aware that she was mighty buzzed from the booze.

Although able to hold her liquor like a professional, it had been a long, long time, and many lost pounds, since Clara had last partaken of anything stronger than a pint or two of Scuppernong, and she'd completely forgotten what it felt like to be even mildly intoxicated. At the moment, it didn't just feel good. It felt freakin' fabulous. It was about darn time she finally let loose and indulged in some real fun, she decided while searching for a paper towel by the bathroom sink. When she couldn't find anything to dry her hands with, she bent over and wiped them on the inside layer of her skirt.

"Good idea," said a woman in a revealing black mini-dress standing at the next sink over, mimicking Clara's impromptu maneuver.

The return trip from the bathroom back to her table was a winding, jumbled journey that involved a narrowly avoided collision with a waitress balancing a tray of flan and an accidental pop into the kitchen as Clara struggled to remember where she and Todd were sitting. Eventually, she spotted the hostess, who kindly escorted Clara to her table, winking. "Trust me, between the killer margaritas and the size of this place, guests get lost here all the time."

"Well, thanks for the assist," Clara said with a smile. "Next time I go to the bathroom I'll be sure to bring my compass!"

After she and Todd had said a quick hello to his friend Luke and finished their last round of drinks, Todd paid the bill, peeked at his watch, and grinned. "Well? What do you say? Shall I take you home?"

Clara thought about it for a moment. She reminded herself, like a good little dedicated voyager, to *sail thou forth* . . . Then, pushing her hair away from her face, she coyly replied, "No."

Months ago, while taking a summer stroll through the Boston Common with Tabitha, she had discussed how strange and unsettling it was to know that the last person she had slept with was dead. "It's a tough feeling to describe. It's just . . . I don't know"—Clara had tightened her face, searching for the right word—"*morbid*, if that makes any sense. I know it sounds like a bizarre concept, but I've spoken about it with other people who've lost their partners, and it's a common issue. You'd be surprised. Don't get me wrong, it's not as if I'm interested in having sex for the sheer sake of having it. That's not it at all. It's just *weird* to know that the last person I did it with is no longer living," she had explained, trying not to remember how wonderful and exciting things had always been with Sebastian in the bedroom. And the shower. And the kitchen. And once in the attic crawl space, but that had been an isolated incident interrupted by a raccoon. Turning to her friend, she had inquired, "Have you ever had sex with a dead person?"

With a horrified look of shock, the elderly gentleman sitting on the opposite end of Clara and Tabitha's park bench feeding the pigeons had stood up and quickly walked away.

"Well, then where would you like to go next?" Todd asked Clara, a look of intrigue crossing his handsome face. "There's a lounge I like called Nightingale's down the street from here. Not that I'm suggesting we need anything more to drink."

"Oh dear, definitely not." Clara giggled, kicking her feet back and forth underneath the table. "Hmmm, I don't know." She shrugged innocently, as if she hadn't a clue in the world. "How about we go back to your place?" She looked him directly in the eyes when she spoke, consciously deepening her seductive smile.

Todd appeared enthralled, as she intended him to be. But, once again, he narrowed his eyes, giving her that familiar, skeptical grin of his. "Those margaritas were *pretty potent*." He enunciated his *t*'s as if he were performing on a stage. "I must say, I've never been one to take advantage of a beautiful woman. And, in case I haven't told you yet, you *are* beautiful."

"Oh, *hot-Toddy*." A blush came to Clara's cheeks. "You say the sweetest things. Don't you want to tune my pipes?"

Todd's brown eyes expanded and his eyebrows arched in a seemingly subconscious gesture.

"*Joking!*" she blurted. Seeing his immediate surprise, Clara bowed her head in a girlish manner, trying, unsuccessfully, to suppress her laughter. "I'm only teasing, of course. Thought I'd throw in a little piano humor for ya there . . ."

"I appreciate that." Todd flirted back, gazing at her. "The world needs more piano humor."

"My sentiments exactly." Clara's smile vanished and was replaced with a serious, sultry visage. "But I would like to go to your place." Biting her bottom lip, she stared at him, waiting.

By the time they arrived at Todd's apartment near the John Hancock Building, Clara had already determined that she had no intention of returning to Libby's. Not that evening, at least.

"I have a confession," Todd whispered, standing just inches away from her in the living room next to his shiny, white, candelabra-topped grand piano that reminded Clara of Liberace. "This is not how I imagined our date ending." He slowly traced his hands up and down her back, causing her to shiver.

"Really?" Clara's mind was swirling. She couldn't think of a single intelligent thing to say.

Reaching out, Todd lifted her chin, examining her in the

glow of the dimly lit chandelier. And then, with a hungry smile, he slowly leaned in for a kiss.

Right before their lips were about to meet, when there was but a fraction of a millimeter between them and Clara could taste his spicy burrito breath, she suddenly snapped her head to the side and grabbed his hand, slurring, "Take me to bread . . ."

13

When on earth did her mother develop an affection for Meat Loaf? Clara wondered, awoken by a dramatic rendition of the stringy-haired musician's famous ballad "I'd Do Anything for Love (But I Won't Do That)" being played on the piano. Cracking one eye a quarter of the way open, she glanced at her watch beneath the covers. And since when did Libby tickle the ivories at seven-fifteen in the morning? This was not at all like her. She wasn't even usually awake at this hour, let alone already fast at work in the music room.

Clara could not only feel her head throbbing, she could actually hear it, as if someone were rhythmically pounding a low-toned tympani drum inside of her skull. She tried to swallow, but her tongue stuck to the roof of her palate, and her chalky mouth was too dry. "Oh God," she muttered out loud, suppressing the urge to vomit.

When Clara finally managed to open both eyes, her vision was blurry at first, but eventually, with some effort, she was able to focus clearly. She saw a familiar old banjo leaning against the wall. It had a brightly colored donkey painted on it. *"OH GOD!"* she said louder, instantly recognizing the homely instrument from Frank's Antiques, where she'd purchased the vase for Lincoln Foster's mother. Never in her life had she seen another mule banjo like it. *"Oh God . . . Oh God . . . OhGodOhGodOh . . . Lord, have mercy . . ."*

Jolting upright in a disoriented, wide-eyed panic, she wondered if she was dead. In her mind, it was a distinct possibility.

Then, feeling a chill on her fanny and noticing that she was naked, she wondered where the hell her clothes were.

And that's when Clara heard the singing.

"And I would do anything for love, I'd run right into hell and back . . ."

Horror-stricken, she covered her face with both hands as she realized that it was not Libby crooning the mushy opus. It was Todd. And she had slept with him. Like a sleazy, margarita-guzzling, two-bit whore. Or even worse—a one-bit whore.

Yearning to curl up into a ball and disappear, she only wished she was dead. How could she have let this happen? How could she have done this to Sebastian? *HOW?*

Queasy and weak, Clara strained to get out of bed, racing around the room as if she were on fire, collecting articles of clothing strewn all over the place as she berated herself. She didn't want to know how her bra had come to be hanging on the plastic window blinds. Nor did she care to learn why Todd had an open can of Cheez Whiz on his nightstand.

"And maybe I'm crazy, oh it's crazy and it's true . . ." he sang in a falsetto as Clara tiptoed down the carpeted hallway toward the front door, praying praying praying with all her

soul that she would be able to sneak out of the apartment un-
noticed.

But when she glimpsed Todd, sitting in nothing but a
snug pair of red, Santa-themed briefs at the Liberace-inspired
piano with an orange juice-box at his side, she couldn't help
but gasp.

"Good morning!" he said, beaming, instantly stopping his
song. "Sleep okay?"

"*Oh, God!*"

"Hey now, are you staring at my instrument?" He quirked
an eyebrow at her.

Quickly shielding her eyes, Clara spun around. "*No!* Not
at all! I wasn't. I was just—I was—"

"Relax," Todd interrupted, laughing. "I'm only teasing. I
was referring to my piano. Remember? *From last night?*"

Clara's expression remained blank.

"Thought I'd throw in a little '*piano humor*' for ya." He
winked.

The previous evening was a blur, but Clara recalled her
off-colored "pipe tuning" sorry attempt at a joke. And she regretted it.

"I always like to start the day off warming this baby up."
Todd patted the top of his piano. "I think it's important to
feel 'one' with your instrument. There's something spiritual
and grounding about it. Know what I mean?"

Clara did not know what he meant. "Was that banjo I saw
in your bedroom from Frank's Antiques?"

"Donkey Strings?" Todd smiled, impressed. "Sure was."
He explained how he had recently acquired "the beauty"
when he spotted it in the Christmas display window of the

antique shop on his way to lunch at the diner next-door. "She just spoke to me. I took one look, and knew I had to have her. The colors are so vibrant and inspiring. I've never seen anything like it."

"Me neither." Clara desperately eyed the front door. "You know, I should . . . I should really get going. I need to take Milk Dud out and feed him—he's probably starving by now—and I still have a *ton* of holiday shopping to—"

"Don't you want a waffle? Or some sausage?"

Feeling her gag reflex activate, Clara fought the impulse to cringe. "*HA!*" She pointed at Todd, forcing a broad, jittery smirk. "More piano humor?"

"Uh, no . . ." He nodded at the platter of waffles and sausages on the marble breakfast bar separating the kitchen from the living room. "I made us breakfast. You know what they say . . . It's the most important meal of the day."

"That it is," Clara concurred, inching her way toward the doorway, pondering whether he'd cooked breakfast wearing only his teeny-tiny Santa briefs as well. "Well, okay then . . . Thanks again for last night. It was—" She lost her train of thought when Todd stood up, facing her directly in all his semi-nude, hairy, stark white glory. "*Oh God!* I—I really gotta go." She threw open the front door, causing the sleigh bells hanging from the doorknob to jingle. "Meat Loaf sounds great!" Gesturing an overenthusiastic thumbs up, Clara made a mad dash for the street, hoping she might have the good fortune of getting run over by a car on the way home.

14

Outside, large, wet snowflakes fell from the gray December sky, and the sharp wind burned Clara's lungs, causing her eyes to tear and her cheeks to sting. Spotting a public trash can at the nearest street corner amidst the winter wonderland, she hurried in its direction, holding her breath. She slid on a patch of ice along the way and nearly tumbled to the ground, but, flailing her arms, she grabbed hold of a nearby tree and regained her balance just in the nick of time. Bending over the cold, metal wastebasket, Clara clutched its paint-chipped rim with both hands as she regurgitated. When at last she was able to catch her breath, she slowly straightened her spine, but another wave of sickness immediately racked her frail body and she began heaving once again before she had a chance to lean over.

"Mommy, look! That lady's barfing! *Ewwww!*" cried a little pigtailed girl in a sled being pulled by her mother.

After several minutes, when Clara was certain that there was nothing left in her system to expel, she cautiously resumed an upright position. Shaking and disoriented, she glanced over her shoulder at the Salvation Army Santa Claus standing on the sidewalk, ringing his silver bell, collecting money for the needy as he openly stared at her.

"You all right, miss?" a concerned man holding a briefcase stopped to ask, startling her.

Embarrassed, Clara wiped her mouth with the back of her hand, nodding, frightened that if she tried to speak she might vomit again.

God, she felt pathetic. "Thank you," Clara managed to respond. "I appreciate your concern, but I'm all right. I really am," she repeated, more to herself than to the worried-looking man with the briefcase. "If you could maybe help me hail a taxi, that would be more than kind of you." Trembling, she tried to smile at him, but she couldn't muster the strength.

"You just hold on right there." The gentleman raised his arm in the air and stepped into the slush-filled street. "I got you covered. This shouldn't take but a minute."

A bright yellow cab came to a screeching halt and the man opened the car door for Clara. "You know where you're going?" he asked when she was safely deposited in the back-seat.

The truth was, Clara felt as if she didn't know anything. Not anymore. Not after what she'd just done with Todd. Nodding, Clara thanked the kind man once again. She wanted to let him know how grateful she was for his assistance, but her stomach still felt queasy, and she decided it was best to play it safe. After all, she wasn't in the habit of up-chucking on Good Samaritans.

"You got enough cash to get where you're going?" he inquired.

Again, Clara nodded. Patting her purse, she whispered "yes," certain that this was one of the most mortifying experiences of her life.

She couldn't help but notice the flash of pity in the man's eyes as he gently closed the car door. "Take good care of her now," he told the cabbie, adding, "You might want to drive extra slow."

"Well, I'd say *someone* had a good night." Libby grinned with a knowing look when Clara arrived home. She set a blossoming, red poinsettia down on the table in the center of the foyer. "If I hadn't known who you were with, I'd have been worried."

"I don't want to talk about it," Clara muttered as Milk Dud, thrilled to see his master, came racing her way, barking up a storm. "Shhhh! Quiet, boy." Her body ached too much to bend down and pet him.

"What's the matter?"

"Nothing." Clara shook her head, turning around and slowly removing her jacket. The last thing she wanted to do was explain to her mother why it was stained.

"I know when something's wrong." Libby shifted the poinsettia an inch toward the right. "Didn't you have a nice time with Todd?"

"That's one way to put it," Clara mumbled, spilling with guilt. Not to mention self-disgust.

"What does that mean?"

Clara cringed. "It means I did something stupid. Okay? Something stupid and terrible. That's what it means." The words came out with a harsher edge than she had intended. Lifting her hand to her forehead, she realized her mother probably wasn't going to stop pressing until she had answers.

Still barking at an earsplitting volume, Milk Dud jumped spastically at her feet, begging for attention.

"Honey, what are you talking about?"

"I slept with Todd!" Clara suddenly snapped, unable to keep this shameful secret to herself a second longer. "There you have it. *We had sex*," she proclaimed. "Possibly with Cheez Whiz." Closing her eyes, she inhaled a deep breath.

Then she noticed that the room had suddenly fallen suspiciously silent.

When Clara opened her eyes again, she discovered Milk Dud licking something seemingly quite tasty off the toe of her boot. "*NO!*" she gasped, shaking her leg. "*No!* Milk Dud, stop it! Stop!" Disgusted, she tried to drive him away as she quickly removed her shoes. "I said NO!"

"Why are you yelling at him like that?" Libby demanded with a reproachful glare, her arms lifting in a gesture of confusion.

"Because it's *vomit* that he's eating off my boots. Why don't you ask me some more questions? Christ almighty! I threw up this morning. On the street! After I had sex with Todd! Who, by the way, plays piano practically *nude*. I'm a cheap, barfing whore!" She stopped herself just in the nick of time before adding, "And I hate myself."

"Clara, you are not a cheap, barfing whore," Libby said calmly. "And those are not *your* boots."

"Oh God," she winced. She had no patience for this. None whatsoever. "I—I'll replace them."

Libby placed a hand on her daughter's arm. "Sweetheart. I was *teasing*. I could care less about those boots."

"I'm sorry, but I really don't have a sense of humor about this." It looked as if Clara was nearing the verge of tears. "You don't understand . . . Todd was the first man since—" She stopped speaking, letting the thought break off in the sudden agony.

Grasping the cast of despair about her daughter, Libby's expression turned serious. "I apologize. I didn't mean to be flip. Really . . . I can see how upset you are. And, contrary to what you may believe, I do understand." She motioned her head toward the cushioned bench in the foyer. "Why don't we sit down and talk?"

Clara drew in a deep breath. "I need to be alone right now." Physically and emotionally spent, she sighed, trying to erase the pervading image of nearly naked, Meat Loaf–playing Todd from her mind. "I'm gonna go take a shower."

She slowly began slogging up the evergreen garland and holly-adorned staircase. "Until June."

15.

"It's *Christmas dinner*, for God's sake. Please don't do this, butt-face." Leo stared at his sister, beseeching. "Please. It won't be the same without you. You *have* to come with us to Aunt Billie's house."

"I'm an adult, Leo. I don't have to do anything," Clara mumbled, lying beneath her covers in bed. Though it was only late in the afternoon, she was already wearing a long, flannel nightgown, a glaring contrast to her brother's tailored sport coat. And an overt symbol of protest.

Standing at the foot of her bed, Leo shook his head and sighed, his cheeks puffing out with air. "I can't believe you're boycotting the holiday. Who does that? You really want to stay home all alone and miss out on Christmas? *Christmas*," he repeated for effect.

"Yes. That's exactly what I want to do. If you all will just let me, that is." Clara realized she sounded as frustrated and melancholy as she appeared. Surviving her first Christmas without Sebastian was turning out to be significantly more agonizing than she'd anticipated. Though she tried her best to block them out, haunting memories of all the jolly holidays they had shared in the past flooded her mind, causing her to feel as if she were drowning, and her wounds were suddenly as fresh again as the glistening snowflakes falling outside her window. She thought about the pink cashmere mittens Sebastian had given her last Christmas morning and how warm and cozy they felt when she slipped her hands through his on the dreamy winter walk they took together shortly after Libby's annual Christmas brunch feast. With the snow gently falling, holding hands, taking in the stunning scenery, and each other, it would have been impossible not to get swept up in the intoxicating, Christmasy romance of the moment— all that was missing was maybe Bambi, a few deer pals, and a blue jay or two to come moseying by singing *Walking in a Winter Wonderland,* and then offer them a thermos of hot cocoa—with marshmallows, of course.

"I told Libby I'm not celebrating Christmas this year. Period. End of story. I just can't do it," Clara said. "I don't know why that's so difficult to understand."

"First of all, because it's your favorite holiday," answered Leo. "You own eighty different Christmas albums that you keep alphabetized, and every December you make your house look like the frickin' North Pole. You live for Christmas. Need I remind you last year at this same time we were tossing back candy-cane martinis in Libby's kitchen and you were trying your best to convince us all to plan a 'family vacation' to Santa Claus, Indiana?" Known as one of the most Christmasy landmarks in the nation, the famous town filled with passionate Santa fanatics draws in more than one million visitors per year. Each local shop and every single street has a Christmas-themed name (Blitzen Boulevard, Comet's Café, and Rudolph's R.V. Resort), and at its annual "Land of Lights," all of the residents of the eight-hundred-house neighborhood decorate their homes with over-the-top light displays in what equates to an epic, 1.2-mile-long, brilliantly blinking holiday adventure. No question about it, the people of Santa Claus, Indiana, love Christmas all year long. Jolly ol' Saint Nick has taken over their lives, and it is a spectacle not to be missed. At least, as far as Clara had been concerned.

"Yeah, well . . . a lot's changed since then," Clara replied in an emotionless tone, as if she were part robot. "I don't get why it's so hard to understand why I'm not celebrating this year."

"Because we're always together as a family on this night," Leo emphasized, incredulous. "That's why. It's a tradition that's never been broken. *We celebrate Christmas together.* We open presents and gorge ourselves on holiday brunch together at Libby's, and then we revisit the insanity all over again for dinner at Aunt Billie's. Together. That's how our family celebrates."

"Don't you get it?" Clara hissed, sitting up in bed. "I have nothing to celebrate! And a major part of my family is gone. You have no idea how this feels. I'm sorry to make a scene, but this is really hard for—" Interrupted by her ringing cell phone, she allowed her thought to trail off as she glanced down at the display screen.

Tightening her jaw, Clara turned off her phone and shoved it aside on her bed.

Leo's eyebrows pulled together. "Let me guess. That was Todd again?"

Clara's eyes squeezed shut as she exhaled. "Please don't say his name. That man's relentless." Consumed with guilt and shame over sleeping with him, she had been ignoring his calls for the past few weeks, praying the persistent piano tuner would finally take a hint and just leave her alone already. "And for the record, I am not proud of the way I'm behaving toward him."

"Then why don't you at least speak to the guy?"

"Because just *thinking* about him makes my stomach turn." Clara shook her head. "I know it's weak—I know *I'm* weak . . . But I just . . . I—I can't deal with him right now. I really can't. My life is complicated enough as it is. *He's* not the one who matters to me."

Leo directed his gaze down toward Clara's pink carpet. He weighed each word before he spoke it. "I know that," he began in a tender voice. "And I know how badly you miss Sebastian. I don't blame you. But the truth—"

"Look, Leo," Clara interrupted, her tormented tone low and gruff, "I do not want to discuss this right now. The last thing I feel is *merry*, and I have no desire to be around people. So please don't make this any harder for me than it already is. I'd rather not ruin your holiday too. Okay?"

Based on Leo's unhappy face, it was anything but okay. "Well, perhaps after you partake of Aunt Billie's super-strength eggnog you won't feel quite so miserable."

Clara rolled her eyes, not at all surprised that her brother was putting up a strong fight. "I'm sorry and I love you. But my mind's made up." Hoping he'd get the point, she turned off the light on her bedside table. Then, as slyly as possible, she slipped her pink cashmere mittens beneath her pillow, hoping that her brother hadn't noticed them.

"All right. You've left me no choice," Leo declared, raising his arms in the dark air. "I was saving this for my closing argument, but . . . Do you *really* want to miss out on seeing Aunt Billie's Christmas sweater? Word on the street is it requires batteries and blinks at two different speeds." Wiggling his eyebrows up and down, he smiled at his sister, clearly trying to lighten the mood.

But Clara failed to crack a grin. "Jesus! I SAID NO, LEO!" she snapped loudly, her fists clenched. "Leave me the hell alone about it!"

Leo stiffened. Unaccustomed to being shouted at by his sister, he looked like a deer caught in headlights. For a moment, he remained at a loss for words.

"JUST GO!" Clara added in a nasty tone, taking advantage of his stunned silence, glaring at him. "GET OUT!"

"Fine." Leo swallowed hard. "Merry Christmas." With an anguished expression, he slipped out of Clara's bedroom, quietly closing the door behind him.

Clara hated hurting her brother—the most important person in her life—especially on the holiday that had always meant so much to them both in the past. But he'd left her with no other option. She knew damn well that in order to persuade Leo to leave her alone on Christmas she'd have to push him over the edge by mistreating him in a truly offensive manner. Even if doing so felt unnatural and wrong. Even if it pained her more than it did him.

Grief-stricken (for multiple reasons), she decided that she would apologize to him about it first thing in the morning.

She just prayed that he'd find it in his heart to forgive her nasty selfishness. Not to mention her pathetic inability to cope.

Clara waited until she heard Libby's car back out of the driveway to allow herself to break down in tears. Sobbing uncontrollably, longing for Sebastian—and for the aching emptiness in her chest to disappear—she removed the pink mittens from under her pillow. Clutching them to her face, she curled up into a tight ball, closed her eyes, and hoped that sleep would come soon.

January

16.

After accepting all *three* of Clara's humble, heartfelt apologies for ruining his Christmas, Leo had accompanied her to take a look at Judge Bennett's available apartment in the city. Upon being in the bright, open space for all of thirty seconds, Clara concluded it would suit her temporary needs just fine. Alas, it's not as if she was a picky renter, or envisioned a specific mental image of "home." No. That had been obliterated long ago. It was a quiet place of her own, and that was all that mattered for now.

As her brother had anticipated, the judge cut Clara a generous deal on the monthly rent in exchange for her assurance that she'd keep the one-bedroom condo tidy and looking "happily lived in" for prospective buyers. To this effect, he left behind an empty dresser, two folding chairs, and a Ping-Pong table for Clara to use. "Really, what more do you need than a Ping-Pong table?" Leo had teased on the elevator ride down from the seventeenth floor to the building's elegant, walnut-hued lobby. "Bed, shmed . . ."

Libby, a self-proclaimed "sentimental pack-rat," had a

bunch of items stored in her basement that she was delighted
to unload on Clara, including an old, brown corduroy sofa, a
full-size bed—which was smaller than Clara was accustomed
to, but she had no problem accepting—and a colossal assort-
ment of kitchen supplies. "I appreciate the offer, but I have no
need for a collection of fancy butter molds or a hand-operated
meat grinder," Clara tried to convince her mother.

"Take them. Trust me, you *never* know," Libby adamantly
insisted. "And Leo says you have plenty of space in that lovely
new kitchen."

"Is there anything else you want me to load into the U-
Haul?" Leo shouted from the top of the basement staircase.
He had offered to help Clara move in on the first Saturday of
the month since he didn't have court that day.

"Take this." Libby thrust a clunky, homemade ice cream
maker into her daughter's arms.

"Oh gosh, I don't even own a table. I don't think I'll use
this. Let me remind you, I have an agenda here. I really don't
plan on spending much time in the kitch—"

"*Take it!*" interrupted Libby.

"Yes, ma'am!" Clara realized there was no use in arguing
with her stubborn mother. Especially when she was holding
a cleaver, which she'd received as a wedding gift many moons
ago and never used.

Lugging her heavy box of impractical kitchenware, Clara
discovered Leo sitting at the dining room table in front of a
wrapped present with her name on it. "What's that?" she inquired, surprised.

"A little housewarming gift I picked up for you. Nothing
major. Just something I figured you'd probably need."

Taking a seat, Clara lifted the present. "Leo, you did not have to do this. Especially after how horrid I've been acting lately. You've done way more than enough for me already. I doubt I'm even gonna be in this apartment for very long."

"It's not a big deal. And for the last time, I have no hard feelings about Christmas. But if you bring it up again, I might have to change my mind." He smiled at her. "Open it."

"I can't believe you." Obliging, Clara tore off a small corner of wrapping paper. She peeked inside and grinned. "You did *not . . .*"

Smirking, Leo reminded her, "Hey, it's on your time capsule list."

"Oh dear. I'm warning you, I'm gonna be rusty. I haven't played this in about twenty-five years."

"Like I have? The last time we played was probably together. Jeez, already with the excuses."

"Know what? You may have always won in the past, but I think the tide is about to turn." Clara ripped off the rest of the wrapping paper, revealing her brand-new, cellophane-sealed game recommended for "children" age three and up. "It's official," she declared, tapping the box, causing the cards inside to rattle. "The Memory battle is *on*." Finding matching picture pairs on a commonly shared board of hidden cards had never been her strong suit; however, sooner or later, she was going to cross **Beat Leo at Memory** off her list. Oh yes, she was.

"Dare to dream," he challenged. "And get ready for some serious card-flipping action."

It was getting late in the afternoon and they were just about to leave for the city when the telephone rang.

"It's for you." Libby handed Clara the receiver.

"Who is it?" she asked.

"He didn't say."

"*No*," Clara mouthed, crisscrossing her arms in front of her body. "I told you, I do not want to talk to Todd. *Please*."

"It's not Todd." Libby rolled her eyes, disapprovingly. "And I don't see why you insist on avoiding him like this. I cannot keep making excuses for you when he calls. You're putting me in a very awkward position."

To Clara's dismay, Todd still had not given up on attempting to reach her. In a recent, rather long-winded message he'd left on her voicemail, he said he had something "important" that he "needed" to tell her. In a subsequent message, he stressed that what he had to let her know "would not take long at all," and he hoped to hear back from her "*soon*, please." When he didn't, he resorted to calling her on Libby's main line at the house, which Clara never answered.

"Well, then, who is it? Mr. Franklin?" Clara hadn't spoken with her boss since she left for the Midwest, and she didn't have the energy to feign a sunny front and play "catch up" at the moment. She knew he would be dissecting her tone and every word, judging how "well" or "unwell" she sounded. Then he'd probably report everything back to all of the other Scuppernong associates, who, having nothing better to do, would gossip about her at the water cooler, just as they'd done with "Psycho Erin M.," who showed up to work one day in the midst of a nervous breakdown wearing cardboard 3-D glasses and carrying a lasso. Waving Libby away, Clara begged her to take a message. "*Please* just do it . . ."

"He sounds younger than The Beer King. Will you stop

behaving like a baby and answer it?" Libby forced the phone into her resistant daughter's closed fist.

Pursing her lips, Clara un-pressed the "mute" button as she rose and trudged defiantly toward the music room. "Hello?"

The last thing she ever expected to hear was the voice waiting on the other end of the line.

"Clara?"

"Yes?"

The man cleared his throat. "Uh, hi. This is Lincoln Foster."

17.

"*Hang in there*. Just a couple more minutes and then we are done!" Nurse Pam announced, examining the needle stuck in Clara's arm.

"A couple more *minutes?*" Clara gasped, her jaw clenched. "Are—Are you sure it hasn't been long enough?"

The jovial nurse let out a little chuckle. "Positive, honey. And, I must say, you are doing an *excellent* job donating blood. If I didn't know this was your first time, I'd think you were a pro."

"You're just saying that to be nice." Clara bit down hard on her lip. "I'm sorry to be a wimp, but I don't know how much more of this I can take."

"Yeah, that's what I told my husband last night a few hours after he polished off a giant bean burrito," joked Nurse Pam in an obvious attempt at distraction. "Lord have mercy, I had to open up all the dang windows in my house! Now why don't you just try to relax and tell me more about this fellow you're meeting after this . . . Lincoln, I think you said his name was? That right? I used to drive a Lincoln. Sweet car."

Swallowing hard, Clara commanded herself to nod. "Is it normal for my arm to be tingling?"

"Common reaction. Nothing to fret about." Nurse Pam squeezed her shoulder affectionately, coaxing, "So *Mr. Lincoln* . . . Is he a friend of yours? Boyfriend? Give me some scoop."

"Um. He's . . . he's just an old friend who I haven't seen in forever. We actually grew up together." Digging deep, Clara inhaled a strained breath. "There was a time when we were very close."

"Do I detect a hint of romance in the air?"

"Oh gosh, no." Clara wondered how it was possible "a couple more minutes" hadn't passed yet.

"You sure about that?"

"I'm sure," she grunted awkwardly, struggling to focus on the conversation at hand and ignore the fact that her body felt as if it were being drained of all life fluid. "Been there, done that."

"*Ahhh* . . . So you used to date, then?" Nurse Pam, an obvious pro, egged her queasy patient on.

"Well, we tried it once, very briefly in high school. But I'd hardly call it serious. We just didn't click on that level. To put it mildly." Wiggling her fingers a tiny fraction, Clara winced as she recalled Lincoln's and her ill-fated—albeit comical—stab at romance. Nothing about it had worked. As in, *nothing*. Which is why she'd quickly put the big kibosh on it in order to salvage their friendship before it was too late. "Glad we got that out of the way!" She'd grinned upon breaking the news to a rather somber-looking Lincoln over unlimited salad and breadsticks at the Olive Garden. Rolling her eyes, she'd breathed a sigh of relief. "Now we can go back to being real friends again. Pass the parmesan cheese, please!"

"*Voila!* That wasn't so bad now, was it?" Nurse Pam adhered a Band-Aid on top of a cotton ball to Clara's arm.

"What?" Clara jumped. "That's—That's it? I'm finished? *Really?*"

"Really and truly. You can even open your eyes now if you want."

"Is my blood still hanging in that bag thing next to me? 'Cause I don't think I can look at that." Clara's eyes remained tightly shut.

"Gee, what a surprise. Just give me a few more seconds here . . ." Moving quickly, Nurse Pam removed Clara's bag of blood from the IV stand and handed it to an orderly, telling him it was O positive. "All right, love, the evidence has been erased. Why don't you go ahead and slowly sit up for me? Take your time now. No rush. Easy does it."

"It's gone?" Clara confirmed.

"Like my girlhood waistline!" Nurse Pam let out an uproarious laugh, slapping her plump thigh. "You hear that one, Marge?" She winked at a fellow nurse, who in turn gave her a high-five. "I'm on fire today!"

Clara opened her eyes and tentatively resumed an upright position.

"Can I get you some orange juice or a cookie? We got chocolate peanut butter chip," offered Nurse Pam.

"No, thank you. I don't think I can eat anything right now." Clara tried her best to ignore all of the other brave people donating blood at the clinic. One woman was actually crocheting with her free hand, and a man was reading a paperback crime novel and sipping iced tea as if he were lounging on a tropical beach. "But can you please do me a favor and hand me my purse? It's right next to the bed."

Nurse Pam passed Clara her handbag. "I'm gonna go take care of some paperwork. When you feel ready, you're free to be on your way, but I'd like you to at least stop by the snack station for some juice before you go. Your blood sugar level is low from the blood loss and you do look a bit pale."

"Okay. I will," promised Clara. She removed her time capsule list and trusty red pen from her purse. "Nurse Pam?"

"Yeah, sugar-pie?"

"Thank you again for your patience with me. I know I acted like a big baby."

"Believe you me, honey, I've seen *much* worse. Clearly you don't know my husband! *Oooooooh weeee!*" she cackled, bending over and slapping her leg again. "I'm telling you, Marge!"

"You're like Eddie Murphy," Marge said, laughing.

Touching Clara's foot, Nurse Pam sparkled. "You did a good thing today, and I know how scared you were. You should be proud of yourself."

Truth be told, Clara was proud of herself. When she'd first spotted the clinic's main entrance, which she equated to Dracula's lair, panic consumed her and she almost turned around and fled. There was a reason she had never done this in the past. But, touching her time capsule list in her pocketbook, she summoned her courage and forced herself to march through that door, knowing full well if she didn't, her mission in Chicago would be good as over, and her final hope would be gone. This grim thought was far more frightening than a blood-sucking man-bat. "Thank you." Clara smiled at Nurse Pam, giving her a little wave goodbye.

"Come back soon. I want to hear all about your reunion with Lincoln!" Collecting a clipboard off a nearby counter, Nurse Pam sauntered off.

What a sweet, warmhearted woman, Clara thought to herself, crossing a triumphant line through **Donate blood** on her list.

Keeping a close look out for Lincoln Foster, Clara strolled through Grant Park, one of the city's loveliest and most prominent public spaces, proudly referred to as Chicago's "front yard." With breathtaking lakefront views, numerous jogging and bike paths, and several notable monuments, it was also the site of three world-class museums, including the Field Museum of Natural History, where Lincoln, a paleontologist, had recently started working. As he explained to Clara during their brief telephone conversation the previous week, he had relocated from Sarasota to the Windy City in September upon being offered a once-in-a-lifetime opportunity to study "Sue," the world's largest, most complete, and best preserved *Tyrannosaurus rex* fossil yet discovered, and an unparalleled international draw. Other than the fact that he would be wearing a gray wool coat and gloves, Lincoln hadn't revealed much else.

Calculating that it had been nineteen years since she last saw her old neighbor and friend, Clara wondered if she'd even be able to recognize him after all this time. True, he'd described his outer garments, and she, in turn, had mentioned that her shoulder-length hair was light brown, and she'd be dressed in a tan coat and pale pink scarf, but still, Lincoln hadn't offered any other physical descriptors to work with, and she couldn't help but worry that identifying him would be a struggle. Last they met—the day before he moved to Sarasota—he'd been covered in acne and wearing a Michael Jackson *Thriller* t-shirt, and Drakkar Noir aftershave, which he'd stolen from his older brother Duncan, despite the fact that he'd yet to sprout legitimate facial hair. Though Libby had maintained some contact with Lincoln's mother over the years, telephoning each other on occasion and exchanging the rare e-mail, Lincoln's name had never been mentioned to Clara. She couldn't even imagine what kind of person he'd turned out to be, though walking through the park toward its main attraction, Buckingham Fountain, where they'd agreed to meet, Clara knew she would soon find out.

The weather forecast had called for sunshine and unseasonably warm temperatures that day, which is why Lincoln had suggested they take an afternoon walk. Of course, Chicago was known for its unpredictable shifts in climate, as made evident by the murky, overcast January sky and arctic breeze rolling off Lake Michigan. Shivering, Clara tightened her scarf around her neck and sank her hands deep into her coat pockets. It looked as if it was about to snow. She hoped Lincoln wouldn't want to stay outside for very long, especially since her toes had started to go numb and she was sure her nose resembled Rudolph's. Plodding her way through the crisp, frost-covered grass, Clara thought she saw Lincoln standing next to Buckingham Fountain where he said he'd be. She squinted just to make sure. But suddenly, the man ripped off his gray coat to reveal a red sweat suit with a neon lightning bolt across the chest, shot both arms straight in the air, somersaulted to the ground, and started breakdancing. Clara watched as a small group of people clapping their hands to the beat encircled him.

Looking around, she spotted another man wearing sunglasses, a gray coat, and gloves, who was about the same height as she recalled Lincoln to be, assuming he hadn't experienced a growth spurt since age fifteen. It was hard to tell because of his shades, but he seemed to be staring directly at her. And then he waved hello. Smiling and waving back, Clara continued toward him with visible pep in her step. That is, until a woman clad in white fur leaped into his arms and began kissing him passionately. *Or not*, Clara thought to herself, averting her eyes from the steamy, semi-pornographic make-out session.

Just then a tall man with dark brown hair sitting on a park bench called her name. "Clara?" he repeated, standing up, brushing a few snow flurries off his gray coat.

She recognized him in a heartbeat.

"Lincoln." She grinned.

"I thought that was you!" he said, smiling back as he approached her.

"Wow. It's really you," Clara marveled, taking him in. How could she have ever believed that she wouldn't instantly recognize her old friend? On second thought, she would have known his familiar face in a sea of a thousand others. In fact, seeing him was like a bizarre déjà vu.

"It's really *you*," echoed Lincoln, staring at her. "Only, all grown up . . ."

"*I know*." Clara ogled back, thinking the same exact thing about him. A passerby unaware of the particulars of their reunion might have looked upon them gawking at each other with blatant wonder and guessed that they were on LSD, about to become enthralled by the mesmerizing sight of their own hands, or lick a tree. "We got old! This is *crazy* . . . I mean, seeing you now," she clarified. How strange and surreal it was to be in Lincoln Foster's presence after all these years. Gone was the gangly young boy she had once played "Olympics" with and given thirteen Snickers candy bars to on his thirteenth birthday. "There's nothing more delicious in the whole wide world," he used to say. The man standing before Clara, with a faint peppering of gray in his hair, new creases in his forehead, and a general thickening of his once-lanky kid frame, was a grown adult—as Clara had expected, but was still somehow surprised to see nonetheless. It was enough to make her head spin. Actually, her head was spinning. A touch dizzy, she glanced down at her feet to make sure she was standing on level lawn.

"What am I thinking?" asked Lincoln. "What kind of greeting is that after all this time?" Hesitating for a split-second, he appeared unsure whether to shake Clara's hand or embrace her.

Clara wasn't certain how to receive him either.

Shifting positions on his feet, Lincoln extended his hand at the precise moment that Clara decided she had better lean in for a hug.

An awkward dance ensued as he modified his salutation into a tentative embrace.

Emitting a shaky chuckle, Clara clumsily arched a little bit closer to him. And then, in the blink of an eye, her head plopped forward and her body fell totally limp, like a rag doll.

"Clara?" Lincoln's arms immediately tightened around her small waist, catching her just before she collapsed to the ground. "Hello?"

There was no response.

Alarmed, he repeated her name, giving her dangling, lifeless form a gentle shake. "Can you hear me?" His voice, drenched with panic, grew louder. "Clara?!" Supporting her full weight in his left arm and deftly sliding his right hand beneath her knees, he lifted her up into his arms so that her body was facing him. "Oh God," he desperately cried, observing that her eyes were closed and her breathing seemed shallow. "Clara! Come on, C.J.!"

Slowly, her eyes fluttered open.

"Clara," Lincoln whispered, out of breath, terrorized, a combination of fear and relief dripping from every pore.

"Lincoln?" She appeared stunned to see him. "I—I didn't drink the orange juice."

- ~~Donate blood~~

18.

Seated at a table for two in the corner of the Mayflower Café, a casual coffee shop which Lincoln stopped by most mornings on his way to work—located just a few blocks away from the Field Museum—Clara finished her apple juice and smiled at him. Though she'd protested, Lincoln had also insisted on buying her an enormous red velvet cupcake, a bottle of water, and, of course, a steaming hot cup of coffee to help warm her up. "Honestly, I feel *much* better now. All I needed was a little sugar," she said, pressing her hand to her forehead and shaking her head in a gesture of embarrassment. "I feel like such an idiot."

"There's no need. I'm telling you, I make women faint all the time. Almost daily, in fact," Lincoln added, clearly trying to set her at ease. "I've been contemplating keeping a tab. I think it may have something to do with the fact that I look like George Clooney."

Clara let out a little chuckle. Lincoln had always been able to make her laugh. And, now that he mentioned it, he did sort of share a slight resemblance with George Clooney.

"I'm just glad you're okay," he said in a more serious tone.

"Lesson learned." She sipped her coffee, keeping her hands wrapped around the oversized mug after she returned it to the table. "Thank you again for being so wonderful about this."

"Well, now we're even."

"What are you talking about?" She appeared confused.

"Remember that time when we were—I don't know—probably ten or eleven years old, and I got that horrible leg cramp while we were playing Sharks and Minnows in Veronica Cooper's pool?"

"*Oh yeah . . . That's right.*" Clara nodded, recalling that fateful summer day. She hadn't thought about it in decades, but suddenly it all came rushing back to her in vivid color.

"I was sinking in the deep end like a ton of rocks, and you grabbed me by the bangs and dragged me out of the water."

"I did." Clara laughed at the memory. "I'd forgotten about that."

"You didn't let me drown," Lincoln stated matter-of-factly, taking a bite of his brownie.

"Nope. I wonder whatever happened to Veronica Cooper."

After they had completed their stroll down memory lane and gotten all of the standard small talk out of the way, Lincoln mentioned how blown away his mother had been by the vase. She'd phoned him right away to tell him about it, marveling at Clara's "unbelievably thoughtful, yet quite unnecessary" gesture. She'd also given him Libby's contact information, because Clara's letter accompanying the vase mentioned that she was currently staying with her mother.

"You really did not have to do that," Lincoln said again. He peered at her with a curious expression. "I can't resist asking, though . . . What made you decide to replace it now, after all of these years, anyway?"

The only natural place for Clara to begin her explanation was with Sebastian. And so she told Lincoln the entire story. When she arrived at the part about her time capsule and what she was doing with it, Lincoln shared that he too had received his time capsule back from Miss Jordain in July. He'd also completely forgotten about creating it in the first place. Although, he insisted its contents weren't very interesting, claiming his relic was filled mostly with silly "little boy junk," like miniature cars and baseball cards.

"So, in a *thirty-minute nutshell*," Clara concluded, "I sent your mom the vase because it was on my list of things to do by the time I'm thirty-five."

"Your birthday's at the beginning of September, isn't it?"

Clara was both surprised and touched that he remembered. "Yes. September second. Which gives me less than eight months to complete my list." She couldn't resist dipping her finger in her cupcake's vanilla frosting. "This is delicious. If I remember correctly, your birthday's in December? Is that right?"

"December twenty-seventh," he confirmed. Then, exhaling, Lincoln gazed down at his empty brownie plate. When he looked at Clara again, his smile had faded, and there was a distinct cast of sadness in his brown eyes. "I wish I'd known about Sebastian."

Clara lifted her shoulders to her ears, trying to think of something—anything—positive or light to say. But, when it came to the topic of her fiancé's death, there was no such thing. "It's okay. There's nothing you could have done. There's really nothing anyone can do."

"I know," he said. "The thing is"—Lincoln tapped his thumb against the round table—"I'm familiar with what you're going through."

Clara was surprised to hear this. "You are?"

He nodded, looking down again. "My wife, Jessica, died five years ago from cancer. Multiple Myeloma."

"Oh, Link," whispered Clara, feeling her heart sink. "I had no idea. I'm so sorry." And she meant it, too.

"I feel the same way about Sebastian. I have no doubt that he was an amazing man."

Again, Clara struggled to find the appropriate response. The last thing she had expected to do was spill her guts to someone she hadn't exchanged a single word with in as long as she could remember. Unloading her problems like this simply wasn't her style, but with shared common ground and a history that spanned decades, it felt natural to let her guard down. "I guess I'm still just trying to find a way to deal with it all and pick up the pieces. I realize it sounds crazy, but I'm hoping maybe my time capsule list might help. I don't really have any other options left." She sighed with a faraway look.

"Believe me, it doesn't sound crazy at all. Your grief is still raw."

"Yes, but it still—"

"I was a *Jurassic* wreck for a long time."

Pausing, Clara gave him a look. "Wait. Was that just a dinosaur joke?"

"Yep," Lincoln proudly confirmed. "Did you like it?"

"*No.*" She couldn't help but laugh in her old friend's face. "That was *bad!*" She covered her mouth with her napkin, trying not to hurt his feelings. Lincoln had never been particularly gifted when it came to delivering jokes.

"What sort of t-shirts do dinosaurs wear?"

"Oh God. I don't even know if I want to hear this."

"Tricera-*tops!*"

She cringed, giggling again.

"What do you call a Stegosaurus with only one leg?" Lincoln didn't wait for Clara's guess. "Eileen! Get it? *I-lean!*"

"Stop!" She leaned forward cracking up. "That's the worst one yet!"

"I know." He laughed. "I made them up myself."

"Yeah, I wouldn't brag about that." Clara wiped her eyes, sure that there was mascara everywhere.

When they had both caught their breath from their necessary emotional release, Lincoln checked his watch and gasped. "We've been here for almost three hours!"

"We have?" Clara was shocked. It certainly didn't feel like they'd been in the café that long. But, sure enough, glancing at the clock behind the bustling bakery counter, she discovered Lincoln was correct. "Oh dear, I have a feeling Milk Dud's probably had an accident in the house by now. Not that there's any furniture or carpet to destroy."

"And I'm late to an appointment with a paleontology professor from England." Lincoln stood up, putting on his coat. "I hate to cut our reunion short like this."

"Short?" Clara wrapped her scarf around her neck.

"Can we get together again soon? I'd love to hear more about your time capsule list—and your family."

"Of course. And I want to hear more about T-rex Sue."

"I know it's short notice, but how about dinner tomorrow? I'm usually off work early on Thursdays." Lincoln began making his way toward the café's exit.

"I'm seeing Leo tomorrow night, but I'm free on Friday if you're available."

"I have an engagement that evening. Saturday too," he said regretfully.

"Girlfriend?" Clara inquired before she had a chance to censor herself. It wasn't her nature to pry into one's personal business, but with an old pal like Lincoln, she figured the usual rules needn't apply.

"We recently started dating. Her name is Meg. She manages the gift shop at the museum. I'll introduce you to her. I think you two would get along well." He opened the door, allowing Clara to exit before him. "How about dinner on Monday?"

"Sounds good." She put on her pink cashmere mittens. "Thank you again for today. I'm so glad you called me. It really was great seeing you."

"You too, C.J." Lincoln smiled, giving her a warm embrace.

To that day, nobody else had ever called Clara James Black by this nickname. Reminding her of a much happier, simpler time, it made her grin.

February

19

In Clara's dream, she had just moved in to a grand, old, Southern plantation that required a complete renovation. Dozens of hired contractors dressed in white protective jumpsuits concealing their entire bodies from head to toe hurried about the vast, dust-filled space overlooking acres of fresh-plowed cotton fields, tending to their various construction duties. Clara had just arrived home via horse and carriage from someplace or other and was upstairs, surveying that day's progress, when a man holding a can of canary yellow paint exited the master bedroom. Setting the paint can down on the tarp-covered floor in the hallway, he unzipped his jumpsuit, revealing his face, and shook a few rogue wood shavings from his tousled hair. Clara froze in place, paralyzed, as her stomach plummeted and a blast of shock electrified her, causing the tiny hairs on the back of her neck to stand straight up. Staring at the man, she tried to say his name, but her breath had been taken away. She couldn't believe it at first. She was afraid to allow herself to even pretend that such a wonderful miracle could possibly be true. But sure as the day was long, there, in front of her very own two eyes, was the one and only love of her life. Trembling, Clara reached out and touched Sebastian's arm to make sure he wasn't an apparition. The handsome figure looked just like Sebastian, he smelled just like Sebastian, and finally, when at last he opened his mouth and said, "Hi, baby. Nice bonnet," he sounded just like Sebastian. Tears welled in Clara's astonished eyes. In that one, single, staggering moment in time, the horrid, gaping hole in her heart was instantly mended, and life's thrilling possibilities suddenly seemed endless again.

"*Sebastian!*" She threw her arms around his waist, weeping with joy, clinging to him like a child. "It's—It's you . . . It's really you!"

"It's me." He held her warm body tightly against his.

Removing her bonnet, he stroked the side of her tear-stained face and passionately kissed her lips.

And then, Clara woke up.

Her eyes sprang open, and she sat bolt upright in bed, her chest heaving. Looking straight ahead, she extended one arm and, holding her breath, slowly, tentatively, felt the empty space beside her, as if maybe, by some small chance, Sebastian might actually be there, sleeping peacefully. But, just like the last time she had this same, strange, yet real-as-can-be, recurring dream, she found herself all alone. Catching her breath, reminding herself that Sebastian was gone and he was never coming back, she glanced about her bedroom. With the exception of a cardboard moving box substituting as a makeshift end table and the judge's wooden dresser, the room was empty.

Wide-awake now, Clara stared at the alarm clock flashing 2:44 a.m. After a few minutes, she flipped her pillow over to the cool side, lay down again, and attempted to fall back asleep. But no matter how hard she tried, she couldn't stop the merciless barrage of images from her vivid dream from invading her mind. Recalling Sebastian's sensual kiss, she touched an index finger to her lips, allowing it to linger, wishing desperately that it could be real.

Soon, a deep, choking, impenetrable sadness set in. Familiar with this middle-of-the-night routine, Clara squeezed her eyes shut, trying to quiet the pervading memories of Sebastian, but it was no use. It was as if she'd been swept up against her will in a vicious, swirling tornado of upsetting thoughts. These were the haunting hours of the day that Clara hated most, when she couldn't escape her own debilitating stream of consciousness, and all hope ceased to exist.

Hearing his master's muffled sobs, Milk Dud came running from his favorite spot under the Ping-Pong table in the living room where he usually slept, and jumped onto Clara's bed, cozying up beside her.

She buried her face in his fur and continued to cry.

Milk Dud placed his paw on her arm as she muttered, "I miss him so much. So much . . ."

"Everything always seems far worse at night," Libby used to remind Clara when she was a child being tormented late in the evening by some seemingly world-ending trouble, such as being told she had a mustache by Maeve, the high school bully who dubbed her "Magnum P.I.," or failing her driver's test for driving on the wrong side of the road. "You'll see, things won't seem quite so bad in the morning," Libby would insist. And usually, she was right. But that was before a truck barreling eighty miles per hour crashed into Clara's fiancé's car, setting the agenda for the rest of her life. That was when she still believed nothing so tragic would ever happen to her. No, not to *her*.

The previous week, while having sushi with Lincoln— the fifth time they'd dined together since their reunion in the park—he'd encouraged Clara to call him any time, day or night, when she was trapped in the brutal grip of a "mean moment," by which he meant a stretch when the unbearable pain of missing Sebastian "threatened to swallow her whole." All too familiar with such dreadful—but fleeting—periods, Lincoln had offered to help Clara through them. "Distraction is key," he'd shared, clinking his cup of hot sake against hers. Staring at the telephone on the judge's old dresser, Clara pondered picking it up and dialing Lincoln's number, but then she thought better of disturbing her friend in the middle of the God forsaken night. What would she tell him? That she just had a puzzling dream where Sebastian was still alive and she resembled Laura Ingalls Wilder's long lost, bonnet-wearing cousin? She remembered Lincoln mentioned that adopting one of the Alcoholics Anonymous mantras had helped him deal with his grief over his wife's death. Rather than focusing on the scary "big picture," he explained, he found it easier to concentrate on "making it through the day, making it though the hour, the minute, the second even." When Lincoln twisted his face into a goofy expression, saying, *"Yard by yard life's pretty hard, inch by inch life's a cinch,"* Clara had laughed and joked that the rhyme would be perfect for one of those cheesy condolence cards with sunshine and rainbows breaking through the foreboding clouds. But weeping in her dark bedroom, consumed with despair and an overwhelming fear that she was doomed to remain a woman who lost her balance and never quite got it back, she realized her friend's philosophy made sense. It was even comforting.

Deciding to wait and call Lincoln when he was less likely to be snoring, Clara lifted from her makeshift end table a framed photograph of her and Sebastian dancing at a black-tie gala for the Boston Philharmonic. She stared at it for a long while before placing it on her chest, directly over her heart, and eventually drifting back to sleep.

She awoke again at 7:15 a.m., and, sure enough, noticed that her stifling sorrow had indeed lifted a bit with the rising sun.

Figuring she might just be able to catch Lincoln before he left for work, Clara brushed her teeth, splashed some cold water on her face, and gave him a ring.

He sounded out of breath when he answered the telephone.

"Is this a bad time? I hope I'm not disturbing you. I know it's early," Clara acknowledged.

"Not at all," Lincoln replied. "What's up?"

"Well . . ." She exhaled, slowly stroking Milk Dud's back. "I kind of had a rough night. Let's just say *mean moments galore*."

"Ugh. I know what that's like. I'm glad you called. But, why didn't you let me know sooner? I distinctly remember giving you specific instructions to come straight to me—*do not pass 'Go,' do not collect two hundred dollars, go directly to Link.*"

Clara chuckled softly. "I take it you're a Monopoly fan?"

"Actually, I'm more of a Scrabble kind of guy. But it wouldn't have made sense if I told you to pick your letters and call me."

"True. I like Scrabble too."

"We should play sometime," Lincoln suggested. "But, tell me, how are you now?"

Clara heard somebody release a dainty, high-pitched sneeze in the background. And that's when she realized that Lincoln was not alone.

A woman with a sexy, raspy voice questioned, "Who is it, love?" Assuming it must be Meg, his girlfriend, Clara suddenly felt guilty about the crack-of-dawn call. "Uh . . ." she stuttered, remembering how winded Lincoln had sounded at first and fearing she'd disrupted an intimate moment. "Actually? I *am* feeling much better. Thank you." She cringed, embarrassed. "But you know what? I have to go make a frittata."

There was a short pause on Lincoln's end. "You have to make a *frittata*?"

"Yes. I do. I love them. And it sounds like you're busy," Clara rushed on. "I'm gonna hang—"

"Wait! C.J. Hang on!" He stopped her just as she was about to end the call. "You're sure you're okay? Because believe me, I know how awful—"

"I'm *positive*. Honestly. I feel a lot better now," she insisted in a deliberately cheerful manner. "Which is why it's frittata time."

After suggesting they get together that evening for dinner, Lincoln told Clara he'd phone her later in the afternoon to iron out a plan. As he was hanging up, she heard

Meg giggle and purr, "Get over here, sexy." Considering it was Wednesday, which meant that Lincoln and Meg were apparently spending weeknights together—coupled with Meg calling him lovey-dovey nicknames—Clara presumed their romance had escalated to a more serious stage than Lincoln initially described. She was happy for her widowed friend; he deserved a second chance at love, and from what Lincoln had told her, Meg sounded like a wonderful woman. Not to mention a horny little minx, based on what she'd just heard.

Clara patted the side of her thigh a few times, beckoned, "Come on Milk Dud," and moseyed toward the kitchen, yawning.

Wearing Sebastian's old Harvard sweatshirt and no pajama pants, she stood barefoot with her arms crossed, assessing a copy of her time capsule list, which was stuck to the otherwise bare refrigerator with a magnet. "What should we do today, boy? What do you think?"

Milk Dud barked.

"Yeah, you want breakfast is what you think," she muttered. After fixing him a bowl of kibble, Clara poured herself a cup of coffee, grabbed her time capsule list off the refrigerator, and proceeded to the living room, which, like the other areas in her apartment, held only a smattering of furniture.

Sitting in a folding chair at the Ping-Pong table, Clara studied her list. Some of the things on it she'd already accomplished in the past, such as **Serve on a real live court jury** (not nearly as "awesome" as a ten-year-old might suspect), **Eat sugar cereal & McDonald's during the week (not just on weekends!)**, **Swim with dolphins** (perhaps something positive came from dolphin therapy after all), and **Ride in a hot air balloon**, which she'd done with Sebastian during their vacation in Tuscany. How romantic she'd imagined it would be, until climbing aboard the balloon's compact, wobbly, wicker basket that seemed more suitable for a couple giant loaves of bread, hitting a few unexpected bumpy air patches, and discovering that she had the ability to scream for surprisingly long periods of time at decibels high enough to make a sweet, elderly, Italian tour guide cover his ears with both hands and swear at her to "Shutta zee foock up!" Clara drew a red line through these items on her time capsule list.

Next, she pondered two of the points that seemed particularly farfetched, if not altogether impossible to accomplish: **Find a cure for heart attacks** and **Become the President of the United States**. Clara knew damn well the only "attack" she was realistically going to be curing any time in the near future was a Big Mac attack, from which she was prone to suffer on occasion. And with minimal interest in politics, she no longer held any desire to become the President of the United States, let alone the P.T.A., which to her felt about equally unattainable.

Eventually, Clara's eyes settled on **Learn Morse code**. Furrowing her brow, she gave this point some serious thought. "Oh, who am I kidding, Milk Dud? What the hell am I doing? This is absurd. Do I *really* need to learn Morse code? Who am I going to use it with?" Clara continued thinking out loud. "My Scuppernong vendors?" She shook her head, wondering if this little plan of hers was as nuts as it suddenly seemed. "But, then again, it *is* on the list," she reminded herself. "Which, I suppose, doesn't give me much choice now, does it?" Her eyebrows pulled together as she chewed her nails, considering it further. Sighing, Clara reached across the Ping-Pong table for her laptop and pressed the power button on. "Well, what do you say, boy? Should we conduct some Internet research on Morse code?"

Raising his only ear, Milk Dud tilted his head to the side and looked at her.

"Yeah . . . I don't really feel like it either," Clara admitted right as her cell phone began ringing. Saved by the bell.

Libby, who had just finished recording a new detergent jingle in the city at a studio in Clara's neighborhood, wanted to know if she was interested in joining her for a winter walk. "Some crisp, fresh air might do you good," she'd persuaded.

"I guess so." Clara shrugged unenthusiastically, to her mother's surprise. Typically opposed to intentional exercise, Clara figured it was better than the alternative. Plus, she hoped it might help her earn a point or two with Libby, who was still furious about and seemed to feel personally responsible for the nasty way she'd avoided Todd. During a recent piano tuning, he'd nervously inquired if Clara was around almost immediately upon walking through the front door, and according to Libby, he acted notably ill at ease the entire time he was there. Though she doubted it would happen, she worried his awkward discomfort might even provoke him to stop working for her. Due to Libby's profession, her piano required fine-tuning every six weeks, and she swore up and down that never had she encountered a more capable tuner than Todd. Or, as Clara now referred to him, "You-Know-Who."

Perhaps Clara wanted nothing more than to remain faithful to Sebastian, and this was her way of doing so: by ignoring other men. She decided she would try to explain this to Libby during their walk.

- ~~Serve on a real live court jury (awesome!!!)~~
- ~~Eat sugar cereal & McDonald's during the week (not just on weekends!)~~
- ~~Swim with dolphins~~
- ~~Ride in a hot air balloon~~

20

"Good Lord . . . Look at the *size* of that thing," Clara whispered.

"I know," replied Lincoln. "I hear that all the time."

Standing in awe as Sue's five-foot-long skull stared her down, Clara smiled. "She's incredible, Link. Absolutely incredible."

"She sure is." He gazed up at the 67-million-year-old fossil with similar wonder. "I never get tired of looking at her. She's from the late Cretaceous period, and if you focus on her massive jaw, you'll notice that most of her razor-sharp teeth are about twelve inches long. Which is more or less average for the T-rex."

"*Amazing* . . . And you said that you're studying her stomach?" Clara's eyes remained fixed on the mesmerizing dinosaur.

"Among other things. Recently, I've been analyzing the material believed to have been Sue's stomach contents from her last meal. It's of great scientific interest because it provides a more complete picture of the ecosystem in which she lived, and reveals secrets that wouldn't be evident from calcareous connective tissue, or *bones*—as we like to call them—alone."

A tall, strikingly beautiful woman with scarlet lips and long, flowing black hair that was a direct contrast to her milky white skin appeared out of nowhere, sliding her arm around Lincoln's waist. "I hope you're not boring this poor, innocent woman to death." She smiled wryly.

"*Who, me?*" Lincoln gave her a quick but obviously heartfelt kiss on the mouth. "Never."

"You must be Clara." The woman extended her hand to greet her. "It's wonderful to finally meet you. I'm Meg."

"Nice to meet you too," said Clara, admiring Meg's navy, vintage-looking polka-dot dress.

"When Link told me you were stopping by on your way to dinner, I warned him not to subject you to a long, academic lecture about—she deepened her voice to mimic his—*the exquisite preservation and invaluable scientific resource that is our dear Sue.*"

Clara grinned, impressed with Meg's impersonation, as well as her spunk. "Hey, that's not bad."

"You know I'm only teasing, love." Meg flashed Lincoln a dazzling smile.

Why this gorgeous woman who reminded Clara of a young Audrey Hepburn was managing the gift shop—as opposed to strutting her stuff on a professional catwalk—was a mystery to Clara. She and Lincoln certainly made a handsome couple.

"Did he show you the *Evolving Planet* yet?" Meg asked her, referring to the museum's popular exhibit that took visitors on an awe-inspiring journey through four billion years of life on Earth, featuring an expanded dinosaur hall, including every major group and the worlds they lived in.

"He told me about it, but we decided to wait and see it with my brother, who's a huge dinosaur fan," Clara explained. "He's a five-year-old boy trapped in a thirty-seven-year-old adult body when it comes to this sort of stuff."

"Hmmm . . . Sounds like someone I know." Meg arched her eyebrows and smirked at Lincoln, who, grinning, appeared altogether enchanted by her.

"Well, I look forward to giving Leo an extra special, behind-the-scenes tour," he announced.

"Oh, he would adore that," Clara assured him, imagining that her brother might need to be shot with a tranquilizer gun at some point during the experience. "I just hope you don't regret making that offer."

"Nonsense," insisted Lincoln. "Leo and I go way back. It'll be terrific to catch up with him and show him around."

"Can you join us for dinner, Meg?" Clara felt her empty stomach begin to grumble. "I think we're going to try a new Chinese restaurant called Syn-Kow over by Wrigley Field."

"I'd love to." She smiled. "I hear their egg rolls are to die for. But I've got a book club meeting this evening."

"Yes, tonight's book is the great *Hollywood Wives* by Jackie Collins," Lincoln revealed.

"We're reading the classics," explained Meg. Placing her hand under his wrist, she lifted it and glanced at his watch. "Oh dear, I'd better get back to the gift shop. I promised I'd be gone just a few minutes. Enjoy your evening—and Clara, I hope we can all get together sometime soon."

"Absolutely," Clara replied.

"I'll leave the door unlocked for you and tell Rodrigo to let you up," Lincoln said to Meg, kissing her ruby lips goodbye.

"*Nicest* doorman in all of Chicago," she told Clara. Then, squeezing Lincoln's hand, she sparkled. "I should be there by ten-thirty, hun."

"Oh boy," Clara groaned, placing her hand over her stuffed belly. "You might need to roll me out of here in a wheelbarrow. I can't have another bite."

"Does that mean your last sparerib's up for grabs?" Lincoln eyed the succulent pork with desire.

"Go ahead. By all means."

Reaching his chopsticks across the table, he lifted it from Clara's plate. "Thank you. And how about that dumpling?"

"Be my guest." She gestured for him to take it.

"You know, I've tried a lot of Chinese restaurants since I've been in Chicago, and so far this one's my favorite by a long shot."

"Me too," Clara agreed. "I'd definitely come back here."

"Deal." Lincoln smiled, popping her leftover vegetable dumpling in his mouth.

After the waitress had cleared their plates, she brought them the bill and two fortune cookies, which arrived on a small green dish that was shaped like a dragon and had dry-ice smoke shooting from its nostrils.

"We have to read our fortunes out loud," Lincoln proclaimed, removing his cookie from its plastic wrapper and snapping it in half.

Clara reached for hers.

"Mine says"—he squinted his dark, chocolate-colored eyes a bit—"*You are gifted at walking.*"

"What?" She giggled. "What the hell kind of fortune is that?"

"A lame one," Lincoln concurred with a chuckle. "But actually, it reminds me of something. By any chance, do you happen to have your time capsule list with you?"

"Always," Clara confirmed.

"May I see it, please?"

"Of course." Grabbing her purse beneath her chair, she wondered what Lincoln was up to.

He gave the list—which had begun to assume a crinkled and shabby appearance due to constant handling—a swift perusal and then announced that he had a proposition for her.

"A proposition? What are you talking about?"

"Well, here's the deal," he began. "At the beginning of May there's a 10K charity race in the city to help raise money for cancer research. It's a fantastic cause. And God knows every cent helps." Lincoln paused, absentmindedly fiddling with his cookie wrapper. "I'm running it in Jessica's honor," he explained. "May's the month that she passed away, so it couldn't be more fitting as far as timing goes. And I know it's something that she would have felt passionately about. Jess was a volunteer for the American Cancer Society right up until the very end." Clearing his throat, Lincoln cast his eyes downward, as if he didn't want Clara to glimpse the shadow of melancholy in them. "I could really use a partner to help me train and stay motivated."

Certain that there had to be some sort of misunderstanding, Clara's eyebrows lifted with genuine surprise. "Are you talking about *me*?"

"No. I'm talking about our waitress. Can you ask her if she's interested?"

Tilting her head to the side, she gave him a look. "Funny."

"*Of course* I'm talking about you. See, I was thinking that if you participate in the race as well, you could simultaneously knock two items off your list." Lincoln looked at it again, reading aloud: **"Run a race (10K like Dad used to run? Find out what a K is!) and Help others through charity like Libby."**

"You do have a point," Clara admitted reluctantly.

"By the way, a *K* is 0.62 miles." He winked.

"And it's certainly a wonderful cause. There's no doubt about that. But, Link, in all honesty, I don't think I have the stamina to even run around the block." Clara wasn't proud of this fact, but, regrettably, it was true. "I mean, realistically, I don't think I'm in the right kind of physical shape to be able to pull off a 10K."

"Neither am I." Lincoln pointed at his sides. "Look at these love handles! Meg calls them Ben & Jerry. That's why I thought that maybe, *if* you were interested, we could help each other train. You know, root each other on? And you could always bring Milk Dud along," he persuaded. "Dogs are 'gifted at walking' too."

Clara did the math in her head. "So that equals 6.2 miles." She passed her fortune cookie back and forth from one hand to the other, pondering the idea. "That's a lot."

"It is." Lincoln sipped his hot tea. "Anyway, no pressure. I figured it couldn't hurt to throw it out there."

Contemplating Jessica and how much she obviously meant to Lincoln, Clara could only imagine the symbolic significance this charity race held for him. She had no doubt that if the proverbial table was turned and she was running a race in Sebastian's honor, Lincoln would support her. He was the sort of man who'd go out and buy matching team t-shirts and possibly even twin sweatbands with a corny message on them. It occurred to Clara that perhaps he needed more than a training partner. Perhaps what Lincoln really needed was a friend who could relate to what he was going through, someone who knew firsthand the indescribable sort of devastating emotional loss that had become a permanent part of his everyday life—not pronounced or glaring in the forefront, but rather quietly existing deep in the background, like an ever-present scab that at any moment could be yanked off a wound that never quite heals.

Studying Lincoln, Clara recognized the heavyhearted flicker of grief in his eyes. She knew that look all too well. She felt it in her gut. And for the first time in almost a year, she was able to feel pain that was not her own. Striking her all at once, it made her want to weep. But, instead, Clara placed her hand on top of Lincoln's, smiled, and softly declared, "I'm in."

He appeared taken aback. "You—You are?"

"I am," Clara reiterated in a stronger voice. "But, I want to make one thing clear."

"What's that?"

"I'm not doing this because it's on my time capsule list."

"You're not?" Now Lincoln sounded *really* surprised.

"Nope."

"Oookay." He seemed leery. "Then, if I may ask, why *are* you doing it?"

Clara grinned, pausing before she answered. "For Jessica Foster."

At first, Lincoln just looked at her without saying a word. And then, swallowing hard, he nodded and smiled gratefully, whispering, "Thank you."

"But *you*"—Clara pointed at him—"are in charge of the training part."

"You've got yourself a deal."

Sitting at a table for two by the window at Syn-Kow, with the entire wait staff clapping their hands and singing a Chinese version of *Happy Birthday* to a mortified-looking diner nearby with a sparkler in his green tea ice cream, they shook on it.

"Okay. My turn." Clara cracked open her fortune cookie, wondering what the hell she'd just gotten herself into. She had no idea how she was going to make it through this race without requiring CPR. Just thinking about it gave her a side stitch! But she knew how much her friend needed her.

"What's it say?" pressed Lincoln.

"Let's see . . ." She unfolded the little rectangular piece of paper, reading, "*One old friend is better than two new ones.*"

"Can't argue with that one," Lincoln agreed, looking at her. "Now how come you get something meaningful and I'm a *gifted walker*?"

Clara forced a small smile. But suddenly, she was far away, lost in her own thoughts.

"Hey . . . You okay?"

"Yeah." She sighed, rereading her fortune. "This just made me think of my best friend in Boston who I'm kind of on the outs with. It's nothing, really."

"Why are you on the outs?"

Clara, visibly saddened by this fact, shook her head. "Oh, it's a long, complicated story. Suffice to say, it's all my fault. And the crappy part is I didn't even realize it until it was too late."

"Well, I've got plenty of time." Lincoln stretched his long legs, leaning back in his chair.

"Are you sure?" Clara double-checked, thinking better of it. "You have to be sick and tired of listening to me drone *on* and *on* like a broken record about *woe is me.*"

"Woe is *not* you," he assured her, threatening, "Would you rather hear my latest dinosaur joke?"

"So, as I was saying about *Tabitha,*" Clara replied instantly.

Summarizing their decade-long relationship, she explained how she essentially dropped off the face of the planet after her fiancé's accident. "It's not like I *wanted* my friendship with Tabitha to suffer. I can't tell you how wonderful she was to me after the accident. Not a day went by that she didn't call, or stop by my house to check on me. She always included me in her plans and extended countless invitations my way. Of course, I rejected them all." Clara rolled her eyes. "Tabitha couldn't have been more supportive, Link. But I was such an emotional wreck I just couldn't handle being around other people. Not even my closest friend. So I pushed her away. Again, and again, and again. Until she finally reached her breaking point." Clara described their tense quarrel shortly before Thanksgiving in which Tabitha, near tears, had stated that whether or not Clara was in mourning, this was no way to treat an acquaintance, let alone her supposed best friend. "Oh, and by the way?" Tabitha had sniffled, "I'm engaged. In case you care." Clara hadn't even been aware that Tabitha was dating anyone special, despite her friend's regular mention of Max.

"Ouch." Lincoln's eyes were filled with understanding. "I felt the same way about being around other people after Jessica died. It was just . . . too hard." He poured himself some more tea. "Life for them was business as usual. But my world was shattered. Totally unrecognizable. I couldn't deal."

"Exactly. I was so out of my damn mind that I wasn't even aware I was shutting people out. Although Tabitha did try to let me know. I can see that now."

"Well, isn't that a step in the right direction?" encouraged Lincoln.

"She was my maid of honor, for Christ's sake! I completely turned my back on her." Ashamed, Clara decided not to share how Tabitha had blown her off for coffee just before she returned to Chicago in December. Clara had hoped to conduct some damage control prior to leaving town and was looking forward to attempting to begin to mend their fractured friendship, but an hour before they were supposed to meet at the coffee shop Tabitha called and claimed that a "last-minute" work meeting had "just popped up," and she was sorry to have to cancel their plans. "Wish I had time to chat. Have a good trip and send me an e-mail or call me sometime from Chicago. If you feel like it," Tabitha had muttered before quickly hanging up the phone.

"It *is* hard not to take that kind of rejection personally," Lincoln conceded. "And let's face it, grief is pretty damn hard to understand and relate to until you've been there yourself. I get that. But I also think you need to cut yourself a break and remember that you were—and still are—dealing with an inconceivable tragedy the best way you know how. We're both aware that nothing, I mean *nothing*, prepares you for handling death. Unfortunately, you don't just wake up one day and say, *Okay, I'm done with mourning, and now it's time to go right back to the normal life I had.* We do the best we can, C.J."

"Yes, but at this point I don't even know what's happening in Tabitha's life. I've missed out on practically a whole *year*. For all I know she's moved to Guam!"

Surprise washed over Lincoln's face. "Really? Tabitha was considering moving to Guam?"

"No." Clara sighed. "I was just proving my point." She shook her head in disgust. "I don't blame her at all for resenting me. I'm a selfish, terrible person. Oh, GREAT!" She threw her arms in the air. "And the snap on my pants just popped open!"

Lincoln gave the man at the next table overtly staring at them a little wave. "All right, A) you're gonna have to stop being so damn hard on yourself, and B) I didn't say anything before, but I undid my top button after the pu-pu platter."

Clara couldn't help but let out a little chuckle.

"Let me ask you this: have you told Tabitha everything you just told me?"

She shook her head. "I tried to, but . . ." Shrugging in defeat, Clara didn't bother finishing the sentence.

"Well"—Lincoln folded his arms across his chest—"what are you waiting for?"

March

It was an unusually balmy afternoon shortly after the first anniversary of Sebastian's death. The sun peeked behind a passing cloud, and the scent of fresh-cut grass and sweet primrose laced the gentle breeze, which carried with it the hopeful promise of spring. Clara, squatting on her hands and knees in Libby's backyard, gripping a pointed, scoop-shaped, silver garden trowel used for breaking earth, dug a fresh hole where she'd remembered burying Leo's recorder when she was a young child.

"I swear this is where I hid it," she said yet again to Libby, who was towering nearby, between the large weeping willow tree and Maple Manor, with both hands on her hips and her eyebrows furrowed. "I'm sorry. I was wrong about the other eight holes I dug." Clara flinched, trying to downplay the fact that she was slowly but surely transforming her mother's meticulously maintained backyard into a crater-cramped zone that resembled a life-size version of Whac-A-Mole, the popular carnival redemption game. "But I have a good feeling about this one."

"Mm-hmm. How much deeper do you plan on digging?" Libby tapped her foot against the soft grass.

"Not much." Clara wiped a thin sheen of perspiration from her brow, fearing her mother was moments away from foaming at the mouth. "It was late at night when I buried the recorder, so it was dark outside, but I don't remember it taking me too long to form the hole. So if I'm not mistaken, it should surface any time now."

"*Any time now . . .*" Libby echoed for effect. "Well, let's certainly hope so."

Ten long minutes of Libby frowning later, Clara was still shoveling at a frantic pace, and her mother was chewing the corner of her bottom lip, watching the unsightly ninth ditch in her treasured garden continue to expand.

"*Uh, one more hole and you get a free sandwich?*" Clara attempted to diffuse the increasing tension in the air.

But Libby just stood there with her arms crossed, unamused.

"I—I don't understand." Clara hurled brown dirt over her shoulder with the trowel. "I could've *sworn* this is where I buried the damn thing!"

"Words every mother longs to hear escape her daughter's mouth."

"I'm sorry. I really mean it. I assure you, I do *not* want to make a monumental mess back here. But you have to understand," Clara pleaded, focusing on one thing and one thing only: her time capsule list. "I need to find that recorder!" She paused for a minute to catch her breath. "Is it okay if I try digging about three feet over to the left? Now I'm starting to think I may have made the hole a little bit closer to the house.

I'm almost positive that was the area." She nodded toward the precise location where she wished to break ground for the tenth time.

"Oh, you're *almost* positive?" Libby emphasized her words with raised arms, exasperated. "Fabulous. I feel much better now. Please, go ahead and form yet another ditch! You haven't destroyed my tulip beds yet. And the hollyhock corner over there"—she pointed west—"looks ripe for the taking."

"I already told you three times that I promise to repair these holes and leave the backyard looking as beautiful as I found it," Clara reminded her, trying to hold on to her last shred of patience, which she felt slipping away. "I'll fix it all."

Closing her eyes and collecting her composure with a dramatic, deep breath, Libby continued in a milder voice, "Honey, look . . . I understand that **Dig up Leo's recorder from the backyard & apologize for burying it** is on your time capsule list. You have given it a *valiant effort*, but listen to me. Listen to me!" She crouched down in the arid soil so that she was at eye-level with Clara. "You do not have to prove anything to your brother. He knows how sorry you are for burying his instrument. You've told him many times. He forgives you. This is *alllll* water under the bridge. The *very old* bridge," she stressed. "Okay? So why don't we just call it a day and go inside. Come on," she coaxed, patting Clara's shoulder. "What do you say about a nice, cold Fudgsicle?"

Clara tightened her jaw and narrowed her eyes in a similar defiant pose that Libby often struck when she was feeling frustrated. Decades earlier, when Grandma Lottie decided to move to Arizona because Chicago's icy winters were too harsh to bear, Libby had broken the news to Clara and Leo

over a delicious, soothing Fudgsicle. When the inebriated
mailman accidentally ran over Clara's brand-new bicycle
with sparkly handle streamers that she'd just gotten for her
seventh birthday, Libby gave her a Fudgsicle before revealing
that her beloved bike now resembled a metal pancake with
half a banana seat. And when Clara overheard some older
kids mention there was no such thing as Santa Claus and
asked her mother if it was true, Libby forked over yet another
comforting Fudgsicle.

"I say that I am *NOT* ready for a Fudgsicle yet." Clara
glowered at Libby. She shoved her trowel into the ground.
"*Please.* I'm telling you, I'm gonna find this fucking recorder!"
Violently stabbing the earth, she immediately felt guilty for
snapping at her mother like a spoiled little brat who wanted a
golden goose for Easter.

"Well, I wish you luck," Libby returned, seeming to accept
that her unwavering daughter was on a hell-bent mission that
she did not plan on aborting any time soon. "I hope you find it
before my backyard resembles an exploded landmine."

"Yeah," Clara-the-recorder-hunter countered, "well, *I*
hope I find it before I have to meet Tabitha in Vegas next
week."

"*Yes, well—*" Libby stopped in her tracks. "What? Vegas?
Wait a minute. You're going to Las Vegas?"

Clara nodded. "With Tabitha."

"But, I thought you said she was upset with you."

"She is. See?" Clara smiled up at her mother. "You're in
good company."

"Stop it. You know I love you. Even when you resemble
Pig Pen from Charlie Brown." Libby referred to the smudge

of mud on Clara's cheek. "When did this get planned? How come you and Tabitha are meeting in Las Vegas of all places?"

"Because that's where the biggest all-you-can-eat buffet in the country is." Clara shielded her eyes from the luminous sun. "It's on my list," she added, "to **Eat at America's largest buffet**. And I really need to clear the air with Tabitha once and for all and let her know how sorry I am about everything."

"I'm sure she already knows that."

"I'm not. I'm just thankful she agreed to come along. After the way I've turned my back on her, I was scared she might not even be willing to consider it. And frankly, I wouldn't blame her."

"So, let me get this straight. You and Tabitha are going to talk and stuff your faces until you're both sick?"

"Yep. That's basically the plan." Clara scooped a new hole in the ground. "It'll be great."

At least, that's what Clara kept telling herself.

22.

Pacing back and forth in the posh sitting area of her luxurious Las Vegas Hilton hotel suite, which encompassed over one thousand square feet of gilded opulence and boasted a wet bar, outdoor terrace, and floor-to-ceiling windows overlooking the dazzling Las Vegas strip, Clara anxiously awaited Tabitha's delayed arrival. Her estranged friend was due at any moment. Tabitha was supposed to have flown into town the previous evening at approximately the same time as Clara, but a violent nor'easter had slammed the Boston area, temporarily shutting down Logan International Airport. "All incoming and outgoing flights were cancelled and I've been rebooked on a Saturday morning flight," Tabitha had explained over the payphone in the crammed airline terminal, shouting to be heard over a crying child, a bickering couple, and a muffled announcement being made over the loudspeaker. "The battery on my cell phone died and there's a long line of stranded, impatient people waiting to use the phone, so I should go, but I'll hopefully be at the hotel tomorrow around noon if all goes according to plan." Tabitha's words had seeped with frustration. "Sorry about this delay. See you then," she'd quickly concluded.

"No, no, no, don't be silly! *I'm* sorry you have to go through this annoying hassle," Clara had tried to squeeze in, but it was too late. Tabitha had already hung up. "Crap," she had muttered, snapping shut her cell phone.

The clock hanging on the gray slate wall with the miniature waterfall told her that it was 12:22 p.m.

"Sorry" didn't even begin to describe Clara's feelings of regret. Saddled with guilt over causing their friendship to disintegrate, she'd originally planned on apologizing to Tabitha the previous evening, at the very start of their trip—for which Clara had happily splurged and covered all expenses—so that they could enjoy the rest of their weekend together and catch up on everything they'd missed in each other's lives. *Well, so much for that idea,* Clara had disappointedly thought to herself while struggling to fall asleep in one of the suite's two queen-size beds, trying to ignore her persistent hunger pangs and resist the urge to pop open a small, fifty-dollar can of "fancy" hotel peanuts. Alas, to allow for maximum food intake and enjoyment, she had decided to fast for a day in advance of hitting America's largest buffet.

Suddenly, there was a knock at the door. Clara jumped.

Rushing toward the door, she quickly reminded herself of several points that she wanted to be sure to apologize to Tabitha for. For the past week, Clara had been carefully considering everything that she wished to say to her best friend, rehearsing the chock-full-o'-grovel monologue in her mind so that when the time finally came, and they were sitting face-to-face, she wouldn't blow it. Pardoning herself didn't seem likely, and Clara prayed that Tabitha's proficiency for forgiveness would be greater than her own.

"Welcome to Vegas!" she exclaimed, swinging open the door and greeting Tabitha with an overly enthusiastic smile.

"Hey there." Tabitha offered a hesitant half-grin in return. Wheeling a small suitcase behind her as she entered the lavish suite, she looked around, seemingly impressed. "Wow"—she marveled at the swanky space—"this had to have cost you a fortune. I can't believe you did this . . ."

"I'm an asshole!" Clara declared (not a part of her rehearsed dialogue), throwing her arms around her curly-haired best friend and hugging her close. "An absolute *asshole*! You have *no idea* how much I've missed you or how sorry I am about everything. I disrespected you and our friendship and that is *not* all right and I feel like a selfish jerk and I really don't know how you'll ever forgive me but I hope you will!" She rapidly rushed on, as if she were trying to squeeze in all her words before a ticking time bomb exploded. "Because I love you! And whether you believe it or not, you *are* my best friend and you mean the world to me but I just couldn't even *begin* to cope with my grief and my messed-up life before but I'm trying my best to pull it all back together now and I need you to know that. I blew it! I blew it *big time*—and there aren't words to properly express how truly, *truly* sorry I am." Clara inhaled an enormous, necessary gasp of oxygen. "*AND I'M AN ASSHOLE!*"

"You are not," Tabitha whispered, her voice thick with emotion. "Stop saying that."

"Well . . . it's true . . ." Clara insisted softly.

When their embrace finally ended, there were tears in both women's eyes.

"Hey—look at you," Tabitha said with a sniffle, taking in her friend whom she hadn't seen since October. "You're lookin' good!"

Overcome with relief, Clara couldn't resist hugging her again.

"Y'all fat, and y'all eat too much!" shouted a belligerent drunk man, covered from head to toe in clam spaghetti, who was being escorted by a bouncer out of America's largest buffet, conveniently located at the Las Vegas Hilton. "Y'all porky piglets!"

"He's not kidding." Tabitha smirked at Clara, taking a bite of buttermilk-fried chicken and eyeing the twisting, turning, 140-foot-long buffet, complete with extravagant ice sculptures, bubbling décor, effervescent columns, and 515 distinct dishes. Combined, the culinary delights represented more than twelve ethnicities and four courses, including over one hundred different salads, forty-five varieties of hot and cold soup, twenty types of meat, thirty kinds of seafood, seventy-five pasta choices, twelve different pizzas, fifty unique cold items, and 150 different desserts. There were two complimentary wine and beer bars on either end of the premiere ballroom. And, to top it off, there was even an Alka-Seltzer relief station. In short, it was everything Clara had dreamed it would be as a child, and more. Much, *much* more.

Three hours of nonstop conversation into their overindulgent meal, Tabitha had just finished describing the trip she and her fiancé, Max, took to Acapulco, when Clara's cell phone rang. "Shoot. I better grab this. It's Leo. He's taking care of Milk Dud while I'm gone." She lifted the receiver to her ear.

"Guess who I'm sitting at a table with?" Leo asked her.

"Who?" Clara heard somebody in the noisy background on his end request a "double, low-fat, no-foam, soy vanilla latte."

"Hang on a second."

"Hi, C.J.," greeted another male voice. "How's the food fest going?"

"*Link?*" Clara was shocked to hear his voice. "It's—It's going great." She glanced at the table, which was laden down with too many little plates to count. "What are you doing with my brother? Where are you?"

"We ran into each other waiting in line at the Mayflower Café. Oh, wait. Hold on a moment. I just heard a weird beep."

Jumping back on the phone, Leo hurriedly explained that he had to take another call coming through. "Lincoln and I are catching a movie after this. I'll give you a buzz later," he said to Clara before hanging up.

"*Oookay.*" She blinked, returning her phone to her purse. "Apparently my brother and Lincoln are having an afternoon play date."

Tabitha took a large bite of beef Wellington. "I think it's nice that they get along so well. Max thinks my brother's a pompous snob. Of course, I do too," she acknowledged.

"I just hope Leo doesn't drive Link up a wall with a zillion pesky questions about his job. I'm telling you, he's got serious dinosaur envy."

"I want to hear more about Lincoln." Tabitha chewed a large mouthful of Thai noodle salad. "What's he look like?"

"I don't know." Clara tasted her chimichanga. "Tall.

Brown eyes. His hair is starting to turn a little bit gray in areas."

"Is he cute?"

Clara thought about it for a moment. "I guess. Kind of. I don't really think of him like that. He sort of faintly resembles George Clooney."

"Are you kidding me? George Clooney's gorgeous." Tabitha sliced her Swedish meatball in half. "It sounds like you two have been spending a lot of time together lately." Shifting her eyes, she hesitated for a moment. "If I may ask . . . is this a strictly platonic relationship?"

"Oh God, *yes*." Clara stabbed a spinach ravioli with her fork. "Lincoln and I go so far back together he's practically like family."

"*Practically* doesn't count."

"Trust me. We tried the whole dating thing once a million years ago and it did not take us long to realize we just don't work on that level. It felt like I was dating my own cousin."

"Yikes." Tabitha cringed.

"Plus, he has a great girlfriend. Meg. I've had dinner with them a couple times and it's obvious how happy they are together. Besides," Clara added with her mouth full of quiche Lorraine, "I'm not ready to think about a relationship. You know, it's only been a little over a year since . . ." Her voice trailed off, for there was no need for her to finish that thought out loud.

"I know," Tabitha said, nodding, munching a miniature falafel. "So Meg doesn't mind that her boyfriend goes for training jogs and out for meals all alone with you?"

"No. It doesn't seem like it. She knows there's no call for concern." Clara, chomping on a sweet potato French fry, further proved her point by sharing, "We're going to the Wisconsin Dells in June and Meg didn't bat a lash. Of course, I told her that Leo and Ava—who he's been seeing on and off—might join us, and she was more than welcome to come along too, but she said that she can't take time off from work. She runs the gift shop at the museum."

"What the hell are the *Wisconsin Dells?*" Tabitha popped a spicy California roll into her mouth.

"You're kidding me. You've never heard of the Dells?"

"Nope."

"Huh." Clara shrugged. "Maybe it's a Midwest thing."

"Could be. What is it?"

"Oh, it's this corny, but charming, Wisconsin tourist town that's basically a children's paradise—sort of like a colossal Coney Island. It's the land of cotton candy, go-carts, haunted houses—that kind of thing. It's actually known as the 'Waterpark Capital of the World.'"

"Sounds great to me." Tabitha slurped her gazpacho.

"I always dreamed of going there when I was a kid," Clara confessed. "I was obsessed with it. Every summer I'd beg Libby to take us, but we never got to go. Apparently, neither did Lincoln. When he saw **Visit the Wisconsin Dells** on my time capsule list, he lit up and said it was also one of his unfulfilled childhood wishes to go there." Pushing her bourbon-glazed ham aside, Clara took a spoonful of banana pudding. "So he's coming too. Trust me, it's not exactly the kind of place that's known to appeal to adults. But, since it's on my list, I'm going." She tasted her fried rice. "I know it sounds like a silly thing to do."

"It doesn't," countered Tabitha, cracking open a crab leg.

"I think your time capsule list and what you're doing with it is fucking brilliant. Brilliant."

"Really?" Clara looked doubtful.

"Yes. Seriously, Clara. Look at how far you've come since Thanksgiving."

"I guess . . ."

"I *know*. And I, for one, am thankful for that list."

Clara smiled. She considered how accurate the fortune from her cookie at Syn-Kow had been. Indeed, she thought to herself, "*One old friend is better than two new ones.*" Tabitha was proof of it.

"Thanks, Tab," she said. "That means more to me than you know."

"I didn't want to harp on anything negative, but things were so bad before you left town"—a serious expression crossed Tabitha's buffalo-wing-sauce-covered face as she ad-mitted it—"you really gave me a scare."

"I know," Clara quietly replied. And she did, too.

"Well," Tabitha said, grinning, wiping her mouth with a napkin and lifting her complimentary beer in a toast, "to the time capsule!"

"To the time capsule," Clara echoed, raising her glass and clinking it against her old friend's.

"*And* to the blessed Alka-Seltzer station," groaned Tabitha.

"Amen!" Clara laughed, leaning her head back. "*We all porky piglets!*"

- ~~Eat at America's largest buffet~~

April

23.

It was an overcast Sunday afternoon and for the third time since Clara had moved into Judge Bennett's condo, his real estate broker had politely requested that she and Milk Dud vacate the premises while he hosted an open house. With the exception of a young couple who had wanted to purchase the home—but put in a ridiculously low bid—there had been no serious takers, and the increasingly disillusioned judge had mentioned to Clara that the marketplace was so grim he was contemplating lowering the price in order to make a sale "and just get it over and done with already."

After meeting Lincoln for an early morning jog along a scenic—but miserably uphill—path in Grant Park known as "The Mountain"—their third training session that week in preparation for the upcoming 10K Race to Beat Cancer—Clara and Milk Dud drove straight to River Pointe. Though her whole body ached from struggling up The Mountain and she'd have preferred to go home and collapse, Libby had invited her and Leo over for a good old-fashioned Sunday supper, and Clara figured she'd spend the day catching up

with her family and hopefully unearthing Leo's damn recorder, which still remained MIA.

When Clara arrived at the house, she discovered a note
from Libby in the kitchen saying that she and Leo were out
running errands and would be back later. "Perfect," Clara
mumbled to Milk Dud, grabbing a bottle of water out of
the refrigerator. "Let's find this thing quickly before your
grandma gets home and has another conniption fit about me
destroying her backyard. What do you say?"

Milk Dud barked and licked his rear end in approval.

Collecting the trowel from the gardening shed near Maple
Manor, Clara returned to the scene of the crime. Or, at least,
to what she crossed her fingers, toes, and spleen was the scene
of the crime. No matter how hard she tried to recall exactly
where she'd buried Leo's instrument, her mind continually
drew a blank, increasing both her frustration level and resolve
to find it. Determined, she pushed up her sweatshirt sleeves,
crouched down on her hands and knees, and got to work.

She dug.

And she dug.

Then, she dug some more.

Two full hours passed without her realizing it.

It hadn't rained in a few weeks, and as a result the ground
was hard and dry, rendering digging more of a physical strain
than it had been during Clara's last ill-fated hunt for buried
recorder. Her knees were beginning to throb and a painful
blister had formed on the palm of her hand where she gripped
the trowel. Concentrating fiercely, she had just formed her
thirteenth crater of the day to no avail. "Dammit!" she cursed,
tossing the trowel aside. "Ridiculous . . ." Short of breath and

perspiring, she wiped her brow with the back of her hand, smudging a gray streak of dirt across her forehead. Her aggravation peaking, fighting the urge to scream, she knew that she needed to take a break.

Sitting cross-legged, leaning back against the sturdy tree that housed Maple Manor, Clara unscrewed the cap off her water bottle and took several big gulps. Then, inhaling a deep, calming breath, she ran her fingers through her hair, leaving behind little particles of dirt in her locks. Milk Dud plopped himself down by her side, resting his chin on her thigh. She gave his head an affectionate pet. "I had no idea how hard this would be," she told him, dejected. "No idea . . ."

The sun was beginning to set, and Clara noticed that the moon had already surfaced in the eastern sky, glowing vibrant white and almost full. She had always loved it when both the sun and moon simultaneously graced the sky. It reminded her of two dear old friends who don't see each other often getting together for a visit. Taking another sip of water, Clara's thoughts turned to Sebastian. If only he could have been there too, relaxing by her side, staring at the sky with her. She often fantasized about sitting on a park bench with Sebastian, gazing up at the moon and stars together. He'd put his arm around her and she'd inch a bit closer to him, leaning her head on his shoulder. If she closed her eyes and focused hard enough, she could practically feel his tall, sturdy body next to her and smell the musky, masculine scent of his cologne. Such a minimal, easy wish it was . . . Some people fantasized about possessing superhero powers, or achieving world peace, or making millions of dollars—owning fancy cars and mansions, circumnavigating the globe in a private plane with a hot

tub and a British butler named Ronaldo who wore a tuxedo
and catered to their every whim. Not Clara. Her ultimate
dream was so much simpler. Yet it was impossible. Shaking
her head at the cruelty of it all, as if to keep herself from falling too deep into melancholy longing with all her heart for
something that would never be, her thoughts instead floated
to something new.

For the first time ever, she imagined what her life might
have been like to be someone else. A whole new person.
Someone who never met Sebastian. Someone less ambitious
to climb the corporate ladder, perhaps an English teacher at
a community college or a grocery clerk, or maybe the wife
of a cattle rancher in a small, rural town in the middle of
Nebraska. Someone whose entire existence wasn't centered
around the endless struggle to accept her soul mate's death
and move on. Someone who hadn't the faintest clue about
the all-consuming, bottomless depth of inconsolable grief.
Clara let out a soft, dreamy sigh, considering how wonderful
it would be to have the chance at a "regular" life. To wake up
in the morning and make oatmeal with raisins, read the newspaper, get dressed, head off to work, and not even once think
about her dead fiancé—because she didn't have a dead fiancé.
How exhilarating and freeing it would be to actually be able
to really "live" life and just be normal! The word "normal"
resonated in her mind. God, what she wouldn't have done to
experience "normal." Yet, Clara feared that she would never
again know the truly amazing sensation of "normal."

Fantasizing about this enticing, grief-free life as someone
else—where happiness was not only real, but also possible for
her too—Clara eventually drifted off to sleep.

May

24.

One Monday morning in early May, Clara received an e-mail from her boss, Mr. Franklin, with the subject line "IMPORTANT" written in capital letters. She immediately felt a strange sense of doom—even before opening the message.

Though they'd maintained a cordial e-mail correspondence with each other since Clara's sabbatical began, they had spoken on the telephone only once during March when Mr. Franklin called to inquire whether she had any idea when she might return to work. Clara doubted that The Beer King, a sympathetic and considerate man, had realized it was the first anniversary of Sebastian's death. Nor did she doubt that he had heard the sadness in her voice, which was hoarse from weeping. Having just hung up the phone with Sebastian's grieving parents in Cape Cod moments before her boss called, Clara was in no mood to discuss business—or anything, for that matter. The whole day had been a relentless *mean moment*, and for once she couldn't help but allow herself to think that nobody—*nobody*—should have to live with the kind of devastation she had suffered, and continued to endure. All Clara wanted to do was just be by herself and not feel like she had to feign strength by putting on a brave face, or apologize for her emotions, including self-pity. She had no desire to hear about how the other Scuppernong account executives were stressed out and overworked from the added pressure of handling Clara's accounts in her absence. "I wish I had an exact answer for you, Mr. Franklin. But the truth is, I'm not sure yet when I'll be back," Clara, clutching the photo of Sebastian and her dancing at the black-tie Boston Philharmonic gala, had told her boss, sniffling. "Do you think it would be all right if we continue this conversation via e-mail either later today or tomorrow? You kind of caught me at an inopportune time." Probably sensing her distress, The Beer King had obliged with a reluctant sigh.

Double-clicking on his "IMPORTANT" message, Clara opened the e-mail and read:

> Clara,
>   I hope you're well. Are you available today for a call? It's urgent. Please let me know at your earliest convenience when works best for you.
>   I look forward to hearing from you soon.

Worried about the "urgent" matter and whether it spelled trouble for her as she feared, Clara decided she best call Mr. Franklin straight away, so she grabbed her phone and took a seat at the Ping-Pong table.

"Good afternoon. Oops! I mean, good *morning*." A bubbly temp filling in for Mandy, The Beer King's usual assistant who was out with the flu, answered his direct telephone line. "Mr. Franklin's office."

"Hi, this is Clara Black calling for Mr. Franklin, please."

"Ms. Black! I have heard so much about you. I know Mr. Franklin is dying to talk to you! Can you hang on a sec? He just went to the bathroom. He had steak and eggs for breakfast," the temp shared under her breath. "Need I say more?"

"Uh, no thank you," Clara responded.

"Oh look! There he is! That was sure quick," the temp whispered into the phone. Then, forgetting to press the "hold" button, she alerted Mr. Franklin, "I have Clara Black on line one for you. She doesn't sound too depressed or whacked out to me. Although, what do I know? Poor thing . . . On a separate note, I think I might've accidentally broken the fax machine. It keeps jamming, and there was some smoke coming out of the top in the paper thingy area, but I poured water on it."

"Not *again*," lamented Mr. Franklin. "I'll deal with it later. Patch Clara through to my office, and hold all calls. I'm closing my door."

Hearing the frustration in his voice, Clara imagined how his lips were probably tightly pursed, and how his chubby, round face had most likely turned a spooky shade of red, as was customary when he lost his patience.

"Clara, my dear!" Mr. Franklin greeted her cheerfully several moments later. "How are you?"

She wanted to answer, "*I'm not too depressed or whacked out*," but thought better of getting a poor temp—who probably needed the money—in trouble, and instead told her boss that she was "doing all right."

"I'm glad to hear it," he responded. "Because to put it mildly, you are terribly missed around here!"

"Well, I miss you all too. I got your e-mail and wanted to get back to you about it immediately."

"I appreciate that, Clara. I hope you'll forgive me for jumping directly to the reason for this call."

"Of course." She prayed his next words wouldn't be "you're fired."

"We need you back!" The Beer King announced. "The Account Executive team is under extraordinary pressure. We have the new light beer entering the market in a few months and have already increased our number of vendors by over ten percent in anticipation of its release. Based on Ron's latest East Coast forecasts, those numbers should continue to rise. We've also got offers in from establishments in California and Colorado, and have drawn up plans to expand west. In short, the A.E. team's plate is spilling over and it's starting to negatively affect their performance and morale. I can't have that."

Clara squeezed her eyes shut. "I'm sorry about this. I feel terrible that I've added to the team's workload when things are so hectic." Releasing a guilty sigh, she still hoped the next words out of his mouth wouldn't be "you're fired."

"I don't want you to feel terrible. I want you to feel like returning to work," he declared. "And I want the old, alert, talented, capable Clara Black that I originally hired back. Not the one who left after Thanksgiving."

Alas, what Clara wouldn't have given to become the "old, alert, talented, capable Clara Black" again. But, like her fiancé, that person was gone forever.

"You know that despite your road bump, Clara, I still believe you can and *will* be an excellent asset to Scuppernong. That said, you've been on sabbatical for a long time now, and I need a more precise sense of your plans for the future so that I can accurately and effectively manage the company's."

"Um . . ." She hesitated, panicking. "Well . . ." She wasn't quite sure how to respond.

After a few moments of awkward silence, Mr. Franklin continued, "I promised you would always have a home at Scuppernong, and I am a man of my word. However, due to the fact that I may need to hire an additional account executive to cover increased business, there's a chance that you may not have a place working on the A.E. team."

Gnawing at her nails, Clara felt her pulse rate quicken. She had been so singularly focused on tending to her time capsule list, giving it one last shot—like "final call" at a bar—to get her life back on track, she hadn't really had a chance to dedicate much thought to her job. Consumed with more pressing issues, the truth was, thus far, her career hadn't registered as a top concern or priority, despite her fondness for her boss, which precluded her from lying to him. And so she told him that although she knew this was not the answer he was looking for, and she hated inconveniencing the A.E. team, the fact remained that she was not prepared to identify a precise date when she would return to work.

"Well, I can respect that, Clara. And, in turn, I hope you can respect what I'm about to say."

Oh, boy. Here it came. Clara, sitting collapsed in her folding chair with her forehead resting on the palm of her hand, thought to herself, *"Hit the road, Jack. You're fired."*

"I cannot continue to ask your overburdened colleagues

to cover your accounts without them knowing there's an end in sight. I'm willing to give you another six weeks to hash out your own personal game plan, but after that, if you're still unable to let me know when you're returning, I'm going to hire a new account executive. I have a business to run here. This isn't personal." Mr. Franklin paused, presumably for Clara to respond.

But Clara, well aware that The Beer King's threat was not personal, remained tongue-tied. This was the last topic she'd been prepared to consider when she'd woken up that morning; yet she knew Mr. Franklin's demand was fair. Sooner or later, this was music she was going to have to face.

"Clara? Are you still there?"

"Oh, I'm sorry. I'm—I'm here."

"Here's my non-negotiable proposal," Mr. Franklin continued in a matter-of-fact tone. "On June fifteenth you and I will speak again, at which point you'll either identify a firm date when you're returning to work, or officially surrender your position. And, like I said, if you choose option two there will always be a job available for you at the company. I just can't guarantee on what level." Mr. Franklin paused again. "Do you have any questions?"

Talk about regressing, Clara shuddered. She wondered why anybody in their right mind would agree to a demotion at a company they'd worked at for years. Especially when they'd previously been the top candidate for a director of sales promotion and there were rumblings of a vice-president position in the "not-too-far-off future." *Great*, she thought to herself. *Just great* . . . Following the helpful AA mantra Lincoln had introduced her to, she was still concentrating on "making it through the day, the hour, the minute . . ." In no way was Clara prepared to plan her future—assuming she had one, which, at times, she sincerely doubted. Making a critical, long-term career decision at this juncture felt premature—unreasonable, even. It was all too much to think about. Deciding she'd cross that bridge *if*, not when, she came to it in June, Clara answered Mr. Franklin honestly, telling him in the most professional-sounding voice she could muster, "No, I don't have any questions."

"Well, I'm sorry it's come to this, Clara. We're understood, then?"

"We're understood," she confirmed, a worried look pinching her face as a new, heart-pounding sense of alarm about her future set in.

Later that evening, Clara met Leo after work outside on the grand, white cement staircase of Chicago's Cook County Circuit Courthouse, Refusing to divulge details of the surprise he had planned, he'd promised her an evening she "would not soon forget." With her mind still reeling from her anxiety-inducing conversation with The Beer King, Clara had considered canceling on her brother at the last minute, but she realized doing so would only incite him to speculate and worry more about her. Something Clara definitely did not need. Thus, she decided it would ultimately be easier to just rise above it and be a trooper. Besides, she was a fan of surprises. At least, in most cases.

"Hi there." Leo, dressed in a handsome navy suit and tie, greeted her with a hug. "How was your day?"

She rolled her eyes. "Don't ask."

"What's wrong?"

Clara sighed. "The Beer King gave me an ultimatum this morning." She provided her brother with an abbreviated version of the stressful phone call as they began walking toward a mystery location, which he said was not too far away.

"Well, the upside is you don't have to make a final decision right now," Leo, ever the rational optimist, pointed out. "You have time to think this through and figure out what you really want."

"True," Clara reluctantly agreed. "But let's not talk about this anymore. It gives me a headache. What I *really want* is to know what the surprise is. Tell me."

"Sorry. My lips are sealed." He smirked. "All I'm willing to say is that you are going to love it. I don't like to brag, but it's semi-genius."

"Oh, *come on!* This isn't fair. Can't you at least give me a little hint?"

"What would the Nestlé Quik bunny say? Where's your patience?" Leo milked the suspense for all it was worth. "Okay. Fine," he acquiesced. "I *will* reveal one last thing. We're meeting Ava at the rendezvous point."

"Ava?" Clara perked up. "That's exciting. So does this mean that things are becoming more serious with you two? Has she decided if she's coming to the Wisconsin Dells with us? How come she didn't meet us on the steps?" Clara asked, referring to the fact that Ava was a courtroom stenographer who often worked on the same cases as Leo.

"Who knows, we're still feeling it out. No. And she took the day off from work. Does that cover all of your questions?"

"No. Where the heck are we going?!" Clara demanded with her fists on her hips.

They continued walking for a while, discussing Leo's latest case, until eventually, Clara noticed a massive crowd of people funneling into the new sporting arena that was home to the Chicago Blackhawks ice hockey team.

And there, before her eyes, was a dazzling, jumbo, lit-up sign, flashing, "*Robots On Ice.*"

"No way!" she gasped, as if Patrick Swayze in the flesh was standing before her with his perfectly muscular arm extended in an enticing invitation to dirty dance. "Are you serious? Are we seeing *ROBOTS ON ICE?*"

Grinning, Leo bowed, making a grand, sweeping gesture with his arms. "Welcome to your surprise."

"Wow." Clara blinked, her mouth hanging wide open. "I don't . . . I don't know what to say. *Robots? On ice?*"

"Indeed. What do you think?" In a swift move, he removed two VIP tickets from his jacket pocket, waving them in front of Clara's flabbergasted face.

"I think it's stupendous," she said, beaming, still trying to wrap her brain around the enchanting concept of figure-skating robots. "I've always wanted to see the Ice Capades!"

"I know, silly. It's on your time capsule list. Why do you think we're here?"

"Well, but where's Ava?" Clara searched the crowd for her.

"She's already inside," Leo explained. "She scored us these box seats. Wait 'til you see them. Our view of the rink is superb! Ava's cousin's a professional skater and is playing the role of the 'Robot Olivia,' who's one of the leads."

"The *Robot Olivia?*" Clara repeated in stunned delight. "This just keeps getting better."

Leo grinned, equally amused. "Right? Apparently, she falls in love with the brooding 'Robot Rodolfo,' who's from the wrong side of the planet and improperly wired."

"Oh my God. I love it. This is going to be glorious."

"I know." He smiled. "We're just lucky to be here."

"*So lucky.*"

"Blessed," Leo said sincerely, leading her toward a special VIP entrance where a midget dressed up like a little green Martian with glittering antennas was shouting into a megaphone, "Welcome, Earthlings! Come, one and all!"

As it turned out, the spectacular show—complete with an elaborate set of the solar system, intricate lighting, cutting-edge, space-age sound effects, flying saucers, holograms, and a chorus of silver, clunky robots who occasionally spoke in emotionless, monotone voices and resembled "Rosie," the lovable robot maid from *The Jetsons*—did not disappoint. In the production's show-stopping finale, when at last the Robot Olivia and the Robot Rodolfo, misunderstood star-crossed lovers, finally found a way to be together, jumping, spinning, and lifting each other around the perimeter of the rink to the song *You Are So Beautiful* in a touching ice dance that was supposed to be romantic, Clara laughed so hard that tears spilled down her cheeks and she nearly upchucked her nachos. And Leo, holding Ava's hand, whispered to nobody in particular, "I hope this never ends."

Needless to say, when the cast of robots took their final, electrifying bow, the entire audience leaped to their feet, whistling and clapping their hands in an unparalleled stand-

ing ovation that Clara knew she would always remember.
Always. And not just because one of the child robots, unable
to bend at the waist in its cumbersome costume, lost its balance, fell forward flat on its square face, and required the help
of several others in order to resume standing—only to fall
right back down again.

After the show, Clara, Leo, and Ava took a taxi to the Wie-
ner's Circle, one of the city's most celebrated hot dog joints,
for a quick bite. When Ava ordered her classic, Chicago-style
dog in monotone robot-speak, requesting, "ex-ter-a mus-tard
please, kind mor-tal," they all burst into hysterics, like slap-
happy children who were up past their bedtime, as opposed
to professional adults—one of whom was so busy enjoying
herself that she completely forgot she'd been issued an ultimatum by her aggravated boss earlier that morning.

- ~~Attend the Ice Capades~~

25

More than five thousand runners with large, black-and-white numbers pinned to their shirts participated in the 10K Race to Beat Cancer, and Clara knew that she would never forget some of them. There was the quartet of siblings dressed in matching green t-shirts that read "In Loving Memory of Our Father, Robert" across the back, the group of women of all ages and ethnicities wearing pink ribbons and buttons that boasted "I'm a Survivor," and the darling little bald girl who smiled and waved at Clara as she galloped past her. There was something about the radiant little girl's infectious, dimpled grin that tugged at Clara's heart. None of this was fair. None of it. And it gutted Clara. Having been primarily concerned with making it to the finish line in one piece without the aid of triage and/or illegal performance enhancing drugs, never did it dawn on her that this race would be a deeply emotional experience. But tied together by the common, unifying thread of suffering, all of these people—*all* of them—had endured unspeakable pain in some form or another, and Clara ached for every last one of them. The remarkable courage, determination, and perseverance of her fellow race mates astounded her, inspiring her with new hope and reminding her that there were people out there who had it worse than she did. Much worse.

Though she fought the growing knot in her throat for as long as she possibly could, eventually Clara collapsed under the weight of her own empathy and began to choke up. Jogging at a slow, labored pace by Lincoln's side, she removed her sunglasses to wipe away her tears.

"You okay?" he huffed, glancing at her, appearing about ready to keel over.

Considering Jessica Foster, Clara nodded, quickly trying to pull herself together if for no other reason than to avoid upsetting Lincoln. "These people are all just so amazing. It really makes you think."

"It does," he agreed. "It helps put everything in perspective," Lincoln added between gasps of air. Suddenly, he bellowed, *"Cramp!"*

Jerking to an abrupt halt, he bent over, clutching his throbbing calf as he grimaced with pain, groaning. *"Bad cramp!* Oh God! Oh GOD! This is bad!"

"Okay, just calm down and try taking a deep breath," Clara suggested, surprised that she'd made it this far without cramping, hurling, expiring (or all of the above) herself. "Take a *nice*, deep breath and try stretching it out—like we do when we warm up."

Obliging, Lincoln inhaled as he contorted his body into an awkward version of a forward lunge. "This isn't helping, C.J. *Craaamp!* It hurts! It really hurts! I've never had a cramp this bad before!"

Flustered by his uncharacteristic hysteria, unsure what to do next, Clara asked, "Want me to rub it?"

"Yes! Yes!" Lincoln eyes were squeezed tightly shut in agony. "Just make it go away. Call somebody. A medic! Lance Armstrong! *Anyone!*"

"You're gonna be fine," Clara calmly assured him, crouching down and massaging his knotted calf as a gray-haired group of senior citizens wearing matching shorts with the message "Kick Leukemia's Ass!" across the derrière zipped past them. "Think of dinosaurs. *Sweet, soothing T-rexes . . .*"

"Oh, that feels good. That's nice," Lincoln said, unscrewing his water bottle cap and pouring its entire remains on his face, sopping Clara in the process. "Don't stop. Please . . ."

Eventually, "the cramp from Hades," as he later called it, subsided, and Lincoln, openly embarrassed about the incident, was able to walk again. Or, at least, hobble. "I can't go any farther, C.J.," he said, defeat written all over his sweaty face. "It'll take me forever. I'm done."

"Come on, Link. You can do this." Clara was not about to let him give up. When she agreed to run this race all those months ago over dinner at Syn-Kow, it was in order to help root him on, and that was exactly what she intended to do.

"No. I really don't think I can. You have to finish without me."

"Like hell I will. This is for *cancer research*, Link. If you can make it up that stinking 'Mountain' I hate so much in Grant Park, you can make it to the finish line. We'll walk slowly if we have to. *We are completing this!*"

"I don't think so, C.J."

Wiping perspiration from her brow, Clara hesitated. "Think of Jessica."

She wasn't sure if Lincoln's wince was a response to her mention of his deceased wife, or the pain in his leg, but he nodded at her. Then, inhaling a deep breath, he said, "Let's go."

About a quarter of a mile later, moments before they strained their way under the multi-colored balloon arch and crossed the yellow finish line that was crowded with spectators, he reached out his hand, and Clara, smiling, instinctively took it.

At eight o'clock that same evening, just as Clara was about to step into a nice, soothing tub of bubbling, hot water, her telephone rang. Utterly exhausted, she almost let the call go to voicemail, but, observing that it was Lincoln, she answered at the last second. And was she glad she did, for he did not sound good. He did not sound good at all.

"What's the matter?" Clara asked, worried. "Is it your leg?"

"No, my calf's actually feeling much better." Pausing, Lincoln cleared his throat. "I'm calling because I'm . . . I don't know. I guess you could say I'm having a *mean moment*. Tough day."

"Oh, Link." Clara sighed, understanding. After their emotional experience at the 10K, she couldn't say that she was surprised her somber-sounding friend was in an especially contemplative state. It made perfect sense. "I'm sorry . . . Is Meg there?"

"No. She's in Minneapolis this weekend at her cousin's baby shower."

"That's right. You mentioned that during the race. I think I was so busy channeling my inner *Dromiceiomimus* that I forgot half the things you said," she joked, injecting her voice with levity as she referred to the speediest of all dinosaurs, which Lincoln had educated her about—at *length*—during their first jog together a few months ago. Clara waited for him to chuckle, sure he'd be wowed by her impressive dinosaur recall, but there was silence on the other end of the line. Crickets. "Oh, come on. I get credit for remembering those things could run at speeds of up to sixty kilometers per hour," she added, hoping to distract him. After all, as he had told her, distraction was key.

"You do," he acknowledged, his voice thick with undisguised gloom, as if he'd given way to despair hours ago.

"I'm coming over," Clara announced, plunging her hand into the tub and opening the drain. "Would it be okay if I bring Milk Dud too? I feel guilty about leaving him alone all day."

"Of course Milk Dud's welcome. But that's all right, C.J.—I don't want you to feel like you have to come over. Really. I know it's been a long day for us both, and you're probably as beat as I am. I'll be fine. I should just—I don't know . . . do a Sudoku, or try to fix the broken air conditioner in my bedroom that feels like the damn Mojave Desert, or . . . something."

"I don't feel like I *have* to come over," Clara emphasized, her mind already made up. "And I don't want you to feel like you *have* to order us a large cheese pizza with pepperoni and onions. Oh! And how about sausage on half too? And maybe some garlic bread if they have it? Or cheesy garlic bread even?"

Now, *this* inspired Lincoln to emit a faint chuckle. "Fair enough," he agreed. "Would you like anything to drink to go with that?"

"Hmmm . . . I'll leave that up to you."

One quick change into her most comfy jeans and twenty-five minutes later, Clara and Milk Dud knocked on Lincoln's door.

When he answered it, dressed in an old-looking t-shirt and mismatched sweatpants, his eyes appeared tired and glassy.

Giving him a warm embrace, Clara couldn't help but wonder if he'd been crying.

"Hey, amigo." Lincoln bent down, petting Milk Dud affectionately on the head. "Good to have you here, buddy." Then, looking up at Clara, he added gratefully, "Thanks for coming over."

She was tickled to see that Lincoln had placed a small bowl of water on the living room floor for Milk Dud in advance of their arrival.

"We get wine," he told her. "Assuming that sounds okay to you?"

"That sounds great." She smiled, intent on keeping him distracted. "Sleeping on the pull-out couch tonight, I see." She nodded at the dark brown, leather sleeper sofa in the middle of the modernly decorated living room, which Lincoln had unfolded into a queen-size bed and dressed in a beige, lightweight blanket.

"I gave up on trying to fix the busted air conditioner in my room. It figures the damn thing would croak when it's ninety degrees outside. Too hot for May . . ."

"Well, at least it's nice and comfortable in this part of the house," Clara, feeling rather like Pollyanna, optimistically pointed out.

"Here"—Lincoln ambled toward the convertible bed—"let me reassemble the couch so we can sit. I'm sorry. I'd meant to do this before you got here."

"Don't be silly. Leave it," Clara said, stopping him. "It's a pain to pull these things out and put 'em back together. No need to do it on my account."

"Really?" He gave her a dubious look. "Are you sure?"

"Positive."

"Because I was actually going to suggest that we eat in front of the TV," Lincoln added. "I could use a little mindless entertainment."

"So we'll be careful not to make crumbs. That is, assuming I don't inhale every last scrap like a Hoover." Clara extended her best effort to evoke a smile. "Personally, I'm pro pizza in bed. Speaking of which, think it'll be here soon? I don't know if it was the race or what, but I have the hunger of ten burly men."

"It should be here any minute now," Lincoln answered with an amused grin—to her delight—just as the doorbell rang, inspiring Milk Dud to bark and charge the door. "Speak of the devil."

Lounging on top of the sofa bed in front of the big-screen television and an excellent bottle of Pinot Noir, they wolfed down the pizza and garlic bread in no time flat.

When Clara, stretched out on her side of the mattress, let out a rather lengthy, unladylike burp, quickly covering her mouth and excusing herself, Lincoln shook his head in amazement. "I can't believe you eat like a man, *and* belch like a man. Outstanding . . ." he marveled. "I salute you."

"Shut up." Smirking, she gave his leg a friendly kick.

"Ouch! *My leg!*" Rocking back and forth on his distinct side of the bed, he winced as he cradled it.

"I'm sorry!" An expression of horror crossed Clara's face. "I totally forgot!"

"Got ya." He winked, pointing at her as he broke into a satisfied grin.

Glaring at him with a dropped jaw, Clara shot him a pretend dirty look. "Oh, that was evil. Sic him, Milk Dud."

With his tail wagging back and forth, Milk Dud did a running leap onto the bed and covered Lincoln's face with wet, friendly kisses.

"What's up, buddy?" Lincoln gave him a thorough belly rub. "Who's the best dog in town?"

"*The One-Ear Wonder,*" Clara said with a yawn, smiling, pleased to see Lincoln doing the same.

"Should we see if there are any good movies on TV?" He refilled her glass of wine, reclining on his back with his legs stretched out and crossed at the ankles.

"Sure. Why not?"

Lincoln was scrolling through the channels when suddenly, Clara gasped. "Go back! Go back, go back!"

He did as he was told until at last she declared, "Stop!"

Lincoln looked at Clara as if she was nuts. "*Mother, May I Sleep With Danger?*" He read the movie's title, which just so happened to be floating across the screen.

"This movie is hilarious." She adjusted the pillows behind her neck. "Pure, campy, made-for-TV cheese. It's so bad it's good. Besides, you gotta love a title that contains multiple forms of punctuation."

"*Mother, May I Sleep With Danger?*" he repeated in a stunned voice, as if there had to be some sort of misunderstanding. "You've actually seen this before?"

"Talk about timing. I can't believe we caught it right at the beginning," Clara said, clapping her hands.

"Neither can I," Lincoln admitted. "You're sure about this?"

She cocked her head to the side. "Do I look sure?"

"All right." He shrugged. "If you say so. Should I turn off the lights?"

"Oh yeah," Clara said, nodding, staring at the television screen.

When Clara's eyes fluttered halfway open at 4:30 a.m., she yawned in a sleepy daze, instinctively snuggling up against the warm body that was spooning her on the sleeper-sofa. What a lovely dream, she thought to herself, luxuriating in its afterglow.

It took her a few drowsy moments to realize that someone's arms really were wrapped around her waist, and someone's breath really was gently brushing against the side of her neck, almost like a soft caress.

And it took her a few languid, dreamy moments more before it eventually dawned on her who, exactly, that someone was.

Too exhausted to think or process the situation, Clara, so comfortable that it required an earnest effort to move an imperceptible millimeter, slowly opened her eyelids all the way—as if needing confirmation that this was not, in fact, another one of her many bizarre dreams—and cast her weary gaze downward to see Lincoln's hand resting on top of hers. How big and protective it seemed cradled against her small, delicate features. Realizing they must have somehow fallen asleep during *Mother, May I Sleep With Danger?*, she noticed Milk Dud snoring peacefully in the corner beside his water bowl, and a late-night infomercial selling something or other undoubtedly exercise-related and available for four easy payments of $19.99 playing on TV. Yawning again as she heard, "But, wait! There's more!" she felt Lincoln's arms tighten around her, pulling her body closer to him in a way that if she didn't know any better, would say almost felt deliberate.

Clara had no idea if he was awake, or if he was asleep, or if perhaps he was floating somewhere hazily in-between, like herself. All she knew was that it was becoming harder and harder, and harder, for her to keep her heavy, drooping eyelids open.

And then, without battle, she let them sink shut again.

Drifting back to sleep with her lips curled upward in the faintest of grins so slight it might have even gone undetected at first glance, Clara voyaged forward, without having to command herself to.

- ~~Run a race (10K like Dad used to run? Find out what a K is!)~~
- ~~Help others through charity like Libby (donate time if I'm poor when I'm old)~~

26

Later that day, Clara found herself absentmindedly turning the pages of *Morse Code for Dummies* without having processed a single word of what she'd just read. She had tiptoed out of Lincoln's apartment at the crack of dawn to take Milk Dud for his morning walk before his impatient whimpering woke Lincoln—still curled up on top of the sofa-bed—out of a sound sleep. Now, lazing on her couch, flipping another page, barely glancing at it, she wondered what he was doing. Was it odd that she hadn't heard from him yet? Was it odd that she would think it was odd that she hadn't heard from him yet? Was that a faint scent of sandalwood soap she'd detected on his body when it was nestled around her? His body had felt stronger and more muscular than she would have thought. Not that she had actually ever given it any thought before. Turning over two pages that were stuck together without realizing it, she couldn't help but reflect on what a strange sensation it had been to wake up wrapped in Lincoln's arms. Not "strange" in a negative way, but rather, in more of an unexpected, bewildering way. A way that felt peculiarly natural, inspiring Clara to pause and consider her old friend. The fact that she was even contemplating him—the same dork who secretly ate glue and had taught her how to moonwalk many moons ago—when she was supposed to be mastering Morse code, gave Clara yet another jolt of surprise.

She closed the thick, yellow manual and sighed, placing it down on her new glass coffee table. Slowly but surely, the judge's condo was beginning to look and feel more and more like home. Rising from the couch, she grabbed her cell phone off the Ping-Pong table and dialed her brother's number. "Sunday Family Dinner" at Libby's house had become a standard, weekly event—or "wonderful, new tradition," as Libby liked to call it—and Clara and Leo usually drove to River Pointe together on Sunday afternoons. In the mood for company, Clara hoped he'd feel like picking her up and heading north a bit earlier than usual. "Sounds good," Leo confirmed. "I'll be at your place in about twenty minutes. Oh! I have to tell you something important before—"

"Sorry, can you hold a second?" Clara interrupted as her Call Waiting beeped. But, observing that it was Lincoln, she changed her mind. "Actually? Gotta go. See you in a few!"

Switching lines, she greeted Lincoln with an intentionally relaxed, "Hello?"

"Clara James." He sounded refreshed and chipper. "How's my race mate doing today?"

"Not bad. And you?"

"I feel like a new man. I slept like I was in a coma. I never even made it under the covers, if you can believe it. Except"—his tone grew more serious—"I'm afraid I owe you an apology."

"An apology? What for?" Clara wondered if he was referring to their accidental cuddle session. After all, Lincoln was in a committed relationship, and she had a sneaking suspicion Meg would probably prefer it if her boyfriend avoided intimately spooning other women, with the exception of Sue (who, at 67 million years old, was not exactly a threat).

"For conking out like a narcoleptic while you were here—not to mention during *Mother, May I Sleep With Danger?* Brilliant movie, by the way," he added, sheepishly admitting, "I can't believe I did that. Clearly, my hosting skills require some honing. I didn't even get a chance to thank you properly for cheering me up last night."

"Please. Don't be silly." Clara had lost count of how many different times and in how many different ways he'd done the same for her in the past five months. She was just happy that for once, she could return the favor. "There's no need, Link. If anything, I'm grateful to you for convincing me to get off my butt and run that race. I needed the experience. I have to say, it really opened my eyes," she confessed.

"I know what you mean," he agreed. "It never ceases to amaze me how we can just go about our standard business and forget to notice the most obvious things. The things that are right in front of our faces every day." He exhaled a contemplative sigh. "I suppose sometimes it takes a certain incident to really capture our attention and help us see things differently. And, of course, we also have to be ready."

"It's so true," Clara agreed wholeheartedly, though it soon dawned on her that she wasn't certain what specifically Lincoln was alluding to. "Wait. You mean, like other people's pain and suffering?"

There was a pregnant pause on Lincoln's end. "Exactly." He cleared his throat. "So, what time did you and Milk Dud take off last night, anyway?"

"Oh, not too late. A little before midnight," Clara fibbed, assuming, based on the fact that he had to ask, he was clueless that she'd quietly maneuvered her way out of his full-body embrace—holding her breath, careful as could be not to wake him—at six o'clock that morning. She had stopped, however, for a few moments to stare at him, lost in thought, before she slipped out the front door

"Well, I owe you a rain check, during which I promise to remain fully conscious."

She chuckled. "Much appreciated."

"Are you free for dinner on Tuesday? I've been craving Syn-Kow."

"Sure," Clara responded, perhaps a bit too quickly. And then, for some reason, she did something she hadn't done before. She immediately asked, "Should we invite Meg?"

"Well, I'd say yes . . . but, apparently, she'll still be in Minneapolis." Lincoln's tone revealed surprise and a minor hint of frustration.

"Oh, I thought you mentioned she was coming back today."

"That was the original plan. But she left a message earlier when I was in the shower saying that her trip was unexpectedly extended and now she's not flying back until Wednesday. It's strange. I know Meg has work tomorrow and Tuesday. I tried returning her call, but she didn't pick up."

"Huh." Clara shrugged, speculating, "Maybe she didn't hear her phone ring."

"I don't know. She has it with her 99 percent of the time. But that reminds me." Lincoln changed the subject, his voice lifting with enthusiasm. "How did the Brachiosaurus answer the telephone?"

"Ummm." Clara pondered the riddle for a few seconds, bracing herself for its punch line. "I don't know. I give up."

"It *didn't*," he said, laughing. "The telephone wasn't invented until 1876."

"Oh, Lincoln." She closed her eyes, shaking her head. "Lincoln, Lincoln, Lincoln. What am I going to do with you?"

It was a sunny, breezy afternoon—eighty degrees outside without a cloud in the sky—and Clara and Leo had opened up all of the windows in his car, rather than turn on the air conditioning, during their scenic ride north to River Pointe. "Shit!" Clara snapped in an instant frenzy as soon as Leo turned into their mother's driveway. For there, thirty yards away, was Todd. Carrying his cumbersome box of piano tuning tools, he had just exited the house, and was taking his own sweet time walking toward his Porsche, which they were about to pull up directly beside.

"*Shit!*" echoed Leo, cringing—a telling sign that indicated he knew he was about to get in trouble. Stomping his foot on the brake, he slowed the vehicle to a crawl, a nervous expression crossing his face as he turned and made eye contact with his panicking sister. "Don't kill me. I *tried* telling you Libby had a piano emergency when we were on the phone earlier, but you hung up on me before I could finish my sentence!"

"Shit, shit, *shit*, Leo!" Clara whispered in a frantic effort to evade the handsome Sears model. Having sex with him—possibly with Cheez Whiz—was regrettable enough, but the way she'd cruelly dodged him ever since, behaving like an immature teenager, was what really turned her stomach, creating a nasty storm of guilt inside her. "Why didn't you tell me while we were driving here, butt-face?!" She punched Leo in the arm. Quickly, her heart banging in her chest, Clara slid her body down the tan, leather seat, curling into a tight ball on the ground, praying she wouldn't be seen.

"I'm sorry. I completely forgot. You had me all distracted, talking about last night's *unintentional*"—he gestured quotation marks with his fingers—"sleep-over party." Leo blamed her in a hushed tone, putting the car in park.

"It *was* unintentional!" Clara peeked under the rubber floor mat, debating whether it might be a good place to hide.

"What the hell are you doing?"

"What are *YOU* doing?! I can't face him!" she scream-whispered, begging, "Turn the car around! Please!!!"

Suddenly, Leo forced a loud, fake cough. "Hi, *Todd*," he said in a most affected manner, attempting to signal to his would-be-invisible sister that the piano tuner was standing right beside her door, peering down at her with a curious expression.

"How are ya?" Todd nodded at him.

"No complaints." Leo stalled. "*Noooo complaints.* Beautiful day we're having . . ." He tapped his hands against the steering wheel.

Feeling Todd's gaze on her, knowing full well that she was busted, Clara looked up at him, forming a strained, guilt-drenched smile. "Hi . . . Todd," she said, giving a little wave.

"What are you doing down there?" he asked.

"I . . . was just . . ." She said the first ridiculous thing that popped into her head. " . . . Searching for my contact lens. It shot out of my eye."

"Need a hand?" he offered.

"Oh, no thanks," Clara resumed a normal, upright position in the passenger seat, adjusting her pretty white camisole and smoothing her tousled hair. "That's all right. I don't think I'm gonna find it."

"Yeah, I don't either," agreed Leo, withholding the fact that Clara was blessed with twenty/twenty vision.

"Okay." Todd shrugged.

"We were just about to head to the store to buy some . . ." Again, Clara, a pathetically unskilled improviser, went with the first ridiculous thing that popped into her head. " . . . Cornish hen."

Leo, who'd been busy picking his cuticles, turned his head and looked at her.

"We're having a big family dinner," she elaborated to Todd.

"I know," he said. "Your mom fried up enough chicken for the whole block. The house smells terrific."

Clara swallowed hard. "We always like to have Cornish hen with our chicken," she explained, drowning in her lousy lie. "Double fowl." She gave him a thumbs-up.

Seeming to recognize that three was a crowd, and enjoying watching his little sister squirm, Leo turned off the ignition. "I'd better go ask Libby how many hens we should buy," he announced, opening his door and slipping out of the car, adding with a dramatic eye roll, "You know how she gets when we're low on hen. I'll be right back." He dashed toward the house.

"See you soon," Clara called out to him through a phony smile and slightly gritted teeth. "*Very* soon!"

After Leo was gone, she hunched her shoulders to her ears and grinned uncomfortably again at Todd, who had set his toolbox down on the pavement and appeared to be waiting for her.

"Got a minute?" he asked.

"Uh, sure." Clara reluctantly stepped out of the vehicle, shutting the door behind her. "What's up?" she said in an overly chummy fashion, standing a few feet away from Todd with her hands shoved deep in her jeans pockets.

"I was just about to ask you the same thing." He stared at her, seeming to anticipate some sort of explanation.

"What do you mean?" She played dumb, trying to calculate her next move and block the haunting mental image of Todd sitting in his tight, Santa Claus-themed briefs at his white piano, crooning a tender Meat Loaf ballad.

"I know it was a while ago that we went out, but I left you more messages than I'm proud of, Clara. You had to have gotten some of them."

With her heart racing, Clara closed her eyes, trying to concoct a believable reason for why she never returned his calls. But she knew there wasn't one. Perpetuating this childish game of cat and mouse suddenly seemed futile and mean. Realizing it would be tactless to present another transparent lie, Clara accepted that she had backed herself into a corner—an undignified, shameful corner. And the only way out was the truth. No more fibs. No more excuses. No more Cornish hens. It was time to come clean.

She took a deep breath. And then, lifting her focus from her sandals, Clara looked Todd directly in the eye, solemnly confessing, "The truth is . . . I didn't call you back because I was acting like an idiot. A *supreme* idiot. The way I've avoided you isn't fair, and it isn't nice, and I sincerely, *sincerely* apologize, Todd." She paused, searching his face, hoping to glimpse some sign of forgiveness. "I should have just been honest with you from the start," she acknowledged softly. "I'm so sorry. I know I've hurt your feelings."

Todd did not look her in the eye. "Well, I have to admit, I *was* a little offended when you told me I was acting *reTodded*."

Clara gasped, horrified. "I didn't!" She took a necessary moment to process this information. "*ReTodded?*" she winced. "Really?"

Todd nodded. "Apparently my name is a lot of fun when you're intoxicated and pretending you're still in Boston."

Appalled, Clara covered her face with her hands. "There's nothing I can say to justify my behavior. I just . . . I guess it comes down to the fact that I wasn't ready to sleep with you. Or *anybody*, for that matter. It honestly has nothing to do with you," she assured him. "It's about my own"—she searched for the appropriate description—"complicated issues."

"We all have issues, Clara. Most of them are complicated."

She exhaled, puffing out her cheeks with air. Dancing the mea culpa two-step certainly was exhausting. "Ain't that the truth."

"And then some," Todd agreed.

Clara hesitated for a moment, summoning the courage to quietly share, "You were the first person I slept with since my fiancé—well . . ."—she paused before she said it out loud for the first time—"he died." Exhaling, she shrugged, trying not to think of Sebastian and how she had failed to remain faithful to him. Though her disloyalty didn't sting as badly as it did back in December, it still hurt.

"Hold on." Todd thrust out his hands. "You don't think we had intercourse, do you?"

Taken aback, Clara cocked her head to the side. "Excuse me?"

"I had a feeling that's what you thought when you made a mad dash out of my apartment. I *knew* it! Why do you think I kept calling you? Believe it or not, Clara, I'm not in the habit of chasing women who obviously aren't interested." Todd absentmindedly kicked his foot against his toolbox while he spoke. "I could tell how upset you were and I figured I ought to let you know the truth about what really happened."

"The truth." She blinked, astonished. And not just by the fact that Todd had used the word "intercourse" in a sentence like a seventh-grade Sex Ed. teacher and somehow made it work. "Wait a minute," she said, narrowing her eyes. "What— What really happened?"

"Well, let's see if I remember . . . You did a clumsy strip-tease, yelled *'Timberrrrr! Look out below!'* as you nose-dived onto the bed, and passed out cold. The end. Next thing I knew, you were snoring."

"Oh, God!" Clara hid her face with her hands again.

"I took the liberty of covering you up with a blanket. And wiping the drool off your face. But that was it."

"*Oh, God!*" She turned her body away from Todd, mortified. For a quick second, she wondered if she had drooled with Lincoln. She sure hoped not.

"Aw, come on . . ." Todd gently nudged her shoulder, spinning her back around so that she was facing him. "It wasn't that bad. I've seen worse."

Stupefied by the fact that he was actually trying to make *her*—a lousy, stripping drooler—feel better, Clara smiled, incredulous. Biting her lip, grimacing, she couldn't resist inquiring, "As long as we're getting it all out there, dare I ask why you had Cheez Whiz on your nightstand?"

"Easy. I was hungry for a midnight snack," Todd recalled. "I sort of have a soft spot for the Whiz."

Clara had to laugh. Now she was the one absentmindedly tapping her foot against Todd's toolbox, looking down as she spoke. "So, then . . . just to be clear . . . There was *no* funny business between us?"

"No, ma'am." Todd shook his head. "I would never take advantage of you like that."

"That's FANTASTIC!" Clara threw her arms around him, beaming with elation that she didn't commit Toddamy. "Thank you for telling me the truth. *Thank you!*" Then, with her arms still wrapped around Todd's neck, she leaned back so that she could look him directly in the eyes. "And thank you for not having intercourse with me."

"My pleasure," he replied. Then, further considering it, he added, "Or not."

June

27

There was a time not long ago when Clara, unable to identify the day or month, could look in the mirror and not recognize who she was, or where she was. Detached and apathetic, nothingness had become her daily routine. But now, examining her reflection in her powder compact after applying a coat of sunscreen to her face, she was present and even a bit excited. She knew that she was the grown woman living a ten-year-old child's fantasy, and that she was sitting in the passenger seat of a black, rented convertible with the wind blowing through her hair on her way to the Wisconsin Dells with Lincoln. She knew that it was the second Friday of June. And, able to read Lincoln pretty well, she knew that he had something on his mind, for he was unusually quiet, and his face was pinched in an intense, contemplative expression.

"It's too bad things didn't work out between Leo and Ava," he declared, driving past a whimsical billboard advertising *Fred's Fishing Bait & Fireworks (The Cheese State's Finest!)*. "It would have been fun if they came along."

"I know," Clara said with a sigh, trying not to worry about

her newly single brother. He'd ended his rocky relationship with Ava a few weeks earlier, offering further support to Clara's theory that he suffered serious commitment issues when it came to women. She couldn't understand why, but for some reason Leo bounced from one fleeting courtship to the next, seemingly determined to deny himself the gift of sharing a true, intimate emotional bond with a partner. Recently, Clara had tried talking about this troubling pattern with her brother, but, in a tone that discouraged further conversation, he'd argued it was "no big deal" and that "there was no point in discussing it any longer. Period. End of story."

"Meg and I broke up," Lincoln said nonchalantly, in the same indifferent manner one might say, "I ate tacos for lunch."

"Think we should stop for some fishing bait and fireworks?" he continued.

Clara did a double take, sure that she'd misheard him— what with the radio playing "oldies but goodies" and the wind and all. "Wait a minute. What did you just say?"

"You never know when bait and fireworks might come in handy."

"*Lincoln.*" Giving him a look, Clara insisted he knew damn well that was *not* what she was talking about.

"Huh." He shrugged, keeping his eyes focused straight ahead on the country road. "I could've sworn I told you that Meg moved back to Minneapolis to be with Roy, her ex-fiancé."

"*Roy?*" Astonished by both this unexpected news and the casual fashion in which it was delivered—as if implying it was a matter of slight significance—Clara demanded without hesitation, "Her *ex-fiancé*? What are you talking about, Link? Are you pulling my leg?"

Promising that there was zero leg-pulling going on, Lincoln recounted how Meg randomly ran into Roy at the Rite Aid when she was in Minneapolis for her cousin's baby shower, and sparks of rekindled love instantly flew. Apparently, they ended up spending the next four days locked behind closed doors at Roy's ranch, after which they agreed, in Meg's own words, that "fate had brought them back together again," and a love as powerful as theirs could not be denied. "Meg's a great person," Lincoln stated. "She told me all about Roy when we first started dating. I have no hard feelings about it."

"Really?"

"If anything, I feel guilty that I don't care more."

"But, I—I thought you two got along wonderfully," said Clara, thoroughly confused. She had not seen this one coming. And, though she'd never admit it to him, she had given Lincoln and Meg's relationship some thought. Especially in recent weeks.

"We got along great. And don't get me wrong, I wish Meg all the happiness in the world. Still, the truth is," Lincoln explained, "we had fun together, but our relationship never delved any deeper than that. There wasn't that real, intense emotional connection, like with—" He stopped himself suddenly, muttering, "Well, anyway, you know what I mean."

Clara nodded. She couldn't help but wonder if he meant Jessica. Or, was it somehow possible that Lincoln could possibly have been referring to . . . oh, never mind—she shoved the unlikely thought out of her head, telling herself it was silly to go there. Silly! *Wasn't it?*

Just then, a Volkswagen convertible filled with loud, giggling women pulled up directly beside them at the stop light. Gawking at Lincoln, the female sitting in the passenger seat gasped, "You're totally right, ladies! He does kinda look like George Clooney during the ER years!" The two girls in the backseat nodded in agreement, and one gushed, "Oh, he *is* cute!"—apparently unaware that Lincoln and Clara could hear them over their radio, which was blasting reggae music. "I definitely would not mind a night out with him," declared the driver as the light changed from red to green. She honked the horn a few times and let out a spirited "Wooooo!" as she sped off, with the women's giddy laughter trailing behind.

His cheeks blushing, Lincoln cleared his throat. "I think they may have been drinking."

Clara smiled. "You're a heartbreaker, George."

"Anyway, as I was saying, it really is for the best with Meg," he concluded. "If she hadn't ended it, I would have. *Check it out.*" Lincoln pointed to a road sign up ahead indicating that the Wisconsin Dells were only forty miles away. "We're getting closer." He smiled at Clara, nudging her arm.

Funny, that's exactly what Clara had told Tabitha verbatim last night on the telephone when her best friend, curious about the nature of her evolving relationship with Lincoln, asked if they would be sharing a hotel room during their "romantic weekend getaway." "While I do admit we're getting closer, we're not *that* close," Clara had countered. "Besides, this trip is about me crossing something off my time capsule list, not romance. And," she'd added, "irrespective of how great we get along, let's not forget that Lincoln has a girlfriend. A *girlfriend*," she repeated with emphasis, for some reason.

"My God. You really do like him, don't you?"

"What? What are you talking about? You sound like Leo. He refuses to accept that Lincoln and I can have a strictly platonic relationship."

After a decade of friendship, Tabitha was quite capable of reading between Clara's lines. "I can hear it in your voice. Don't deny it."

"Oh, I . . ." Clara considered denying it. "I . . . I honestly don't know," she finally confessed. "It's complicated, Tab. I shouldn't even be thinking about this."

"Why not?"

"Because it's *Lincoln Foster*, for God's sake! I've known him since he was a little boy who secretly saved his boogers in a jar! Our history goes way too far back for this kind of thing. Besides, we already tried it once before and it didn't work out."

"Please. That's not a good excuse," Tabitha insisted. "You were fifteen. You also had a crush on *Teen Wolf*. Let me ask you, do you enjoy spending time with Lincoln?"

"Of course I do," Clara admitted, reluctantly. "He's just so easy to be around. And we always have a great time together. But I could also be confusing genuine friendship with something more," she rationalized, more to herself than to Tabitha. "After all, it's been a long time since I spent any quality time with a man who's not my brother. *AND*"—her voice raised a notch—"let us not forget, please: *Lincoln is happily committed to Meg*"—she repeated for the third time—"which definitely renders us just good friends."

"Who spoon," Tabitha had slipped in. "I say go for it. You only live once."

"No way. I've been through more than enough drama as it is. I'm not about to get involved in something messy."

"Why does it have to be messy?"

Clara groaned. "You're incorrigible. I'm hitting the sack. Link's picking me up early in the morning."

"What are you gonna wear? Is your bathing suit one piece or two?"

"*Good niiiiight*, Tab. I'll call you on Sunday when I get back. Tell Max I send my best." She quickly snapped her cell phone shut, shaking her head with an exasperated little grin, deep in thought.

If one leaves the Wisconsin Dells without taking a scenic tour, one can't, in all honesty, say one has experienced the Dells. Thus, the first thing Clara and Lincoln did after checking into their cozy, two-bedroom suite at the Historic Chippewa Inn, a luxurious bed-and-breakfast surrounded by country gardens and flowing springs, was take a Wisconsin River tour. Journeying on a famous "Original Wisconsin Duck," a green-and-white amphibious army vehicle used during World War II, they traveled by land and water on trails tucked away among the natural beauty of the Dells, squeezing through the narrow walls of Red Bird Gorge, plunging into the winding river, spying flora, fauna, and breathtaking views from towering sandstone cliffs to picturesque wilderness trails.

After their tour, as the radiant summer sun began its slow descent in the western sky, Clara and Lincoln took a leisurely stroll down the Waterpark Capital of the World's thriving Main Street, where swim apparel was abundant, along with yellow foam "Cheesehead" hats shaped like wedges of cheddar, frosty snow cones, and moccasins, a time-honored Dells tradition. At one of a dozen old-fashioned candy stores, Lincoln handpicked and purchased a giant bag of sweets for him and Clara to share, including everything from pastel-colored saltwater taffy, chocolate fudge, and a variety of scrumptious penny candy, to the best melt-in-your-mouth homemade peanut brittle either one of them had ever tasted.

They were deep in conversation when they approached the   Guess-Your-Weight-or-What-Month-You-Were-Born Girl's busy, red-and-white-striped booth, situated on a long, bustling block of classic carnival games where cheerful circus music being piped through loudspeakers filled the seaside air. Clara grabbed Lincoln's arm, pulling him to a halt. "We have to do this in Libby's honor! *Come on.*" She grinned, pointing to the sign that read $2 For 3 Guesses! "What do you say?"

"I say she can guess my birthday, but there's no way in hell I'm stepping on that giant scale that looks fit for a velociraptor." Lincoln popped a handful of sour cherry balls into his mouth, followed by a miniature chocolate-covered pretzel, followed by a root beer barrel. "Nuh-uh. No way."

Clara eyed him, smiling as she stuck her hand in the candy bag, removed a turquoise chunk of rock candy, and ate it. "Maybe you'll be able to stump her." She wiggled her eyebrows up and down in a devious fashion. "I'll go first." Clara flagged down the busy Guesser Girl and handed her two crisp one-dollar bills.

"Ladies and gentlemen," the buoyant employee blared into

her microphone, "we have another contender! That's right, you heard me! A fine, young woman who dares to challenge the great and powerful Guess-Your-Weight-or-What-Month-You-Were-Born Girl! She's a brave one, that's for sure!" Ultimately, Clara wasn't surprised when the undeniably skilled Guesser Girl nailed her weight perfectly in a scale-free moment that would have made Libby proud, nor was she surprised when she discovered that she'd gained nineteen pounds since returning to Chicago seven months ago. "Oh well. No crappy stuffed unicorn for me, I guess," she said, pouting at Lincoln.

"Yeah? Don't be so sure." He raised two dollars in the air, challenging the Guesser Girl to identify what month he was born.

First, she insisted that he had the "unmistakable aura of a Libra" and that he was a "classic" October baby. Next, she suggested that she'd "misread his aura" and "on second thought" he was born in ... April. And finally, after examining Lincoln long and hard with one index finger pressed against her chin, she took a wild stab at ... August.

"Not even close." Lincoln triumphantly shot both arms in the air. "December twenty-seventh!" Removing his official Illinois state driver's license from his wallet, he presented it to her.

The Guesser Girl slammed her palm on a button causing a red light on the booth's wall to flash and the winner's siren to whirl. "*Hot dog!*" she proclaimed into her microphone. "We have ourselves a *WINNER*, ladies and gentlemen! This tall, handsome Capricorn—who looks an awful lot like George Clooney, if I do say so myself—is a definite keeper. Don't let him go!" She winked at Clara. "Please take your pick of prizes, sir." She gestured behind her toward the wall of crappy stuffed animals that cost about a nickel each, but were considered priceless in more meaningful ways by a lucky few.

Lincoln chose a silvery white unicorn, which, with a twinkle in his eye, he promptly bestowed upon Clara, grinning, "A unicorn for the lady!" Then, his voice growing tender and lowering a notch in volume, he said, "I'd win you the moon if that's what you wanted."

There was a thoughtful pause before a shy smile crossed Clara's face, and her gaze met his.

By the time they exited the popular Ghost Out-Post Haunted House attraction, laughing at its corniness, night had fallen, and the clear, June sky was peppered with dazzling stars so bright they appeared close enough to be able to reach out your hand and touch. "*Wow . . .* I'd forgotten how beautiful Wisconsin is." Clara stared up toward the heavens with her mouth gaped open. She linked her arm through Lincoln's. "What a gorgeous evening." They ambled slowly in no specific direction until eventually they happened upon Mama Mary's, a charming little Italian restaurant with an outdoor patio illuminated by candles and paper lanterns. "Let's eat here," they both suggested at the same time.

After a relaxing and delicious meal, which included a bottle of Chianti and a shared slice of tiramisu, Clara and Lincoln, exhausted from their first, fun-filled day, returned to the Historic Chippewa Inn, and, after a long, end-of-evening embrace, retreated to their private bedrooms, closing the doors behind them.

"*Good night, Link!*" Clara, tucked snugly in her bed, called out across their silent, darkened suite. They'd already wished each other good night, but, laying there thinking about him—wondering what it might be like to *intentionally* fall asleep in the same bed together—she couldn't resist saying it one more time.

"*Good night, C.J.!*" Lincoln, also beneath his covers, returned in a loud but gentle voice, which brought a subtle smile to Clara's face. "*Sweet dreams . . .*"

"*Good night!*" hollered some guy from across the hall with a very deep voice like James Earl Jones.

- ~~Visit the Wisconsin Dells~~

28.

After a hearty, early-morning breakfast, Clara and Lincoln—well-rested and prepared to *"soak up the sun and waterpark fun"*—headed directly to Noah's Ark, best known as "America's Largest Waterpark!" A full-day event, this was not only the Dells' premiere attraction, it was what Clara had specifically been dreaming of as a ten-year-old waterslide fan composing a mandatory list to stick in her fifth-grade time capsule.

Upon paying the price of admission and entering the spectacular, over-the-top waterpark where the constant sound of rushing water and children's laughter pervaded the hot, summer air, Clara—stunned by its glittering enormity—slowly turned to Lincoln. "Holy crap." A growing smile spread across her face. "We're really here. *Look at it*, Link. It's—It's a literal wet dream!"

"It sure is." He grinned, his mouth slightly agape. "I've never seen anything like it. No wonder I wanted to come here so badly when I was a kid! Uh, for the record, C.J., your time capsule list *rules*."

"And here we are, twenty-two years later," she marveled. "Together. Who would've thought?"

"I know." Lincoln beamed at her for an extended moment before urging, "*Come on*. Let's go get changed!"

When Clara exited the women's locker room, barefoot and wearing her new, lemon yellow bathing suit—a two-piece tankini that she'd purchased especially for the trip—Lincoln, waiting for her by a giant, mushroom-shaped fountain in his plaid swim trunks, appeared to stop himself from doing a double take.

"*Wow.* You look—You look fantastic." It seemed as if he was trying to make a concerted effort not to let himself stare at Clara's body, which had resumed its standard healthy and enticing womanly form.

"Thank you." She felt her cheeks flush, keenly aware of his eyes taking her in. Perhaps she was mistaken, but she could have almost sworn that she'd detected a glimpse of desire in them. "You don't look too shabby yourself." She grinned, noticing that the alleged love handles Meg had previously dubbed "Ben & Jerry" seemed to have disappeared. Then, worried that she might have been caught checking him out, Clara cleared her throat. "I vote we ride Black Anaconda first," she suggested, referring to the longest water coaster in the entire country, which was over a quarter mile long, and boasted six hair-raising climbs and spiraling, thirty-mile-per-hour drops that inspired the ride's menacing motto: "*You can't scream long enough!*"

"Excellent call." Lincoln raised his hand in the air, waiting for Clara to give it a high-five, which she did with noted enthusiasm. "I think it's this way!" He bolted toward the bustling Paradise Lagoon Activity Pool, where shrieking toddlers splashed their way across a lily pad trail leading to a shallow swim area.

They were waiting in a long line to ride the wildly popular Flash Flood—their seventh thrill ride of the day—when Clara, soaked to the bone, began to shiver, despite the fact that it was eighty-five sunny degrees outside. "*Brrrrr!*" Her teeth chattered as she wrapped her arms around her chest. "They should give us towels while we w-w-wait."

Standing behind Clara, watching her quiver, Lincoln inched forward and enclosed his arms around her so that the front of his body was pressed against the back of hers. "Better?" He gently ran his hands up and down her chilly arms.

It was a caring gesture as opposed to a sexual advance, but still, Clara turned her head, water dripping off her ponytail, and smiled at him with her heart suddenly racing. "Much. Thank you . . ."

"You're covered in goose bumps!" he noted.

Clara wasn't sure if they were a result of being drenched in freezing water, or being held against Lincoln's warm, wet body—which felt surprisingly muscular—but suddenly, she didn't seem to mind the long line quite as much.

After a few more water coasters and a lunch break, Clara and Lincoln, ready to relax and let their burgers digest, hopped on individual inner tubes and took a long, leisurely float along the snaking Endless River.

Unable to recall the last time she'd gotten a tan, Clara luxuriated in the sensation of the sun warming her exposed body. Drifting languidly along the water, her mind was not beleaguered with what she was going to tell The Beer King during their scheduled phone call next week when she was required to reveal her future plans regarding Scuppernong; it was not fretting about what might happen if a buyer decided to purchase the judge's condo that she'd grown attached to; it was not worrying about where the Sam Hell she'd buried Leo's forsaken recorder and whether or not Libby was going to forgive her for annihilating her backyard; it wasn't contemplating the last few remaining items on her time capsule list, or "The Untold Want," or even Sebastian. Rather, Clara was lost in deep thought about her old friend, Lincoln Foster, and her unexpected, new feelings for him, which, she realized while floating *"the carefree waterway,"* had been slowly blossoming for some time now.

"Should we take The Plunge?" Lincoln, lounging in the raft slightly ahead of hers, grabbed hold of her foot and gave it a wiggle, knocking Clara out of her reverie. She gasped with surprise.

"I'm sorry!" He laughed, still holding on to her toe. "Didn't mean to scare you."

Catching her breath, Clara covered her chest with her hand, smiling. "I'm sorry, what—what'd you say?"

"The Plunge," Lincoln repeated, raising his eyebrows up and down while pointing toward the north end of the park. "Are you ready to take it?" He was talking about Noah's Ark's highest, steepest, undisputedly most terrifying water ride: a fierce, old-fashioned, extreme vertical-drop slide, "ten stories up, five seconds down." The Plunge challenged the bravest of thrill-seekers, *"Do you dare to drop?"*

Though she was feeling adventuresome, Clara wasn't

quite sure if she had the guts to "dare to drop." "Oh gosh"—
she swallowed—"I don't know, Link. It looks scary."

"*Come on,*" he persuaded. "When are we ever going to
be back in the Wisconsin Dells at Noah's Ark again? This
could be a once-in-a-lifetime opportunity. What would Walt
Whitman say?"

Knowing Lincoln was right, Clara dipped her hand in the
Endless River and splashed him in the face. "He'd say: *Now,
Voyager, let's go to the arcade first while I build up my stinkin'
courage.*"

After a jaunt in one of the park's three classic arcades,
complete with Ms. Pacman—Clara's favorite video game, involving fruit—followed by a raucous ride on Bumper Boats,
Clara and Lincoln proceeded to the Holy Mother of all water
rides: The Plunge.

During their twenty-five minute wait in the winding line,
Clara's nervous stomach did somersaults, her anxiety level
increasing with each rider's haunting scream as they plummeted down the radically steep slide. Beginning their slow
climb up the wooden, ten-story staircase, Clara and Lincoln
passed a menacing plaque that warned in bold letters, **THE
POINT OF NO RETURN: FOR YOUR SAFETY, RIDERS
ARE NEVER PERMITTED TO WALK DOWN STAIRS!** "No
problem," Clara mumbled to Lincoln. "I can do this."

Only, when she finally reached the top of the staircase and
was asked by a Plunge Boy—a handsome young man in his
late teens who resembled David Beckham—if she wanted to
ride on her mat "feet- or head-first?" Clara instantly froze,
paralyzed with fear, stuttering, "I—I can't do this!"

"Sure you can." The encouraging Plunge Boy grinned, well

accustomed to this sort of P.P.H. (Pre-Plunge Hesitation, as it was known among seasoned park employees). "I promise, you're gonna have a blast. And it'll be over in *five* measly seconds. Bam!" He clapped his hands together. "Piece o' cake! So what'll it be"—he nodded at the mat—"feet- or head-first?"

Biting her lip, wide-eyed and visibly trembling, Clara stared down at the bottom of the aqua slide, ten *looooong* stories below, and shook her head. "No. No way, man. This is *CRAZY!*" Spinning around, she started toward the staircase.

"Sorry. Can't let you do that." The agile Plunge Boy lunged to the side, blocking Clara with his bronzed, muscular arm.

"This is nothing, C.J.," Lincoln chimed in, attempting to comfort her. "It'll be *fun!* Here"—he stepped in front of her—"would it make you feel better if I go first so you can see there's nothing to it?"

"*No!*" Clara grabbed his hand, her wobbly knees clanking together as she desperately pleaded with him, "Don't leave me up here! *Please! I can't!*"

Suddenly, a little girl with black braids standing in line with her father behind Clara shrieked, "I can't either, Daddy! I wanna get down! I wanna get down *NOW!*" She began to wail.

"Miss, I appreciate that you're nervous," the well-trained Plunge Boy stepped in, "but the staircase is wet and slippery and way too dangerous for me to let you climb down. Not an option. So you're gonna have to take a seat on the mat and—"

"And what?" Clara interrupted, her voice growing louder and more hysterical by the second. "*Dare to drop?* Hell no, Plunge Boy! *I wanna get down!*"

"*I WANNA GET DOWN, DADDY!*" screamed the little girl with black braids.

"It's okay, it's okay . . ." Lincoln gave Clara's hand a gentle squeeze.

"It's not okay!" Clara hollered. "Look how freakin' high we are! This slide is for *LUNATICS!*"

"*This slide is for LUNATICS!*" sobbed the little girl with black braids.

"Fuckin' A. *She's right!*" said the teenage girl standing in line behind the little girl with black braids, shuddering.

"Miss, you're holding up the line and starting a riot. I'm gonna need to ask you to please sit down on your mat and enjoy your ride down the slide now," said the Plunge Boy. "Come on." Crouching, he gave her mat a welcoming pat.

"Oh my *GOD*, Link!" Clara clung to him.

"*OH MY GOD, DADDYYYYYYYYYYYY!*" sobbed the little girl with black braids.

"FUCKIN' A!" gasped the teenage girl behind her.

"All right, *look*," whispered the Plunge Boy to Clara and Lincoln. "Under normal circumstances we don't allow two riders on one mat, but how about if I bend the rules to prevent mayhem and let you go down together? Will you get on the mat then?" he implored Clara.

"Together?" she repeated, shaking.

"*Yes.*" Lincoln smiled appreciatively at the patient Plunge Boy. "Thank you. That would be wonderful. Right, C.J.?" He curled his arm around her shoulder, offering reassurance.

Blinking, Clara made a strange, undecipherable grunt.

"That means *okay*," Link explained as he lowered himself

down onto the red foam mat, beckoning for Clara to come join him.

"Now you sit between his legs and lean your back upright against his chest," the Plunge Boy instructed her. "No problem. Fun stuff . . ."

Holding her breath, looking like a deer stuck in headlights, Clara followed his directions.

"Good girl." Lincoln smiled as she tightly grasped hold of his thighs, clinging on with white knuckles for dear life. "I've got ya," he whispered in her ear. "I've got ya now . . ."

"Ready?" asked the Plunge Boy. "On the count of three. One . . . Two . . ."

Like a wild banshee, Clara started screaming at the top of her lungs.

"*THREE!*" Giving Lincoln's back a friendly push, he sent them shooting down the slide.

And together, Clara and Lincoln took The Plunge.

That evening, they dined at one of the nicer restaurants in the Dells, the Edgewater—a charming, rustic spot with dim lighting and a hundred-year-old oak tree located smack dab in its center, which a full bar, also made of striking oak, had been built around. There was a jazz quartet playing old standards in the corner near the bar, and several couples swayed to the music, as if in a different era. Over a meal of savory seafood and delicious vodka cocktails known as "Oak Cars," Clara and Lincoln laughed until their eyes watered about how loud she had shrieked the whole way down The Plunge, and how his aching ears were still ringing. "Your brother might have to teach me sign language when we get home," Lincoln teased.

"I really am sorry." Clara giggled, dabbing at her eyes with her napkin as their waiter approached their table with their third round of "Oak Cars."

"Can I interest either of you in some dessert this evening?" he inquired.

Lincoln looked to Clara for a response before answering, "No, thank you. I think these drinks will do us well."

"It's been a hell of a day," Clara elaborated to the waiter, proudly sharing, "We took The Plunge."

"Ahhh," he nodded. "What did you think of Noah's Ark?"

"Awesome!" Clara and Lincoln replied in perfect unison, as if they'd rehearsed the moment.

"I couldn't agree more," said the grinning waiter before bouncing to a new table of diners that had just been seated.

"I really did have a wonderful time today." Clara removed the straw from her beverage.

"Me too." Lincoln raised his glass, smiling at her. "To the Dells."

"To the Dells." She happily clinked her "Oak Car" against his.

"*And*," he added, softening his voice, still holding her gaze, "to the wonderful creator of the list that brought us here."

Clara's cheeks flushed a rosy shade of pink as she smiled bashfully. "Well, thank you for believing in it."

Lincoln placed his glass back down. "I've always believed in you, C.J." Then, forming a fist, he began tapping the table.

Clara sipped her drink, admiring the artistry and care that had gone into the bar's thoughtful construction. Growing up,

Maple Manor had always been one of her most favorite places on earth—her own private spot where she could seek sanctuary when she needed to be alone with her thoughts, and over the years, she'd come to consider the wise, old tree that housed it a dear friend. Busy considering the beauty of both trees, it took Clara several moments to realize that Lincoln was still tap-tap-tapping his knuckles against the table. And it took her several moments more to realize that his deliberate, rhythmic knocking possessed a familiar ring. "Wait a *minute* . . ." She narrowed her eyes, leaning forward, listening harder, examining Lincoln more closely.

Looking into her eyes, he continued tapping the table.

A smile spread across Clara's surprised face as her jaw dropped. "*Link!* You speak Morse code!"

"So do you," he fired back. "Told you it wouldn't take you long to get the hang of it."

"Well, *Morse Code for Dummies* was a major help." After studying the thick, yellow manual daily over the last two weeks, Clara had finally been able to cross a red line through **Learn Morse code** on her time capsule list. Apparently, to her delight, she'd retained more knowledge than she realized.

"*So?*" pressed Lincoln. Tapping his knuckles against the table, he repeated his question for Clara.

"Um"—she hesitated—"*well* . . ." And then, concentrating ardently, she answered him with a slow and deliberate series of knocks.

"I was hoping you'd say that." Smiling, Lincoln rose and extended his hand to Clara, which she promptly accepted.

"But I'm warning you"—she stood up—"I'm an awful dancer."

"That makes two of us," he assured her, leading her on to the dance floor where a smattering of couples swayed to a breezy rendition of *Embraceable You*.

"I'm clumsy enough I could even fall," she advised with a smirk.

"I already have," he confessed softly.

A pleasurable shock passed through Clara, collecting in a knot in her belly.

They danced, holding each other close, for one brief song, before the band announced it was taking a "quick, fifteen-minute break," and Lincoln and Clara, wiped out from a memorable day complete with Plunge Boys, Oak Cars, and Morse code, returned to the Historic Chippewa Inn.

Standing in the middle of their cozy suite's shared sitting room, they gave each other a long, end-of-evening embrace, just as they'd done the night before. Only this time, Clara's rapidly beating heart did flip-flops as she prolonged their charged hug for as long as she could, hoping perhaps Lincoln might choose not to release her. But, eventually, to her disappointment, he let her go, his arms falling limp at his sides.

Clara had to stop herself from frowning. "Well"—she smiled up into his eyes, still standing close enough to smell the lingering scent of sandalwood on his body—"I guess . . . this is good night."

"I guess so." Lincoln stared at her longingly, not moving a muscle.

"Okay then." Desire swelled within her. She resisted the urge to leap on top of him.

"Good night," he whispered.

"Good night." Turning around, Clara slowly began walking toward her bedroom. She told herself that it was completely ridiculous to feel let down that Lincoln hadn't made a move. Of course he hadn't. What was she expecting? After all, like she'd insisted to Tabitha, they were friends. *Just friends*. The "F" word. Besides, Clara reminded herself, just because she harbored a sincerely surprising, unexpected growing attraction toward him, in no way, shape, or form did that mean it was reciprocal. Not at all. Maybe he'd been talking about something else earlier that evening when he mentioned he'd "fallen." Maybe he'd been referring to some kind of enchanting herbivore with scales and a beak from the Cretaceous period. Alas, if only she were a T-rex, perhaps things would be different, she thought to herself.

"C.J.?" Lincoln suddenly called out just as she was reaching for her doorknob.

Halting, Clara's pulse rate skyrocketed, and she felt her breath catch in her throat.

"Forgive me if I'm out of line," Lincoln's voice trembled. "But . . . you have no idea how badly I want to kiss you."

He stepped forward, and before Clara could respond Lincoln had gathered her up in his arms, his lips hovering just inches from her own. Clara swallowed hard. Her heart was beating so fast that she could actually hear it. "You—You do?" she somehow managed to whisper.

Link's eyes stared into hers with smoldering intensity. "Hell yes, I do."

Clara recognized the hungry gleam in his gaze. She had no idea how her legs were still holding her up. She tilted her head up ever so slightly, moving her lips even closer to his.

"God, you're beautiful," Link whispered before at last closing his mouth over hers.

Clara instinctively wrapped her arms around his neck, pulling him even closer. Lincoln kissed her with such passion that she weakened all over and he had to support her. "Link," she whispered breathlessly, returning his deep, affectionate kisses as a lovely warmth spread throughout her body and left her head reeling. "Is—Is this really happening?"

He nodded, covering her face and neck in intoxicating kisses.

Clara's lips explored his until eventually, she leaned her head against his chest, letting her weight fall against him as she closed her eyes.

With one arm wrapped snugly around Clara's waist, holding her body pressed close against his, Lincoln gently placed his other hand on her crimson cheek, stroking it with his fingertips.

Clara felt like she was melting into him.

"You lied to me," he whispered.

"What?" She had no idea what he was talking about. Shocking as it was to her, all she knew was that folded in his arms, feeling the strength of his shoulders, she was exactly where she wanted to be. Exactly.

"You did not leave my apartment *just before midnight* the night of the race." Lincoln slowly traced his hand up and down the length of her spine. "Liar, liar . . ."

Clara's brows shot up. "Lincoln Foster!" Astonished, she leaned back so that she could look him directly in the eye. "*Scoundrel! You were awake.*"

Flashing a sheepish, guilty-as-charged grin, he shrugged, entwining his fingers with hers.

"I can't believe you!" Clara kissed him long and hard for it. What a strange, phenomenal sensation this was!

"I was secretly hoping you and Milk Dud would be swayed by the staggering powers of the sofa-bed and wouldn't leave," Lincoln admitted.

"I was secretly hoping you'd kiss me ever since we left the Edgewater," she confessed, surprising even herself with her daring honesty.

"Believe me, I've wanted to."

"Really?" She smiled.

"God, yes."

Taking Clara's face in both hands, Lincoln slowly leaned in and kissed her lips with such tenderness and love that she let out a soft little gasp before she could stop herself.

She knew she still had a lifetime of mourning ahead of her. But for this moment—at least for this brief and priceless moment—she was happy. Truly happy. And so Clara retreated to Lincoln's bedroom with him.

And together, Clara and Lincoln took the plunge.

- ~~Learn Morse code~~

29.

"This is wonderful!" Tabitha squealed into the telephone. "I hate to toot my own horn, but I had a strong feeling something would happen between you and Link this weekend. Just like I had a strong feeling Meg, *lovely* as she may be, wasn't destined to remain in the picture for very long. It's so obvious how crazy you two are about each other." She took a quick inhalation of breath. "Okay, okay, so tell me what happened next. *Wait 'til Max hears about this!*" she shrieked with joy. "All right, you woke up this morning after a toe-curling, fabulous night, went out for a lumberjack breakfast in the Dells, drove back to Chicago, and then what happened? What next, *what next?*" At last, Tabitha paused with bated breath.

Just thinking about the magical weekend caused Clara, lounging on her couch with a Sunday-night steaming hot cup of chamomile tea, to break out in a sparkling grin. "Uh, let's see . . . We stopped at Leo's to pick up Milk Dud, visited over there for a while; both he *and* Lincoln creamed me at Memory. It was pathetic. I swear to God, I have zero short-term memory. And then Link dropped me off at home. That was basically that."

"*That was basically that.* Listen to you! Do you know I can actually hear your smile over the telephone?"

"You can?"

"Oh, yes. So tell me, when are you seeing each other next?"

"Dinner tomorrow night."

"And *after* dinner?" Tabitha pressed.

"To be honest, I'm still trying to wrap my brain around the last three days," Clara admitted. "I'm telling you, Tab, I was not expecting this at all. The whole weekend was the kind of thing you see in a movie. A *cheesy* movie! Only . . . it was . . . real."

"*Awww,*" cooed Tabitha. "I am so happy for you. *And* Link."

"*Me . . . and Link . . .*" Clara repeated slowly, her voice revealing genuine surprise. "Jesus. Who would have ever thought?"

"Well, let's see . . . Me, Max, Leo . . . your mother, I suspect . . . Meg probably had an inkling . . . and then of course there's Lincoln and—"

"All right, all right, I get the picture," Clara interrupted, chuckling. "I'm clueless."

"Well, to be fair, you *have* had a few other minor issues on your mind. Speaking of which, I hate to bring up a stressful topic, but have you decided what you're going to tell The Beer King of Boston?"

Running her fingers through her hair as she immediately plummeted from Cloud Nine, Clara let out a weighty sigh. "Our call is scheduled for Wednesday. Just thinking about it makes me nauseous." She paused. "It's crazy to consider how your life can change so drastically. I think I've put this off long enough, Tab."

The first grief counselor with whom Clara met shortly after Sebastian's fatal accident shared with her an Abraham Lincoln adage that he suggested was "profoundly inspirational." Gazing up from his little black notebook where he'd been jotting down notes, and sticking his chewed pencil behind his ear, the grief counselor quoted, *"People are just about as happy as they make up their minds to be."* Nodding, as if she understood, Clara thought to herself, "What a trite load of flaming donkey crap." Aching, she longed to counter, "Yeah, doc, how about you and I discuss the wisdom of Honest Abe after you receive a random phone call from the Boston police department telling you that the love of your life—the soul mate you planned to grow old with and can't possibly imagine existing without—was just brutally killed in a freak accident nine days before your wedding. How about we talk then?"

The second psychiatrist Clara sought for help offered her a "powerful" quote from Aristotle, citing in a terribly serious voice and questionably authentic British accent, *"Happiness depends upon ourselves."* Once again, Clara's eyes glazed over as she pretended to comprehend the ancient philosopher's message. In reality, however, she was thinking, "So Aristotle was a cliché-spouting philosopher like Abraham Lincoln . . ."

The third and final psychiatrist Clara met with—an unnaturally tan man with a bright orange glow whom Leo dubbed "Dr. Oompa Loompa"—told her, "A very wise man once said, *'In three words, I can sum up everything I've learned about life—'*"

"'*It. Goes. On,*'" Clara interrupted with a blatantly dismissive eye roll, adding, "Robert Frost." She exhaled a troubled sigh, wondering if this orange fellow really believed he could help solve her problems by presenting to her a quote that she knew like the back of her own hand. "I know about poetry," Clara muttered to Dr. Oompa Loompa.

But sitting there at the Ping-Pong table, holding her cell phone, gathering the courage to dial The Beer King's telephone number for their scheduled 2:00 p.m. call to discuss her future at Scuppernong, Clara found herself contemplating all three quotations that the various doctors had shared. And suddenly, they not only rang true—they made sense. The great Robert Frost had hit the nail right on the head. Life does go on. However, as Clara had come to learn, sometimes it's just too damn painful and difficult—if not altogether impossible—to recognize it.

Once upon a time, Clara's promising career at Scuppernong had been exactly what she wanted, and it brought her great joy. For too long she had clung to the fading illusion of that joy. Frightened and disoriented after her fiancé's death turned her world upside-down, she had desperately grasped on to every last remaining shred of the comforting life she once knew. But that old life was nothing more than a beautiful part of the past. A memory to be cherished. Clara finally accepted not only this, but also that she was a different person because of it. A different person with different desires and needs. Sitting at the Ping-Pong table, contemplating her long, enlightening odyssey, she was struck by the incompatibility of her past with her future. Clara knew in her heart there was no going back. What's more, she no longer ached to go back.

Thus, with a new glow of aspiration, Clara told The Beer King that she loved him and the company dearly—there was no denying it had played a critical role in her life and provided her with a strong sense of both direction and satisfaction. But part of conquering grief, and growing up in general, was accepting that things change. Adjusting and adapting is necessary, because if you don't, it's not long before you're living a lie. And, as Clara had learned the hard way, life's just too short for that. She was not quite certain yet what her future held, but she was sure of one thing. Scuppernong was an important part of her past.

And then, having made up her mind to be happy, Clara tendered her resignation.

July

30

After their trip to the Wisconsin Dells, Clara and Lincoln spent almost every night together, making up for lost time. Milk Dud's water bowl in Lincoln's living room was transferred to the kitchen, becoming a permanent fixture, and Clara left a toothbrush in his bathroom, as well as an extra copy of her time capsule list amidst a stack of old science journals and *Fossil News* magazines in his entryway.

Late one scorching hot evening shortly after Independence Day, while Clara and Lincoln were zipped inside of an old camping tent erected in the middle of Lincoln's comfortably air-conditioned living room, he brought up Clara's list. "There can't be much left on it," he supposed, lying on his side next to Clara on top of a green sleeping bag built for two.

"Nope," she confirmed, resting on her back. "In fact, now that I get to cross off **Sleep in a real tent**, I have only seven items remaining." She proudly held up seven fingers.

"Seven items!" Lincoln placed a gentle kiss on her bare shoulder. "Good for you. That's terrific." He kissed her right cheek. "Let's hear them." He kissed her left cheek.

"Well, I still have to find Leo's damn recorder that seems determined to stay buried," Clara began, having committed her list to memory by this stage. "I'm seriously contemplating snapping that bastard piece of plastic in half when I get my hands on it. And then there's **Grow my own garden with an avocado tree.**"

"Mmmm, I like avocados." Lincoln kissed her forehead.

"I like *you*," Clara twinkled, continuing. **Find a cure for heart attacks, Beat Leo at Memory.**" She let out a soft little moan as Lincoln traced a sensual trail of kisses down the side of her neck.

Morphing into a science geek, he stopped lavishing her with affection. "You can do it. It's all about math and strategy."

Clara wondered if she'd misheard him. "Math and strategy? Memory?"

"Absolutely. Based on your dubious tone, I'll assume the strategic value of different Memory moves may not be obvious, so I'll share some basic game mechanics."

"Oh, by all means." Clara couldn't believe how serious he'd suddenly become. "Please do."

"The first key is to memorize the grid's four corner cards. They're critical. It's easier to remember other cards if you can relate them to a corner card. And then you have to master the efficient use of the 'match' versus the 'miss.' The 'match' being the intentional reveal of an unknown card that makes a pair together with a previously known card. The 'miss' being the intentional reveal of an unknown card that does not make a pair with a previously known card. The unknown card is all about risk. When do you turn one over? When do you choose *not* to turn one over in order to advance your position?" Lincoln paused. "Do you follow?"

Clara's head was starting to reel. "Christ, what did you do? Write your graduate thesis on Memory?"

"I grew up playing it with my brother. Besides, it never hurts to apply a scientific approach."

"Right. Got any other helpful tips? Perhaps something just a *touch* less scientific?" Clara smirked. It turned out Lincoln was even nerdier than she'd given him credit for.

"As a matter of fact, yes, I do." He kissed her belly button. "Repetition. Let's say you flip over a 'red apple' card in the bottom left-hand corner on one turn, and then on your next play, you flip over a 'blue bird' card that's just a few cards away from the red apple. What you need to do is mentally repeat 'blue bird/red apple, blue bird/red apple, blue bird/red apple'—just keep repeating it again and again in your mind. Then, the next time you flip over a blue bird, your temporal lobe will subconsciously connect blue bird and red apple, and you'll know you need to turn over a card that's near the red—"

"Okay, okay, okay! My brain hurts!" Clara laughed. "I think I got it."

"Really?" Lincoln quirked an eyebrow. "Good. Then I can go back to doing this . . ." Pushing up Clara's camisole just far enough to expose her abdomen, he covered it with light kisses. "Oh!" He stopped kissing her. "Typically, the player who takes the last turn and scores the final collect sequence wins." He inched her camisole up even higher.

"Ooooh, I love it when you talk Milton Bradley to me! It's strangely alluring." She flashed an amused smirk, delighting in the thrilling sensation of his lips on her body.

"Yeah? Wait 'til you hear my hypothesis on Chutes and Ladders." He grinned mischievously. "But back to your list . . ."

"Yes! Please! Back to my list," Clara chuckled, trying her best to remain focused, which Lincoln certainly wasn't making easy. "Next is **Apologize to Stella for stealing her Twirly Curls Barbie & give it back to her** . . . as well as **Apologize to Stella for stealing her Chia Pet (and accidentally killing it).**

He kissed her right thigh. "Jesus. Now I know who to blame if any of my stuff goes missing."

"Yes, I'd suggest you hide your Barbie dolls," Clara warned. "And, finally, last, but not least, **Become a teacher.** *Voila!*" She beamed. "That's the whole list."

"I have a brilliant idea." Lincoln kissed her left thigh. "You can teach people Memory strategy for winners!"

"Not bad . . ." She mulled it over, challenging with a smirk, "Perhaps I'll do just that. Oh yes, perhaps I will."

"Well, it sounds to me like you've got this in the bag. You should be able to accomplish all of that before you turn thirty-five. You still have—what? Six and a half, seven weeks? I think you're gonna do it." Lincoln planted a deep, passionate kiss on Clara's lips, pressing his body against hers.

"Mmmm." She emitted a little gasp, wrapping her legs around him. "I think *we're* gonna do it."

"By God, I think you're right." He gave her a long, probing kiss. "That, my dear, is what you get when you *sleep in a real tent.*"

"In that case"—Clara giggled—"we might have to go apartment camping more often."

The next day, back at her apartment, Clara sat down at the Ping-Pong table in front of her computer, logged on to the Internet, and got down to business. First, she conducted some basic research on the American Heart Association. As a child who missed her daddy something fierce, she had always dreamed of discovering a magical cure for heart attacks so that other kids wouldn't have to grow up without parents who suffered the same, cruel fate as James Black. As an adult who missed her daddy something fierce, Clara knew, sadly, that there was no such thing as a magical cure for heart attacks. Since she was not a doctor—hell, she could barely even draw a convincing heart on paper—she had no choice but to accept that her options were limited regarding **Find a cure for heart attacks** on her time capsule list. Thanks to Sebastian's hefty life insurance policy, however, her funds were not limited. Thus, with the goal of doing everything in her power to help prevent heart attacks, Clara jotted down the mailing address of the American Heart Association, retrieved her checkbook from her purse, and made an extremely generous donation in her father's name, saying a silent prayer that somehow it might make a difference.

Second, Clara conducted some research on Stella Hirsch, her elementary school classmate with enviable toys from whom she occasionally pilfered. A Google search yielded a list of nine different people. Clara had no idea if any of them was actually the person she was looking for, but, figuring it couldn't hurt to try, she sent each of them the following message with the subject line, "STELLA HIRSCH FROM RIVER POINTE, IL?":

Dear Stella,

Please forgive the intrusion if I've got the wrong "Stella Hirsch," but by any chance might you have attended River Pointe Elementary School and had your Twirly Curls Barbie and Chia Pet stolen from you as a child?

If so, I hold important information concerning the abovementioned burglaries and would appreciate it most sincerely if you could reply to this e-mail at your earliest convenience.

Thank you in advance and I hope to hear from you soon.
Sincerely,
Clara Black

P.S. I feel compelled to add that I am of sound mind and mean you no harm.

"Well, all we can do now is wait and see if anybody responds," Clara said to Milk Dud, who was lying by her feet chewing on a plastic cheeseburger toy. "What do you think, boy? Will we hear back from Stella?"

Milk Dud barked.

Leaning back in her folding chair, she stretched her arms and exhaled as her mind turned to her conversation with Lincoln inside of the tent. How astonishing it was to consider her dwindling time capsule list had only a few remaining tasks! Soon, Clara knew, she would accomplish them. And then, at long last, she'd be done. Her list would be conquered. That would be that. She could retire her trusty red pen, for she'd have succeeded in what she set out to do. Only, wondered Clara, *then what?*

For the first time, it began to sink in that the finish line truly was in sight. She didn't even have to squint to see the proverbial light at the end of the tunnel, and somehow, this shocked her. In a way, it felt to Clara like ages ago that she had shared her magical, gay kiss with Billy/William Warrington and then joked about doing everything else on her "silly" time capsule list. Yet, in another way, it felt like only yesterday that she and Leo were sitting at that old kitchen table after Thanksgiving, reading the Saturday newspaper, discussing the unlikely possibility of Clara registering for Chef Guillaume's gingerbread class. Pondering her long, surprising journey, again Clara asked herself, *THEN WHAT?*

Scrunching her eyebrows, deep in thought about what form her life was supposed to take next, she realized how much she would miss carrying the old, worn-out piece of paper around with her in her pocketbook, crossing a triumphant line through the goals she accomplished—one by one—feeling a sense of achievement as she watched her list gradually decrease over time. As Leo had hypothesized over half a year ago when Clara resembled the walking dead trudging morosely through life, her list had indeed given her a sense of purpose. It had provided her with desperately needed direction, serving as an unusual form of security and comfort. It did not happen overnight, but as the days turned into weeks, and the weeks turned into months, Clara had come to revere that list because of it. It occurred to her the issue wasn't really completing everything on it. She had lost herself. And the *real* issue had been finding herself again. The time capsule list was simply an end to that means. And now it was all coming to an end. For some reason, this made Clara anxious as well as sad.

Turning off her computer, she let out a heavy sigh.

And then, out of nowhere, she had an epiphany.

Clara leaped from her chair and hurried to her bedroom, where on her nightstand she kept a spiral notebook that served as a journal to keep track of her strange and vivid dreams. After tearing out a piece of paper at its perforated edge, she returned to the living room.

Concentrating fiercely as she tapped her pen against the Ping-Pong table, she thought long and hard for a long while before writing anything down.

And then, Clara began composing a list of goals that she hoped to accomplish in the future.

Unlike her first list, this new one did not include a finite deadline, for Clara hoped that she would have many years ahead of her to accomplish its items. Nor did this new list occupy merely the front of one page, but rather it snaked along the margins, ultimately concluding at the bottom of the page's backside. Clara's first list was public knowledge, and over time, many interested pairs of eyes had perused it. Her new list, however, would be private. It was for her, and only for her. Clara knew that she would never share it with another living soul. Not even Leo. For there was no need, really. All that mattered was that she knew the list was there. And the fact that it was made Clara smile.

- ~~Sleep in a real tent~~
- ~~Find a cure for heart attacks~~

August

31

The moment Lincoln and Clara sat down to Thursday night dinner at Syn-Kow, Lincoln, wearing an enormous grin, announced that he had "big news." And then, practically bouncing in his seat, far too ecstatic to let anticipation build, he blurted, "I'm going to Argentina!"

"*No*," gasped Clara, immediately suspecting what the trip was about. "Lincoln! Tell me you're going to see the Argentinosaurus!" By this point, she too was practically bouncing in her seat.

"*I'm going to see the Argentinosaurus!*"

Clara squealed, quickly covering her mouth with both hands. She'd only been listening to him chatter about the remarkable, staggering Argentinosaurus—the world's largest known dinosaur for which there existed good evidence—for three months straight now. "Holy crap, Link! This is huuuge."

"I know," he said, nearly bursting with excitement. "Sayid invited me to fly out there a week from Monday to help with the dig. Check it out!" Retrieving an official itinerary from his sport coat's inner pocket, he handed it to Clara. "Can you believe it?"

She glanced at the piece of paper. "I sure can." She rose and embraced Lincoln, her fingers sliding into the soft, thick hair at his nape before she planted a steamy, celebratory kiss on his lips. "Nobody deserves this more than you do. I am so thrilled for you."

"Aw, thank you," he said, blushing. "*And* thanks, *Sayid.*"

South America had become paleontology's newest hot zone—its dusty, eroding slopes producing an explosion of finds—and Sayid, Lincoln's good friend and colleague at the American Museum of Natural History in New York, was a member of a renowned team of scientists working to excavate the Argentinosaurus, named after the location where its fossil was first discovered in Argentina's sprawling Patagonian province of Neuquén. Lincoln had mentioned to Clara on multiple occasions that he hoped Sayid might invite him to visit the site and possibly even ask him to lend a hand. He'd said that merely having the rare honor to glimpse the fossil still buried in the earth would be not only one of the highlights of his career, but of his life.

Back in her seat, Clara perused Lincoln's itinerary. "Wow. So you'll be gone for two weeks? That's a long time." Silently acknowledging she'd miss him while he was away, she attempted to return the document to him, but he told her it was hers to keep.

"Oh, get this! I still can't believe this part," Lincoln admitted. "I'm staying at the camp *on-site.* It's literally situated right in the middle of nowhere. Nothing as far as the eye can see except for monstrous, 95-million-year-old bones."

Clara realized she had never seen Lincoln this excited about anything before. "Oh, Link . . . It sounds like heaven." She smiled, knowing that to him it was. And besides, spending two whole weeks apart wouldn't be *that* difficult, she told herself. Alas, as the old saying went, "Absence makes the heart grow fonder."

"I'm glad you think so. Because there's one more part to my news." Lincoln reached into his jacket pocket and pulled out an envelope. Holding it in his hand, he paused for a quiet, extended moment, not saying a word, just smiling at Clara.

"What?" she asked self-consciously, noting his penetrating gaze. "Why are you looking at me like that? Do I have something on my face?"

"No. There's nothing on your face. You look gorgeous. As always." Lincoln took a deep breath, the gleam in his eye still shining. "Okay . . ." He fidgeted a bit with the envelope, tapping his thumb against it. "Are you ready?"

"Am I ready for what?" Clara gave him a playful look. "What are you talking about?"

Then, handing the envelope across the table to her, he explained, "This is for you."

"What's this?" She eyed the sealed white envelope inquisitively.

Lincoln, almost on the edge of his seat now, watched her closely. "Well, go on. Open it."

Following his orders, Clara ripped open the envelope. Her expression of curiosity quickly changed to one of confusion. "Wait . . . I don't understand. Why—Why are there two plane tickets to Argentina in here?"

Once again, he flashed her a beaming grin. "Because you're

coming with me," he replied softly. Lincoln allowed a few seconds for this to sink in. "You're going to Argentina, too, C.J.!"

Clara was speechless.

It was clear by the proud sparkle in his eyes that Lincoln was thrilled to be able to share this moment and this special experience with her. "Surprise! That's the second part of my news." He rose out of his chair to gather her in a joyful embrace. "Well? What do you think?" He squeezed her closer. "Isn't it great?"

There were a few moments of stunned silence before Clara answered, "Uh, yeah . . . It's"—she hesitated, still processing this unexpected development—"great."

His arms wrapped around her waist, Lincoln leaned back, looking Clara in the eye. "Well, you don't have to sound so exuberant about it," he teased. "We're just going to see the Argentinosaurus." Taking her shocked-looking face in both hands, he kissed her lips. "In *Argentina!* The whole trip's planned out and paid for." He stopped briefly to reiterate before kissing her again with increased passion.

"It—*It is?*" Clara managed between kisses. She pulled her mouth away from his. "Wait. When did you buy these tickets?"

"Yesterday. You might notice they're first class."

Only, Clara, with her brain reeling at a million miles per minute, was too busy thinking to notice anything.

"What's the matter? Don't you like first class?"

"Yes, yes, of course I do. I'm just . . ." Raking her hand through her hair, she remained at a loss for words. "Wow. I'm a little surprised, I guess, that you booked such a huge trip without mentioning anything about it to me first. You know what I mean?"

Obviously astonished, Clara sat back down, and Lincoln, following her lead, returned to his chair across the candlelit table from her.

"I know. I realize it's a big step. Absolutely. But I thought you'd be happy about it." He studied her closely, a look of hesitancy clouding his face. There was a moment of silence. "I wasn't mistaken. *Was I?*"

"No. No," Clara responded, perhaps a bit too quickly, fearing she may have hurt his feelings with her lack of initial enthusiasm. "That's not what I'm saying."

"Good." Lincoln exhaled a sigh of relief. "Because this is going to be an incredible experience. Once in a lifetime, really! A bunch of the other guys are bringing their wives along, too," he added brightly.

Clara gulped. For her, time seemed to grind to a halt. *Wives? Had he just said "wives"? The last time she checked, there was not a ring on her finger. She was definitely not Lincoln's wife. Never before had they even discussed the topic of marriage. The thought hadn't so much as crossed her mind. There was only one person in her life with whom Clara associated the word "marriage," and that was Sebastian.*

"Don't worry, there's a nice hotel not too far off," Lincoln continued. "That's where Sayid's wife, Holly, is staying. You'll love her. Think about it, C.J. We've never done anything remotely like this together before."

"I know." She blinked. "That's kind of my point."

"What do you mean?" he asked, puzzled.

Fingering her cloth napkin, Clara picked at its edge. "I mean . . . like you just said, taking a trip of this magnitude is a big deal." She'd never even gone on a two-week-long vacation with Sebastian, and she couldn't help but wonder what the implications of accepting Lincoln's invitation might be. Sure, she enjoyed spending time with him, but was she really ready for this next step? A *two-week* trip halfway around the world? Were there invisible strings attached? Surely this significant trip would be a symbol of their commitment to each other and where their relationship was headed. Was she moving too fast with Lincoln? Why hadn't he consulted with her first before making arrangements? Did he really assume she wouldn't have to give it any thought whatsoever? Why had he used the word "wives" so casually? Why was she suddenly plagued with uncertainty? And why hadn't their waitress come to take their cocktail order yet? Eventually, as the confusing seeds of doubt continued to blossom in her mind, Clara realized that Lincoln was staring at her. She didn't know quite what to say. "Don't get me wrong. I'm honored you'd even think to take me with you." She placed her hand over her heart in a gesture of sincerity. "Oh, I don't know . . . I suppose I'm just—"

"You're just"—Lincoln interrupted—"not looking excited like I hoped."

"*Well . . .*" Guilt washed over Clara for being the obvious cause of the deflated expression now pinching his face. "I have a lot of thoughts racing at me all at once here. A couple minutes ago I was debating whether I want shrimp or pork lo mein, and now I'm just trying to"—again, she paused, wringing her hands as she searched for the right words—"process . . . *this*," she said, nodding toward the plane tickets on the table.

"I know I took you a little off guard, but what exactly are you trying to process?" Lincoln folded his arms across his chest.

Where was she supposed to begin? "Well, for starters,

there's Milk Dud," she stuttered. "I—I don't know what I'd do with him for two whole weeks."

"Libby loves that dog more than life itself. I'm sure she'd be glad to watch him."

"Libby works," Clara reminded him. "I can't just expect her to be available all day and night for two whole weeks. That's not realistic."

"So we'll find a great kennel."

"I don't even know where my passport is. Not to mention my big suitcase from Boston is still filled with stuff I haven't bothered to unpack yet. And, besides, I'm not sure I can just drop everything to jaunt off to Argentina for two whole weeks."

Lincoln's eyebrows pulled together. "Why do you keep saying *'two whole weeks'* like that?"

Clara hurriedly took a sip of her ice water, wishing their waitress would come and take their darn drink order already. This unexpected situation definitely called for a mai tai. A strong one. Or four. "Because two weeks is a long time, Link," she answered truthfully. "And, you have to admit, you haven't exactly given me a whole lot of advance notice here."

"I didn't realize that much advance notice was needed." A slight, yet notable, edge of defense had crept its way into Lincoln's tone. "I figured it's not like you punch a clock or anything. You're not working at the moment. You know?"

"Yeah, I know." Clara, increasingly uncomfortable with the direction their discussion seemed to be heading, swirled around the ice cubes in her glass of water.

"Forgive me, but I think your time capsule list can wait a couple weeks. Big deal." He shrugged his shoulders. "Does it really make a difference? It's not exactly a critical matter of life or death."

However, for Clara, that's precisely what her time capsule had become: a matter of life or death. She winced at his dismissal. "Actually"—she blinked, both surprised and hurt by his belittling jab—"I have only one month left to finish everything on it." She adjusted her napkin on her lap. "And, you obviously think differently, but it's critical to me." Wounded, Clara looked away from Lincoln. "I thought you knew that," she said quietly.

Lincoln swallowed hard, his expression softening. "I'm sorry. I didn't mean to imply—"

"It's fine." She saw the regret in his eyes and didn't want to make things worse by escalating the awkward conversation.

"No, that came out wrong," Lincoln insisted. "I know how important your time capsule is to you, and believe me, I totally respect it."

Clara sighed, forcing a small grin, though she could feel herself shutting down, as was her habit when she was officially done discussing a difficult topic or had reached her breaking point and could no longer deal with the situation. Doing her best to conceal her panic, she plastered on an even bigger smile. "It's *fine*. Really. It is." She did not want to get into this any further with Lincoln. Not tonight, at least. Not while she was still struggling to make sense of his unexpected invitation and the sudden, unexpected feelings of doubt and confusion it had stirred inside her. "But I say we change the subject. Is that okay?"

"Yes." Lincoln nodded. "Of course." He quickly swept up the envelope and returned it to his jacket pocket.

"This is supposed to be a happy occasion, and that is *exactly* what it's going to be!" Clara declared, picking up her menu and flipping it open. She pretended to be engrossed in it. "I'm starving! Do you want to pick out a couple main dishes to share? We could each choose one?" She kept her eyes focused on the print, not pausing to let him respond. "Oh, look at this! *'Chef's Special Celebration Delight'* sounds like a perfectly appropriate entrée. We have to order that. Don't you think?"

Lincoln's eyebrows lifted in what appeared to be baffled surprise. And not the good kind of surprise. He nodded. "Uh . . . sure. That sounds great." He found the dish on his menu. "Should we get it with jumbo prawns?"

"Absolutely," Clara responded, a bit too enthusiastically. "You know what they say—*the more prawns, the merrier!*"

Lincoln let out a little chuckle. "In that case, maybe we should order *'From Dusk Til Prawn'* as well?"

Finally, the waitress, who had served them on many occasions, appeared at their table. "*Hello!* It's my favorite happy couple." She grinned widely. "Can I start you off with drinks tonight?"

"*Yes!*" both Clara and Lincoln answered together.

Clara and Lincoln were in his car, driving back to his apartment, when a song came on the radio that instantly caused Clara's heart to stop beating in her chest. It hit her like a sudden painful combination of mace and electroshock therapy, overwhelming her to the point that she had to consciously remind herself to continue breathing.

As Lincoln rambled on about how one of the Argentinosaurus's back vertebrae had a "shocking" length of 1.3 meters, Clara, suddenly desperate for fresh air, lowered the passenger-side window all the way down.

Frank Sinatra's *Night and Day* was the first song that she and Sebastian had ever danced to. Swaying beneath the light of a full moon at a mutual friend's engagement party on a private beach, they held each other close. Months later, they both confessed to falling in love with each other during that memorable dance on the sandy shore. Throughout their years together, Clara and Sebastian shared countless special moments to "their song," and when their wedding coordinator asked if they'd chosen the music they wished to use for their first official dance as husband and wife, it was a no-brainer.

In those first, dark, horrible weeks after Sebastian's accident, Clara listened to their song often—hundreds of times: late at night when she was tossing and turning in bed, trying to fathom falling asleep without him; early in the afternoon when she was sitting on the couch, trapped in the numbing haze, doing absolutely nothing. It comforted her, and helped her feel close to him.

It had been a long, long time since Clara last listened to their song. Too long, she berated herself, gazing out the window of Lincoln's car while it played in the background.

And that's when she remembered.

Clara felt her chest constrict as an overwhelming sense of guilt and confusion engulfed her. How on earth had it failed to cross her mind until now that tomorrow was August 3? *August 3!* The anniversary of Sebastian's and her first date. For ten happy years, they'd celebrated their very first lunch together at the Sandwich Shack, a surprisingly nice restaurant to include the word "shack" in its name. August 3 had always been an important date that Clara typically looked forward to well in advance, making special dinner plans, getting all dolled up, buying Sebastian a little gift—nothing fancy or expensive, just a trinket to remind him how much she cherished him. Last year, she'd given him a funny magnet of a foot with googly eyes that she knew he'd appreciate. And there it was, 10:00 p.m. on August 2, and it had only *just* dawned on her what tomorrow was! Clara's stomach turned at the realization that perhaps, if she and Lincoln hadn't been listening to the radio, their anniversary might have passed without acknowledgement. August 3 could very well have come and gone with nary a blink. This distressing thought hit Clara like a kick in the gut, shaking her to the core. But even worse, in her mind, was the fact that she was so busy pondering going on an adventure-of-a-lifetime, two-week dream vacation with another man that she'd started to accidentally lose track of what had always mattered to her most. Or, perhaps more precisely, *who* had always mattered to her most.

Never had Clara felt farther away from Sebastian.

"I love this song," said Lincoln, checking his rearview mirror and switching lanes. "Old Blue Eyes is the best."

Suddenly, it seemed to Clara that the oxygen in the car had been sucked away, and its walls were closing in on her. All she wanted to do was get the hell out of that car. And quick.

"Don't you think?" Lincoln glanced at her. "Hey—you okay?" He placed his hand on top of hers and began singing along with Sinatra.

Clara fought to stifle the rumbling threat of tears. "No,

I'm—I'm not okay," she mumbled, her face twisted in anguish. Abruptly pulling her hand away from his, she leaned forward and changed the radio station.

"What's wrong? Why do you look like that? And, why are we listening to polka music?"

Clara glanced uneasily at him, but all she could see was Sebastian's face. Inhaling a deep breath, confounded, she asked herself again how she could have been so distracted, so *selfish* that she almost forgot about August 3?

"C.J., what—what is it?" Lincoln's face was contorted in obvious worry. "You look pale. You're not gonna faint again, are you?"

"*Night and Day* was the song Sebastian and I chose for our first dance," Clara blurted. "Tomorrow is our anniversary. And I forgot. I *forgot* . . ." She shook her head in shame, squeezing her eyes shut. "I just"—it was hard for her to form a coherent sentence—"I think I need to be alone right now. It's been a long night. Could you take me home, please?" Her voice was meek and detached.

"Wait." Lincoln appeared incredulous, as if perhaps he had missed something. "I don't understand what's happening. I know I threw you for a loop earlier and our evening got off to a shaky start, but I thought we'd gotten past it and were having a good time," he said. "We were laughing a few minutes ago. And now you want to go . . . *home?*"

Clara nodded. The last thing she wanted to do was hurt Lincoln again. Yet, she knew that there was no way she could return to his apartment and climb into his bed. Not tonight. Not when the only person she could think about—the only person she *wanted* to think about—was Sebastian. "I am so sorry, Lincoln. *So sorry.* I don't want to cause any more trouble. Especially after the whole Argentina thing. Please just understand that I really need to be by myself right now. Okay? I just—I can't do this . . ."

Wearing a shell-shocked expression, he pressed, "You can't do what?"

Clara's eyes couldn't seem to find his face. "God . . . let's not make this a big deal. It's your special day, Link, and I've already ruined it, and I feel *hideous* about that. I feel hideous about a lot of things." Again, she closed her eyes, covering her face with her hands. "It would really just be best if you took me home."

"Best for who? You're shutting me out." He turned off the radio. "Please, just talk to me, C.J. Talk to me."

"I *can't* talk right now!" Clara snapped, her voice catching in her throat. "Please," she whispered as a tear dripped down her cheek, the absence of Sebastian slicing through her like a cleaver. "Take me home. I—"

"Fine." Lincoln cut her off, his voice husky and low. The growing tension in the car was almost palpable.

"Please don't be mad," Clara begged. "I promise you, this is not what I meant to happen." She paused, trying to collect herself. "This is not how it's supposed to be . . ."

"Not how what's supposed to be?" Now Lincoln really seemed confused.

Clara couldn't help but note the impatience in his voice. "I don't know," she said, struggling to put her swirling, complicated thoughts and emotions into words. "All of this, Link. You. Me. *Us.* Sitting here in this car with you right now. Being in Chicago. *None of this* is what I had planned."

"Jesus, C.J.," Lincoln replied, as if he couldn't quite believe what he was hearing. He turned and looked at her, obviously baffled. "Don't you get it by now? None of this is what anybody planned. Whose life actually turns out the way they planned it? You think I planned for my wife to die a painful death? Do you think I planned to get offered this job in Chicago? Do you think I planned to fall in love with you? Of course not! Stuff happens!" he declared in an escalating, powerful voice. "Like it or not, sooner or later you're gonna have to face up to that. It's what life's all about."

A stark silence followed.

"You're"—a pair of dazed, brown eyes lifted to Lincoln's, and Clara felt herself at a genuine loss of words—"in love with me?"

"Forget it," he glowered. "I don't know why I said that. I was on such a rampage it just flew out of my mouth." He turned left on to Clara's street.

"Okay," she said quietly, looking down at her lap, tears streaming down her face.

Lincoln pulled his car up in front of Clara's building, put it in park, and shut off the engine.

Neither of them moved.

He waited a tense minute or two before asking in a dejected tone, "So . . . what now?"

The truth was, Clara didn't have an answer for him. At least, not one that she suspected he'd like. Slowly, she lifted her shoulders to her ears. "I don't know." She wiped her eyes. Though it crushed her to admit it, she felt the least she could do was offer Lincoln honesty. And so she told him, "I think . . . maybe I need some space to figure some things out."

Lincoln seemed as surprised by this as Clara herself.

For a moment, it looked as if he was going to protest. He opened his mouth to say something, but apparently thought better of it. Instead, he stared at Clara in silence with a pained expression.

She had the distinct feeling that he was exerting every ounce of his control to keep his emotions in check.

"I can't believe you just said that," he eventually mumbled so softly she could hardly hear him. "I take it Argentina isn't happening." This was more of a statement than a question.

Clara shook her head.

"I get that you're upset, C.J. I assure you, I get it all too well. *Because I've been there.* But, do you really think pushing me away right now is—"

"That's not it," Clara countered, her voice strangled with shame and self-loathing. "You don't understand."

"Of course I understand. That's exactly my point!" Lincoln argued with unintentionally increasing force. "You think I'm not familiar with how it is to fear that you're beginning to forget about the single most important person in your life? The person who *was* your life? I let Jessica's birthday pass last year without any acknowledgement whatsoever. I didn't even realize it until almost a week later. Do you think I don't know how confusing it is to feel like that at the same time you're moving forward, you're also slipping further away from that person, and there doesn't seem to be a damn thing you can do about it? You believe I don't know how scary it is to realize your life has suddenly taken a whole new crazy direction that you never even saw coming?"

Lincoln's jaw had clenched in a taut line, his face hardened, and Clara could sense by the intensity of his emotion that their conversation was quickly spiraling to a point she had not originally anticipated. "No. That's—That's not what I'm saying, Link."

"But you *are* saying that despite everything we've been through together, despite what we have"—his voice cracked—"you . . . need time away from me."

Torn between guilt and desire, Clara still couldn't bring herself to look him in the eye.

"Who can possibly understand what you're experiencing right now more than me?"

"*God.*" He certainly was not making this any easier for her. "I know you understand, but—"

"But, rather than trust me to relate and support you," Lincoln interrupted, bewildered, "your natural instinct is to close me out." Appearing as if he'd just been slapped in the face, he looked away from her. "Do you have any idea how that makes me feel?"

Clara's heart constricted with an emotion so intense that it made her ache. Trying her best to keep from crumbling to pieces right there in the car, she reiterated in a small, contrite voice, "I didn't say that I never want to see you again. All I said was that I need some space to figure some—"

"Yeah. I got that part," he clipped. "And I hope you'll forgive me for taking it personally. Although . . . maybe . . . it's what's best. I have no interest in arguing with you about the fact that you're letting the past hold you back and interfere with the future." He shook his head, his eyes filled with melancholy. "I can't make you see that, Clara. Even though I wish I could." Lincoln cast his gaze downward, pausing. "And, space or no space, I can't move forward with someone who's obviously not ready to let go of the past and let me in." He shrugged. "It can't work . . . I know that."

Clara looked at him through eyes spilling with tears.

"I think you should go," Lincoln muttered. His tone was not angry. It wasn't hostile. It was just sad.

"Please don't hate me," she whispered achingly as she slipped out of the car and hurried into her building.

32

Resolved, come hell or high water, to **Dig up Leo's recorder from the backyard** once and for all and then never, ever again mention the frustrating debacle, Clara arrived at Libby's house early in the afternoon prior to "Sunday Family Dinner." Busy catching up on some work at the courthouse, Leo planned to drive to River Pointe separately later in the day.

After saying a preoccupied "hello" to her mother, Clara made a beeline for the backyard and went straight to work, grateful for a legitimate distraction to hopefully help take her mind off Lincoln.

She had been digging to no avail for two hours, working up a good, angst-fueled sweat, when Libby, wearing a floppy, wide-brimmed sunhat and a scowl, arrived in the backyard with her fists planted on her hips. "*Mary, mother of Christ.* I cannot believe what you've done to my yard," she stammered in a visible state of shock, slowly spinning around, taking in the muddy eyesore. "It looks like a goddamn golf course!"

In no mood to resume this ongoing squabble, Clara, irritable to begin with, rolled her eyes. "I've told you a zillion times, *I'm sorry. I will fix it.* I don't know what else you want me to say about it."

"Hey"—Libby held up a disapproving hand—"watch your tone," she warned. "I've been nothing but patient and understanding about this entire recorder fiasco and I am about ready to put my foot down." She shook her head, peeved. "Probably in a stupid golf hole."

"You think what I'm doing is stupid?" Clara challenged.

"I did *not* say that. What is wrong with you today?"

"Nothing," insisted Clara. She hadn't discussed Lincoln's and her breakup with anyone yet, and as she was trying with every fiber of her being not to think about it, she quickly changed the subject, inquiring in a disinterested tone, "What's on the dinner menu for tonight?"

"Okay"—Libby made a vague gesture with her hands—"now you're really worrying me."

"Why?" Squatting in the dirt near Maple Manor, Clara put down her garden trowel, staring up at her mother, confused.

"Because we discussed this last night on the phone. We had a whole conversation about it. Remember?" When Clara didn't respond, Libby continued, "I asked if you'd like barbecue ribs or steak for dinner and you told me you just saw a delicious-looking rib recipe on the TV show *Heavenly High-Rise?* And then we talked about how we're both big fans of Delilah White?" Libby was referring to the charming domestic diva and host of *Heavenly High-Rise*, the popular do-it-yourself program. "*Remember?*"

"Oh, yeah. That's right." Clara recalled that when she'd first heard her phone ring, her pulse rate skyrocketed, for she hoped it might be Lincoln. But alas, no luck. "I'm a little spaced out today."

Tilting her head to the side, Libby paused to examine her daughter. "Clara-pie," she said in a much gentler tone. "I think I know what's going on here."

"You do?"

Libby nodded, a compassionate look of understanding spreading across her face.

Clara picked up the garden trowel and began digging again, wondering how her mother had figured out her relationship with Lincoln was over. Was it that obvious?

"There are still days when I miss your father so badly it's literally all I can think about. Days when something out of the clear blue reminds me of him, and the next thing I know, I'm sobbing over some silly cat food commercial . . . or a song playing in the background at the mall . . . or the sight of a complete stranger in a parking lot who happens to look just like him . . . or even a random scent, like toasted pumpkin seeds, his favorite, which—as you know—make me gag. And you know what?"

"What?" The hostile chip remained on Clara's shoulder.

"I remind myself that it's *normal*. It's healthy. It's what happens when someone you love dearly passes away. You miss them every moment of every day. There's no escaping it. The pain never goes away. You just learn how to live with it. Sometimes, it all boils to a head and the pent-up emotion needs to come out." Libby released a slow, contemplative sigh, choosing her words carefully. "I know how much you miss Sebastian. And it's *okay*. It's okay, honey. You don't have to fight it."

"Christ! I know that!" Clara replied in a much harsher

tone than she'd intended. Currently, she lacked both the patience and desire to discuss Sebastian.

Narrowing her eyes, Libby straightened her spine. "You know what? I give up. I don't know what's the matter with you, but you better have that attitude changed by the time I get back from Foodthings. I'm out of butter," she mumbled. And with that, Libby turned around and began marching toward the house.

"Fine," Clara glowered, already feeling guilty about the repellant way she'd behaved toward her mother, but too aggravated and discomposed to do anything about it.

"And find that recorder because I've had it!" Libby shouted over her shoulder.

A few minutes later, Leo arrived in the backyard. "*Whoa.*" His eyes widened like saucers. He stopped to assess the landscape, mouth agape. "What just happened between you and Libby? I bumped into her on my way in and she warned me to keep a safe distance from you because you're *in a mood.*" He gestured quotation marks with his fingers.

Clara made an unattractive sound as if something were caught in the back of her throat. "Don't ask." She shoved her digging tool into the ground, hurling dirt over her shoulder. "She's pissed about the mess I've made back here."

" 'Mess' is definitely one way to put it," Leo agreed. "Actually . . . It sort of reminds me of a golf course. We should get some clubs. And maybe a concession stand? I could go for a nice, cold beer right about now."

Clara was too annoyed to crack a smile.

"All right. Spill it," he demanded. "Something's obviously going on."

Finally putting down her garden trowel, Clara rubbed her eyes with both hands and rose, standing a few feet away from her brother.

She exhaled an anguished sigh, looking off toward the house. "I think I ended it with Lincoln on Thursday night."

Leo practically did a double take. "*What?* You broke up?"

Clara nodded solemnly.

"But *why?* What happened? And, on a separate note, why am I only hearing about this now if it happened on Thursday? That's *three days* ago."

"Because I wasn't even sure what was going on—or if it would really last. It's extremely complicated. And it all happened so fast. Frankly, I'm still not sure what exactly happened, or how everything escalated to the point that it did. It's crazy . . ."

"That's usually how it goes." It was clear by Leo's tone, he could relate.

Clara described Lincoln's surprise invitation to Argentina, followed by the painful experience of hearing *Night and Day* in his car, and the upsetting sequence of unexpected events and emotions it triggered. "I didn't say anything to you about it because I had to process it all," she rationalized in a small, spiritless voice. "And, I feel like a fool for admitting it, but I thought maybe there was a slight chance I might possibly hear from Link yesterday or Friday, but—"

"No word?" Leo interrupted, a crestfallen air about him.

Clara shook her head. "Which should not surprise me in the least, based on the look in his eyes when I left his car." If only she could erase from her mind that awful, haunting image of Lincoln sitting in the driver's seat staring at her, heartbroken and confused.

"Well, if you want to talk to him, then why don't you just pick up the phone and call him?"

"Oh, because I can't, Leo. It wouldn't be right."

"Why not?"

"You don't get it. I made it *abundantly* clear how I need my space. He tried to talk me out of it, but I refused. I have zero right to complain now that he's giving me exactly what I asked for," lamented Clara. "Especially after what I just put him through. No way. Trust me, it was horrible, Leo."

"So, let me get this straight. You're gonna sit back and let your own stubborn pride get in the way of what you really want?"

"It's not stubborn pride," Clara argued. "For crying out loud, he offered me a once-in-a-lifetime dream trip, told me he *loves* me for the first time, and I told him I need space! I might as well have pulled a *'Say Anything'* and given him a pen! What am I supposed to say now? *'Oops? Just kidding! Sorry for making you jump through all my cuckoo-for-Cocoa-Puffs hoops. Changed my mind!'*" Clara sighed, shaking her head. "'Cause, see ... That's my whole problem, Leo. I really don't know that I have changed my mind. I don't know anything anymore. Other than the fact that I'm conflicted as hell about what's right. Well, *that*, and I hurt Link. I hurt him bad ..."

"To be fair, you did rip the rug out right from under his feet without warning," Leo agreed. "You can't blame the poor guy for being upset or not calling you immediately after a double dose of that kind of rejection. Especially after telling you that he *loves* you for the first time?" Leo ran his fingers through his hair, imagining it. "*Man . . .* Talk about harsh."

"Great. Very helpful. Whose side are you on anyway?" Clara scowled, knowing that Leo and Lincoln had developed a solid friendship. She'd suspected that her brother might not take this disappointing news very well.

"This has nothing to do with sides. You know I'm always on your side. And I completely get why you'd want to give the Argentina trip some thought, and why hearing that song hours before your anniversary you almost forgot would be distressing. Absolutely . . . But, still—let's call a spade a spade."

"*Meaning . . .*" Clara prompted.

"Well, you have to admit, whether or not you had some understandable soul-searching to do, you did have a major meltdown and push Lincoln away." Considering it, Leo shook his head in what Clara, feeling as if she'd been accused of a crime, interpreted as disapproval.

"Yeah. Like you're one to talk," she automatically charged, hearing the frustration in her own voice.

Leo winced, taken aback. "What's that's supposed to mean?"

"Oh, *come on*, Leo. You're the undisputed master of pushing people away!" It was as if an internal censuring filter in Clara's brain had suddenly fractured, allowing her words to spew effortlessly from her mouth.

"Why?" He folded his arms across his chest. "Because I ended things with Ava?"

"Ava, Anne, Layla, Harper, Joanna, Eleanore"—she was on a roll now—"Kristin, Victoria Lynn—"

"*Okay . . .* Clearly, I should have taken Libby's advice," Leo grumbled to himself. "Look, I'm sorry that you're hurting, Clara. And I am genuinely sorry if you messed up the best thing that's happened to you in a long time because you're afraid, but that does not give you the right to take it out on the people who care about—"

"*Please!*" Clara flew off the handle like a camel that just had its back broken by a flimsy straw. "*I'm* 'afraid?' That's laughable. *You're* the one who's terrified, Leo."

"Of what?" He raised both his hands and his resentful voice to match Clara's.

"Good question! You tell me," she welcomed without pausing to let him speak. "Ever stop to think that you avoid giving your heart to someone because you fear something bad might happen to her? Like it did to Dad? And Sebastian? Better not to take any risks and play it niiiiice 'n safe to prevent getting hurt, right? Ever stop to think maybe *that's* why you run away like a scared little boy the moment you finally let your guard down and start getting close to a woman? Maybe *that's* why you consistently cop out? News flash: *you're* afraid, Leo!" Clara was about to say something else, but the expression on her brother's face suddenly stopped her.

"And you're the one who just crossed a line," he said, his voice shaky and gruff, almost a whisper. "Real nice . . ."

And then, with his head hung low, he walked away.

"I can't find your sister anywhere," said Libby to Leo as she entered the kitchen. "It's almost dinner time. Have you seen her?"

"Not in the past few hours," he answered, feigning interest

in *The New Yorker* spread out before him on the kitchen table.

"This is the strangest thing. She's not in the backyard—
thankfully," Libby added under her breath. "She's not anywhere upstairs as far as I'm aware of. I just came from there.
And she's not down here. I looked in the music room and
dining room. All of the bathroom doors are open. Huh."
Her eyebrows pulled together as she tapped her fingers on
the kitchen counter. "*Clara? Honey?*" she hollered loudly, her
voice echoing throughout the house.

"Maybe she's in the basement," Leo suggested with his
nose still stuck in his magazine.

"Good idea. I'll go check." Libby meandered off.

She returned to the kitchen several minutes later. "No
sign of Clara in the basement. This is very odd. Where could
she be?" And then Libby's brows lifted and she raised an
index finger in the air as if she'd solved the mystery. "Her car!
Maybe she's outside getting something from it. I'm gonna go
see." Again, Libby walked off in search of her daughter.

When she returned to the kitchen a little while later, the
look of bewilderment plastered across her face revealed a
growing sense of unease. "It's not like Clara to disappear like
this. I'm starting to worry, Leo. I checked the garage and she
wasn't there either. Did she mention to you she was leaving
the house? Going out for a walk or something?"

"Not that I'm aware of," he replied in a deliberately disinterested tone.

"Will you please stop looking at your magazine for two
seconds and help me find your sister? I'm concerned. Frankly,
I'm surprised you're not. Clara's in a vulnerable place," Libby
stressed. "She's extremely upset about Sebastian."

This got Leo's attention. "She is?" He closed *The New Yorker*, surprised.

"I think that's why she's in such a foul mood."

"You *do*?"

"She's having a very hard time. She misses him desperately. And she has come so far, Leo. She's practically like a new person." Libby sighed. "Of course there are road bumps along the way with grief. They're to be expected. But I would really hate to see her stumble and fall too far off track now. Not after all the progress she's made," she muttered more to herself than to her son. "Do you think she might be in the attic?"

"Uh . . . I think there's definite call for concern if Clara's fiddling around in the attic considering she's never been up there before in her life."

"Well, then we have a problem, son. Because your sister is gone."

"No, she's not," Leo reassured Libby with unmistakable confidence, rising from his chair. "There's one place we haven't looked."

33

Dusk had fallen, and the low, constant hum of crickets buzzing pervaded the cool, August night air. "Knock, knock!" Leo called out, tapping his knuckles against the old, weathered ladder of Maple Manor as he ascended it slowly. "May I have permission to enter?" he asked before he reached the top and had even confirmed that Clara was inside. Waiting for a response, Leo knocked on the ladder again, his other hand grasping the tree's thick, gnarled bark.

"*Enter,*" replied Clara, sitting crossed-legged on the wooden floor beneath a window where a blue and white gingham curtain that Libby had sewn once hung. Her eyes were puffy and red, and she was fairly certain she had a splinter in her left cheek that was not located on her face.

"I had a feeling I'd find you here," Leo said as his head emerged inside of the tree house. He hoisted his tall body inside of the empty, square-shaped room that smelled like ancient, musty forest.

"How'd you know?" Clara sniffled.

He shrugged. "Brotherly instinct. Well, that, and it's where you always hid out as a kid."

Indeed, Maple Manor had long been a sacred place of solace for Clara, a special space high up in the branches where she could come to escape the troubles of the mean world below, or to dream.

Hunching over, for Maple Manor's roof was too low for Leo—or most grown adults—to stand up straight, he looked around. "Did this place shrink?"

Clara nodded. "I think so."

The brown, wooden floorboards creaked as Leo maneuvered his body across the tree house, taking a seat beside Clara with a muffled grunt.

A tear trickled down her cheek as she stared straight ahead, exhausted.

Leo gave her knee a friendly pat.

"I am so sorry about before," Clara choked, spilling with guilt as she turned and faced her brother, unable to stand the unbearable feeling of being at odds with him for another minute longer. "I was way out of line. *Please* forgive me." Her bottom lip trembled.

She extended both arms, seemingly desperate for a hug, and Leo immediately embraced her.

"It's okay," he said quietly. "Please don't cry."

"I didn't mean those awful things I said." Clara hugged him tighter. "They weren't true. They weren't . . ."

After a moment, Leo pulled away from her. "I'm not so sure about that. I've been thinking about what you said," he admitted, "and you might have had a valid point."

"But the way I attacked you was cruel," Clara adamantly

insisted, not about to let herself off the hook. "You were the one who was right about me taking out my problems with Lincoln on the people I love. I acted like a beast. I swear on our siblinghood"—she shuddered, wiping her eyes with the back of her hands—"I'm so sorry, Leo."

"I know," he soothed, offering her a reassuring smile.

He reached his hand into his sweatshirt pocket. "How about a Fudgsicle?" Producing two sunshine-yellow-wrapped, frozen dessert bars, Leo offered one to Clara.

She nodded. "Yes, please."

Sitting side-by-side in their old tree house while the troubles of the mean world stirred below, Clara and Leo ate their frosty treats.

"Oh yeah. I almost forgot." Clara grabbed something from behind her back. "Here's your recorder." She handed it to Leo. "I'm sorry I buried it and let you stay punished for losing it," she quoted from her time capsule list.

"Not a problem." He grinned. "Apology accepted."

Holding her chocolaty Fudgsicle, Clara took a big, deep breath, bowing her head as she slowly exhaled. "Tough week . . ."

"It sure was," her brother affirmed. "It's gonna be okay . . ." Leo put his arm tightly around her shoulders and didn't say another word.

No words were needed.

- ~~Dig up Leo's recorder from the backyard & apologize for burying it (& letting him stay punished for losing it!)~~

34

One week with no word from Lincoln told Clara that he had meant business when he said he took her rejection personally and "couldn't move forward with someone who was obviously not ready to let go of the past and let him in." In retrospect, Clara realized this had been Lincoln's own way of saying goodbye to her. As in, *goodbye for good*. Adios. Game over. She didn't know how exactly she had expected him to react when she insisted, out of the clear blue, that she needed her space, effective immediately. At the time, she hadn't the wherewithal to properly think it through. But, Clara did know one thing for certain: she had not expected to miss Lincoln as much as she did. Not by a long shot. His sudden absence stung, leaving her feeling strangely off kilter. Still, she was determined not to let it get the best of her. She'd made her decision, and now she had to live with its consequences. After all, she'd already inflicted upon Lincoln enough unpleasant emotional drama and felt strongly that it was selfish and unfair for her to ask any more of him.

At first, Clara tried to ignore her pangs of sorrow by indulging in good old-fashioned denial, justifying that it was only natural to miss Lincoln in light of the excessive amount of time they'd been spending together lately. They'd practically grown inseparable over the past month. *Of course* it was normal for her to miss him! She'd get over it, move on, and that would be that. At least, that's what Clara kept telling herself.

Suppressing her feelings, she threw herself into the last few remaining items on her time capsule list. Though it wasn't very big, the judge's concrete balcony—located off the living room—contained just enough space, and received enough afternoon sunlight for Clara to plant a tiny, aboveground garden. At her local green nursery, she purchased an array of herbs, including parsley, basil, oregano, and mint, which Alejandro—the knowledgeable, apron-clad employee assisting her—stressed was "next to impossible to kill" and "delicious in cocktails."

"Sold," Clara had declared, forcing a small smile, striving to sound cheerful. Since it was already August and the weather would soon turn colder, her options were limited with regard to late blooming flowers that would thrive. Thus, Clara stuck with her old, hearty favorite, the chrysanthemum, choosing two different jewel-toned varieties.

"The chrysanthemum represents the light of hope in dark times," said Alejandro, unaware that this was the precise reason why Clara appreciated it so.

"Maybe I should buy another," she joked, her voice faltering despite her effort to sustain an upbeat tone.

After adding autumn crocus and purple ornamental kale to Clara's cart, he suggested she also try planting asters.

"They're taller than the mums so they'll add an extra dimension of height to the garden," he explained.

"And, just so we're clear, all of this stuff will actually grow *aboveground*? In a balcony garden?" The crimped expression on Clara's face revealed her skepticism.

"*Yes*," reiterated Alejandro. "Absolutely. Why do you look so doubtful?"

"I don't know." She shrugged, lifting her hands. "I guess . . . it's just my nature?"

"Well, you better change that." He grinned, winking at Clara. "Hesitation and cultivation are not friends. The garden *knows* . . ." He nodded. "You'll see. Believe in it and it'll grow. Simple, really."

"Believe in it and it'll grow," Clara repeated, suddenly thinking of "Audrey II," the man-eating, jive-speaking plant in the play *Little Shop of Horrors*. "Got it. Good advice."

"And don't over-water it. That's the most common no-no."

"I will avoid that *no-no*. Oh! One last question . . . Do you sell avocado seeds?"

"We do. But unfortunately avocados can't grow in this varying climate. They require steady heat."

"I hear you. But I have to give it a try, Alejandro," declared Clara, adding with a lackluster fist pump, "Believe in it and it'll grow."

"See?" He smiled. "You're learning. But you're still gonna need *un milagro* to grow an avocado in Chicago."

"*Milagro*?"

"A miracle!" Alejandro translated.

"Terrific . . ."

Clara spent the next three hours on the balcony with Milk

Dud, planting away as the sun streaked westward over the steely city skyline. She attempted, without much success, to avoid thinking about Lincoln, who she imagined was probably busy preparing for his Argentina adventure, looking forward to having the time of his life excavating ancient bones on the other side of the globe. Well, at least one of them would be enjoying themselves, she reflected with her hands elbow-deep in dirt.

When the last seed had finally been covered with soil and sprinkled with water, Clara wiped her brow, dusted off her hands, and took a seat on the balcony's only chair. She crossed a thick red line through **Grow my own garden with an avocado tree**, as the tears she'd been fighting not to shed blurred her vision.

The next day, after Clara and Leo lunched at a little outdoor bistro in her neighborhood, they returned to her condo to resume their ongoing Memory battle. Clara may have been beaten by love, but she had no intention of being vanquished by her brother at the children's pair-matching game. No way. Determined to finally show him who was boss and cross off one of the last items on her time capsule list, she was sitting cross-legged on the floor in front of the coffee table, staring at the board with her eyes on the prize—the picture of fierce concentration—when suddenly her cell phone rang. Remembering Lincoln's theory on the game, she quickly flipped over two of the grid's "key" corner cards, failing to make a match, shot out of her chair as if her backside were ablaze, leaped over Milk Dud, and sprinted toward her pocketbook on the windowsill ledge. She hurriedly grabbed her cell phone from it, glancing at its display screen.

And then, like an overcooked soufflé, Clara's face fell.

She released a sigh, unable to mask her disappointment.

"I don't understand why you don't just pick up the phone and call him." Leo turned over one card with a picture of a cow and another card with an ice cream sundae on it. "It's obvious that you want to talk to him."

"I don't even know what I'd say to Link at this point, Leo," Clara said sullenly, returning to her seat. "I really don't." She hadn't admitted to her brother that she'd stopped by the Mayflower Café earlier that morning, secretly hoping she might have the good fortune of "coincidentally running into" Lincoln. For two whole hours she'd nursed a cappuccino at the same round table where she and Lincoln had sat seven months ago after she fainted in Grant Park. Each time the little bell attached to the café's front door jingled, Clara felt a flutter of hope as she glanced toward the entrance as casually as possible. But Lincoln never walked through that door. And eventually, Clara, feeling rather foolish, gave up her table so that an elderly couple holding hands could sit down. Wondering if this qualified her as a stalker, she watched as the white-haired gentleman gallantly pulled out the chair for his wife to be seated, feeling a familiar lump beginning to form in her throat.

"Go. It's your turn," Leo reminded her.

"Oops! Sorry." Clara thought for a moment, and then flipped over a card that happened to match one of the corner cards she'd already revealed. She collected the pair and took another turn. "Anyway, it's been nine days. If Lincoln had something he wanted to say to me, he would have done so by now."

Leo took his turn. "Not necessarily. Don't forget you asked for your space. Link's a stand-up guy. All he's doing is honoring your request. Doesn't mean he likes it."

She made a clicking sound with her tongue, frowning. "You're my brother. You have to say that. Besides, he's probably so excited for Argentina that I haven't even crossed his mind. He leaves the day after tomorrow." Hesitating, Clara stared at the slowly shrinking board, calculating her next move, tapping one of her already-collected cards against the table before she flipped over two more cards, successfully making yet another pair.

"All the more reason to call him," urged Leo. "You could say that you know how much the Argentinosaurus means to him, and you just want to wish him a quick *bon voyage*. Keep it nice and light. *Enjoy Dino-Land.*" He took his turn. "*Happy bone digging.*"

Clara considered it. "Yes, but then what? I wish things were different, Leo, but I still feel torn about everything. I—I really don't know what exactly I want from Lincoln or what I'm ready for," she claimed, making her move. She shook her head, dejected, sick and tired of trying to make sense of her conflicting emotions. "That's the problem. And it's not fair to him."

"Guess what? You don't need to have all the answers right now." Studying the board, Leo furrowed his eyebrows. "Who knows what Lincoln might say if you give him a chance to open the floor for discussion?"

Clara exhaled, flipping over two matching "bicycle" cards.

She took her next turn, revealing two identical "pencil" cards. "Yes! It's about time I got those stupid pencils considering I've been chasing them half the game."

"*Uh . . .*" Leo blinked, appearing dumbfounded as he eyed what little remained of the grid. "You've got this. There are only six cards left. You're gonna sweep the board."

Positive she'd misheard her brother, Clara eyed him dubiously. But when she assessed the grid, sure enough, to her own surprise, she discovered that she did indeed remember what each of the final cards was. She actually did have Leo cornered! Her memory had prevailed! At long last! Victory was hers. Wasting no time, Clara quickly turned over all three pairs, her smile expanding with each card she revealed and collected.

"And, after countless losses over too many years to even count, she finally makes a clean sweep! Better late than never," Leo announced in his best sports commentator voice. He extended his hand. "Good game," he conceded as Clara, visibly shocked, shook it.

"Wait. Are you serious?" She cocked her head to the side, brimming with skepticism. "I swear to God, Leo . . . did you throw the game because you feel sorry for me?"

"No," he insisted. "And I hate to break it to you, but I think *you* might be the one who feels sorry for you."

"I won?" she quietly confirmed.

"You won."

"Holy Moses. *I won!*" Clara victoriously shot both arms in the air. "No way! I did it, boy!" she alerted Milk Dud.

Raising his only ear, he barked in celebration.

"*Finally!* Lincoln was right."

Leo folded his arms across his chest. "What do you mean, *Lincoln was right?*"

"He said to first memorize the four corners, and then base everything else in relation to them." Clara grinned. "And that's exactly what I did!" She pointed her finger at Leo. "I schooled you, butt-face!"

"Oh boy. I forgot what a great sport you are."

"You know what?" On a rare, Memory-inspired high, she picked up her cell phone and rose.

"You're gonna do a victory dance?"

"This is a sign, Leo. I think maybe I will call Lincoln to wish him *bon voyage* after all. Worst-case scenario? It'll be awkward and we'll hang up."

"*Now* you're talking."

"All right . . ." Clara took a deep breath, adrenaline pumping. "I'm doing it before I chicken out. Wish me luck."

"Should I leave the room?"

"No, no, no—stay! *Stay!*" With her heart pounding in her chest, Clara dialed Lincoln's phone number.

Leo watched his sister's facial expression as she waited, and waited, and waited for Lincoln to pick up.

After a minute, still clutching the phone to her ear, Clara slowly lowered herself down on to the couch. And then her shoulders slumped.

"What's wrong?" asked Leo.

Crestfallen, she snapped shut her phone, muttering, "It's . . . it's too late." She closed her eyes for a moment.

"Why? What do you mean?"

"He's"—Clara swallowed hard, lifting her chin in an effort not to appear as wounded as she felt—"already gone. His outgoing message said he's out of the country and unreachable until he returns." Feeling a thousand times worse than before she made the call, she immediately regretted dialing Lincoln's number and acting on her foolish impulsiveness.

"Huh." Leo cast his gaze downward, fidgeting with a Memory card. "He must have decided to leave a few days early. Still, I—I reckon you *had* to have been on his mind."

"Yeah," whispered Clara, feeling her heart sink even further. "You *reckon* . . ."

- ~~Grow my own garden with an avocado tree~~
- ~~Beat Leo at Memory~~

35

The moment she read the e-mail reply from Stella Hirsch, Clara automatically shot out of her chair, grabbed her phone, and began dialing Lincoln's number. After a week and a half during which she had given up all hope on hearing back from her old friend, Stella had finally responded. And for the icing on the cake? Her automatic signature had even included her full mailing address. Grinning, Clara couldn't wait to share the great news with Link! It wasn't until she was just about to press the last digit of his number that it finally dawned on her, with the forceful power of an unexpected punch in the face, that he was in Argentina. Not to mention, they weren't on speaking terms. And he probably hated her. A sharp, searing pang of disappointment swept through her, followed by a dreadful sense of sadness. In a short period of time, she had grown so accustomed to sharing everything—both big and small—with Lincoln, that it had become second nature. Like blinking. She didn't just miss not communicating with him, she hated it. Clara didn't know if it hurt him the way it hurt her. But she knew if she dwelled on the pain, she'd break down in tears. Again. Silently commanding herself to keep it together, reminding herself that hearing back from Stella was a wonderful thing and it brought her one step closer to completing her time capsule list, she tried calling Leo. But he wasn't home. Last, but not least, she rang Tabitha.

"Score!" replied Tabitha upon being brought up to date on Stella. "Now all you have to do is send her a Barbie doll and you can cross that off your list too."

"Yep," said Clara.

"This is fantastic. You're practically done!"

"Yeah."

"And you certainly waited long enough to hear back from Stella. I probably would have all but given up on getting a reply too."

"Yeah."

"So enough with the depressed '*yeahs.*' You should be celebrating this moment of triumph! I wish I wasn't all the way in Boston. Why don't you grab a drink with Leo?" Tabitha suggested. "Or maybe see if Libby wants to meet for dinner? It sounds like you could use some company. You should go out, have some fun, take your mind off things."

"Yeah . . ." Clara agreed, sullenly. "I know. I just don't feel like it, though."

Noting that Clara's mood seemed to have progressed from situational discontentedness to something darker, Tabitha cut to the chase and asked if she was okay.

"I'm really trying my best not to let this whole Link thing get me too down," Clara admitted with a heavy sigh that seemed to carry the weight of the world. "But it's so much easier said than done. I miss him. I really do."

"Call him, Clara."

"I told you last time we spoke, he's in Argentina and un-reachable."

"So leave him a message," Tabitha urged. "Enough is enough. I'll put it this way: at least you have the opportunity to speak with him and make things right."

"Yes, but—"

"No 'buts.' " Tabitha cut her off, demanding, "What did you tell me when we were in Vegas?"

"Uh . . . Pass the Alka-Seltzer?" Clara extended her best attempt at levity.

But Tabitha was not having it. "We were discussing Se-bastian, and you told me in no uncertain terms that it might sound cliché, but we need to cherish the relationships and friendships we have now, because we honestly never know what tomorrow may bring. We may *think* we know. But that's just 'comforting ignorance,' as you called it. Because no matter how much we'd love to believe otherwise, we can never really know. That person could suddenly be gone in an instant"—Tabitha snapped her fingers—"permanently. Never to be seen again. And then what?" She paused, allowing her words to sink in. "Lincoln is still here, Clara. That is a gift that you of all people should recognize."

Dabbing at her wet eyes with her sweatshirt sleeve, Clara reflected on her friend's powerful words. "I know," she snif-fled. "I know. You're right."

"Of course I'm right. Where do you think I got all my wisdom?"

Clara let out a soft chuckle. "Thanks, Tab." She blew her nose. "I needed that."

"No problem. Oh! And by the way? You did tell me 'pass the Alka-Seltzer,' too. But that was more of a desperate plea than a comment."

Clara laughed, harder this time. "Oh gosh, my stomach hurts just thinking about it!"

While navigating her way through Toys "R" Us toward its massive Barbie doll section, Clara passed an aisle of merchandise that caught her eye. Deciding to take a small detour, she slowly ambled down the row of dinosaur-themed toys, coming to a halt in front of a tall, metal bin filled with stuffed sauropods. She picked up a fluffy green Brontosaurus with pointy teeth and googly eyes, and stared at it. "Don't be scared. It's not real. He can't hurt you," said a little, freckled-faced boy wearing a Superman cape with the price tag attached to it.

Though putting on a happy face was getting harder by the minute, Clara dredged up a smile.

"My favorite dinosaur is the Allosaurus," he shared, sticking his finger up his nose. "What's yours?"

"Hmmm"—Clara thought about it—"that's a very good question. I like the Giganotosaurus a lot, but think I'm gonna have to go with the classic T-rex."

"I'm gonna be a paleontologist when I grow up!" The little boy examined a booger on his fingertip.

"Is that so? I happen to know a paleontologist." Clara returned the Brontosaurus to the bin.

"*Really?*" The little boy's eyes lit up. "Is he the neatest, coolest, most awesomest?" He wiped his booger on his cape.

Clara smiled. "Yeah. He is."

Upon returning home, she fished out a box of stationery from under her bed, and wrote a concise, heartfelt letter of apology to Stella. Next, she tucked the folded note inside of the brown cardboard mailing box containing the brand-new Twirly Curls Barbie doll she'd just purchased, sealed the box closed with packing tape, and addressed it to *Ms. Stella Hirsch.*

"Well, Milk Dud"—Clara exhaled, tapping the box a few times—"*that is that.* What do you say? Shall we bring this package to the post office and call it a day?"

Milk Dud barked.

"Let's do it. Come on, boy." Clara patted her thigh, collecting her purse, Milk Dud's leash, and, of course, the most important item of all: Stella's box.

Later, toward nightfall, Clara sat down at the Ping-Pong table with her time capsule list, her red pen, and a stiff rum cocktail garnished with a sprig of fresh mint from her balcony garden. Slowly, she drew a line through **Apologize to Stella for stealing her Twirly Curls Barbie & give it back to her**, as well as **Apologize to Stella for stealing her Chia Pet (and accidentally killing it)**.

Then, leaning back in her chair, feeling a sense of amazement, Clara's lips curled upward into a grin, for although she could hardly believe it herself, only one item remained on her list.

That evening, in Clara's dream, she was once again back inside of her grand, old Southern plantation. Though it was still in the process of being renovated, Clara, all dolled up in a green satin gown with a bustle, was hosting a big, festive party in the grand ballroom for an eclectic group of dear friends.

"Haven't you learned anything?" Billy/William Warrington, holding hands with his husband, Hans, asked Clara.

"Yeah, haven't you learned anything, honey?" demanded Nurse Pam with her hands on her hips.

"*Ms. Thing*, haven't you figured it out yet?" wondered Greg, the pint-sized Pottery Bin employee with stiff bangs hair-sprayed perfectly in place.

"Don't you know? Don't you knowwy wowwy know?" cooed Jane, the overzealous animal lover from For Pets' Sake.

"Think about it, Clara," encouraged Patrick Swayze, wearing a black leather jacket fit for a dancing renegade.

"Doubt is *all* up here," Frank, the kind proprietor of Frank's Antiques, reminded her, raising an index finger to his head.

"Can't go back—enjoy your ride!" urged the bronzed, teenage Plunge Boy from Noah's Ark.

"*Sí, señorita.* Believe in it and it'll grow," reiterated Alejandro from the green nursery, carrying a giant avocado tree covered with plump fruit.

"I can talk," admitted Natalie Marissa, Clara's Cabbage Patch Kid, sipping a martini with olives.

"Would you like me to help you figure this all out?" asked the Good Samaritan who hailed a taxi for Clara the snowy, winter morning after she did not have intercourse with Todd and Cheez Whiz.

Out of nowhere, the darling little bald girl who had smiled and waved at Clara during the 10K Race to Beat Cancer sprinted across the ballroom, grinning as she gave Clara a thumbs-up. Only, Clara almost didn't recognize her, for she had a full head of thick blonde curls.

Suddenly, Sebastian, dressed in Confederate army regalia, stepped forward from the mass of hungry guests huddled around the hors d'oeuvres table.

The band in the corner, being conducted by James Black, stopped playing music, and the room fell completely silent as Clara's astonished eyes filled with tears. She stood there, staring at her fiancé, paralyzed, as if suspended in midair.

Smiling at her, Sebastian whispered, "Hi, baby. Nice bonnet . . ."

"What—What's going on here?" she asked him, trembling. "I don't understand."

This time, Sebastian did not kiss her lips, but rather, covered her hand with his. "You know what to do . . ." His brown eyes twinkled. "You know." Giving her hand a tender squeeze before he released it, he reminded her, *"The untold want, by life and land ne'er granted, Now, Voyager—"*

"Now, Voyager—" echoed the whole group.

Winking, Sebastian began walking backward, grinning lovingly at her. *"—sail thou forth, to seek and—"*

And then, Clara woke up.

Her eyes sprang open, and she sat bolt upright in bed, her chest heaving.

She didn't bother reaching out her hand to feel the empty space beside her in bed. For Clara knew Sebastian was not there. She knew it all too well. After experiencing more of these strange dreams than she could keep track of, she had this disorienting middle-of-the-night routine marked down to a science by now. Only, this particular dream had been dif-

ferent from the usual. Very different. "You know what to do,"
Sebastian had told her. "*You know what to do . . .*" Glancing at
her alarm clock flashing 1:25 a.m., Clara wondered what he
was talking about. What exactly had he meant? Again and
again, she replayed this line in her mind, remembering the
strong look of assurance on Sebastian's face, and the bright,
powerful sparkle in his eyes that she loved and missed, in-
comprehensibly beyond words. "*You know what to do . . .*"

Clara did not know what to do.

Tossing and turning, she struggled to deconstruct her dream
in an effort to understand it. But she was at a loss. A complete
loss. And now, to her dismay, she was wide awake, with a palpable sense of unease growing inside the pit of her stomach.

It did not take long for Clara's mind to spin into overdrive,
and soon her stream of consciousness swept her up and away
in an anxiety-fueled storm of swirling, complicated thoughts.
She envisioned each raindrop of this storm to have a face.
There was Sebastian, and her father, and all of the other
people who had appeared in her odd dream. And then, of
course, there was Lincoln. Lincoln, who had left the country without saying goodbye. Lincoln, who probably despised
her. Eventually, all of the raindrops in this storm reflected his
face. And soaked in restless agitation, Clara knew it was unlikely that she'd be falling back asleep anytime soon.

Holding Milk Dud in her arms, she watched the alarm
clock flash 3:30 a.m.

She watched the alarm clock flash 4:30 a.m.

Then it was 5:30.

And 6:30.

The sun was now shining. Clara couldn't take it anymore.

Antsy and distraught, she threw back the comforter and slipped out of bed. She needed air—fresh, cleansing air—to help clear her mind. Without really giving it much thought, Clara changed into her running gear, laced up her sneakers—which she had to locate first at the bottom of her cluttered bedroom closet—and headed over to Grant Park. Although she had not gone for a jog since the 10K Race to Beat Cancer, she decided that perhaps a healthy dose of exercise would help tire her out—such was usually the case—so that she could finally get some real sleep.

"What could be more exhausting than this?" Clara asked herself, staring at the menacing, uphill path laid out before her. If battling The Mountain didn't help wear her out, then surely nothing would. It was a strenuous climb for Clara, and she remembered all of the many times she labored on up this trail with Lincoln huffing along at her side.

As Clara started up the incline, she replayed her last date with Lincoln in her mind, recalling almost verbatim the raw, painful conversation they'd had inside of his car. "I can't move forward with someone who's not ready to let go of the past and let me in," he had said, his eyes spilling with melancholy.

Clara's feet pounded against the pebble-and-dirt-covered path.

She wondered what Lincoln was doing at that very moment, and envisioned him in a large, dusty expanse in the middle of nowhere unearthing ancient dinosaur bones. The idea of him engaged in an activity that brought him such pure joy made Clara smile.

She continued upward, and The Mountain grew steeper. Working hard, Clara felt beads of perspiration sprouting on her forehead. Never in her wildest imagination did she fore-see herself continuing to jog after she had successfully crossed a line through "Run a Race" on her time capsule list. But then, never did she visualize herself doing most of the things on her list. That is, until she was so lost and low that she felt she had no place left to turn.

Mindlessly, Clara picked up the pace. Hammering up The Mountain she felt a warm, satisfying heat spreading beneath her skin. Perhaps this is why her father had always enjoyed running so much, she thought to herself, grateful that Lincoln had encouraged her to give the sport a try.

Clara's breath grew shorter, and she accelerated. Soon she wasn't jogging. She was running.

The ascent triggered something inside of her. As she climbed upward, she thought about how her time capsule list had not only served as a catalyst in her life, but how it had changed her. And Lincoln had been there, rooting her on almost every step of the way. Perhaps she was too exhausted to wrestle against the truth any longer. Or, perhaps it was the primitive act of running that helped Clara confront the issue she'd been evading for weeks. It was time to accept her true feelings for Lincoln, she realized. *Finally*, it was time for her to advance forward. She was ready.

As she continued upward, moving almost effortlessly now, she saw the purpose in everything she had done since return-ing to Chicago. It had been a long, hard climb, but she was still there. She was still fighting. And at long last, she felt as if she were winning the battle.

"*Go, go, go!*" She heard Lincoln's voice driving her on as she approached the summit.

By the time Clara reached the top of The Mountain, a weight she had been carrying with her for many, many months was no longer there. It was simply gone.

A slow, knowing smile spread across her face. Suddenly, she understood what Sebastian had been trying to tell her in her dream.

Indeed, Clara knew what she had to do.

- ~~Apologize to Stella for stealing her Twirly Curls Barbie & give it back to her~~
- ~~Apologize to Stella for stealing her Chia Pet (and accidentally killing it)~~

36.

According to the bright blue arrivals and departures monitor on the wall at O'Hare International Airport, Lincoln's return flight from Argentina had just landed at Gate K13. Clara, pacing back and forth around the perimeter of the crowded baggage claim area, keeping a close eye out for him, felt her knotted stomach doing flip-flops as her pounding heart threatened to burst right through her chest. Any moment now, Lincoln would appear. *Any moment.* The nerve-racking suspense of waiting for him to finally surface was almost too much for Clara to bear! She was certain this had to be why tranquilizers were invented.

She could not believe she was really doing this. She didn't even know what she was going to tell Lincoln. All she knew was that seeing him as soon as possible was more than a desire. It was a necessity. She had to let him know that she realized she'd made a monumental mistake. She was sure of it. As sure as she'd ever been of anything in her life. And filled with a new, unwavering sense of purpose and determination, Clara was prepared to do anything she could to communicate to

Lincoln how she truly felt about him—even if it meant taking a bold risk and showing up at the airport unannounced in a t-shirt that was stained with ketchup and looked like crime scene evidence.

Although, over the past few days since her eventful climb up The Mountain she'd been too busy tending to important business to allow time for sleep, Clara had never felt more alert, or more alive. Now, if only Lincoln would just come retrieve his damn luggage already! What was taking him so long? Standing on her tiptoes, biting her bottom lip, feeling almost dizzy from the heightened sense of escalating anticipation, Clara searched the growing sea of faces for him.

Suddenly, she felt a light tap on her shoulder.

Her pulse rate skyrocketed, and the muscles in her stomach instantly clenched. For a brief moment, the only sound Clara was able to hear was that of her own rapidly beating heart.

Holding her breath without realizing it, she turned around.

And there, to her relief, stood Lincoln. An overt look of astonishment was plastered across his suntanned face.

"Hi . . ." Clara swallowed hard, staring up into his eyes, feeling slightly light-headed. "I—I thought of one," she declared before he had a chance to speak.

Lincoln's expression of obvious surprise was replaced with one of confusion.

Shaking, feeling the weight of the moment's significance, Clara took a deep breath. Here went nothing . . . "What do you get if you cross a pig with a dinosaur?"

Silence ensued.

Placing his carry-on bag down on the ground, Lincoln considered it. "I don't know." His voice was tenuous and low, even slightly hesitant. "What . . . do you get?"

"*Jurassic pork*," Clara answered, hoping that he might crack a smile, which, to her relief, he did. As is turned out, inventing these lousy jokes was more challenging than she'd suspected.

"You made that up?" Lincoln blinked, as if he still could not quite believe that she was actually there in the terminal standing before him.

She nodded.

"Not bad. What—What are you doing here?" He paused. "And is that *blood* on you?"

"Oh, gosh!" gasped Clara, looking down at her white shirt at what appeared to be a gunshot wound. "*No. It's ketchup.*" She smiled nervously, clutching her purse, fighting the urge to throw caution to the wind, wrap her arms around Lincoln and plant a huge, passionate kiss on his lips. "I ate a hot dog while I was waiting for you. And I was such a clumsy wreck I dropped it. Little known fact: grace eludes me when I'm nervous. I should have known that I was in no condition for condiments, but"—Clara stopped herself, closing her eyes, aware that she was rambling like a jittery basket-case—"*not the point.* I'm here because . . . *because* I was wrong, Lincoln. So wrong. I don't need my space." There was no other way to say it. "I need *you.*"

"C.J., I—"

"No, wait. You have to let me finish before I lose my nerve. Or throw up on you," Clara continued rapidly, her words practically running together. "I apologize for everything, Link. God!" She rolled her eyes. " 'Apologize' doesn't even begin to cover it. You were right to feel rejected and hurt. And you were absolutely right when you said that I was letting my past interfere with my future. I see that now. And I don't want to let it hold me back. And I *certainly* don't want to let it come between us! Because, contrary to what I may have led you to believe, you mean the world to me." She rushed on breathlessly, bringing her hand to her chest in a gesture of sincerity. "You have to believe me. I admit it, I *was* afraid to put the past behind me and move on. Just like you said. But, I swear to you, Link, I am not afraid anymore. The only thing I'm scared of is losing you." She stopped to take a deep breath.

"Who said anything about losing me?" Lincoln's eyebrows pulled together. He shifted positions on his feet, hesitating. "I'm the one who should apologize for being harsh and impatient with you, C.J. I was hurt that you'd even consider walking away from something as special as what we have." He looked away from her. "It was wrong of me to demand something from you that you're clearly not ready for. To expect you to move forward with our relationship at a pace you're obviously not comfortable with."

"That's just my point, Link." Clara shook her head. "Yes, I had some things that I needed to figure out, but I'm *not* uncomfortable with it. It's . . . what I want." She stared into his eyes, resolute. "*You're* what I want. And I don't need any more space, or any more time to know that for a fact." Dropping her purse on the ground next to Lincoln's carry-on bag, Clara could not stop herself from throwing her arms around him.

This seemed to be all the encouragement Lincoln needed to tighten his arms around her waist, tilt his head down, and finally, press his lips to hers.

A shudder ran through Clara, and she clung to him even tighter, returning his kiss with equal fervor.

When at last she pulled away, there were tears in her eyes. Only this time, they were tears of joy.

In the next moment, Lincoln was cradling his hand around her head and holding her face pressed to his chest, as if he still found it difficult to believe that she was actually there in his embrace. "I have a great idea," he whispered. "Let's never do this again."

"Hell no." Clara closed her eyes, savoring the gift of being exactly where she wanted to be. After what felt to her like a long while she added, "I guess it's a good thing I bought a place here, huh?"

Lincoln released her, doing a veritable double take. "Come again?"

"Oh yeah," said Clara in the most nonchalant tone she could muster. "Didn't I tell you? I bought the judge's condo. The terms were finalized yesterday. It should work out well with school."

"But—But, what about your home in Boston? You love that house."

"I'm thinking I'll probably put it up for rent. I'm not ready to sell it. And it's a prime piece of real estate, so it's a wise investment to hold on to."

Blinking, Lincoln beamed. "*Wow*. I don't even know what to say. This is unbelievable news!"

"I know!" Clara smiled unabashedly at him.

Lincoln placed his hands on her cheeks and brought his hungry mouth to hers for another deep, affectionate kiss. But, after a moment, he suddenly disengaged, leaning back.

"Hold on. Rewind. Did you just mention something about *school?*"

"Oh yeah." Once again Clara used the most casual tone she was capable of employing under the exciting circumstances. "Didn't I tell you? Northwestern and the University of Chicago both have fantastic masters programs for English. I'm crossing my fingers that I might hopefully have what it takes to get accepted to one." She shrugged. "I was thinking I could probably make a pretty decent poetry teacher."

Lincoln just stared at her in wordless awe.

"Might as well do something that I love, right?"

"Okay. Now hold on one second," he demanded. "Are you seriously telling me that you figured *all* of this stuff out while I was in Argentina?" His voice could not have sounded more incredulous.

"Well, there is one more thing," Clara admitted.

"Let me guess! You solved the space-time continuum."

"Still working on that one." She giggled. "*But,* now that I've officially decided what I want to be when I grow up, I *did* take the liberty of crossing off the last item on my time capsule list: **Become a teacher.** Which means"—she paused for dramatic effect, smiling—"I'm all done! *And,* might I add, I still have one full week before I turn thirty-five."

Lincoln's jaw fell open.

For a moment, there was silence.

He shook his head, amazed. "Sweetheart . . . *Congratulations!*" Gazing at her with blatant wonder, and love, Lincoln leaned close to Clara, touching his forehead to hers. "I am so proud of you," he whispered. "I know how much that list meant to you."

Indeed, the time capsule that Clara made when she was ten years old was more than just a reminder of who she once was. It was a reminder of who she had wanted to become, and it was a life preserver, a bridge from Clara's past to her future when she had none. It was the beacon of hope that guided her back home, where she knew, without doubt, she belonged. And it was what ultimately helped her rediscover not only how to smile, but also true love.

"Hey Link?" Clara slid her arm around his waist.

"Yes, C.J.?" He draped his arm around her shoulder.

"Remember that one time when you went to *Argentina* to dig up a 95-million-year-old dinosaur?"

"Well, a lot's happened since then. But, now that you bring it up, why yes, I do vaguely recall this trip you speak of."

"Good," Clara said, smiling. "My car's parked in Lot Q. How about we grab your luggage off the carousel and you tell me all about it on our ride back to your place?"

"Sounds like a plan." Grinning, he kissed the top of her head.

"I want to hear every last detail starting with when you got off the plane in Patagonia."

Clara and Lincoln were standing at his kitchen counter, having just opened a celebratory bottle of wine, when she heard his stomach grumble.

"You haven't eaten dinner yet," she said. "You must be starving!"

"Well, I'd be lying if I said I haven't been threatening to kill for a slice of pizza for the last—oh, I don't know . . . *week*."

That was all she needed to hear. "Done."

Gliding to the opposite end of the kitchen, Clara opened up the "junk drawer" where Lincoln kept a large stack of local restaurant menus, along with a menagerie of random knick-knacks.

Atop the pile of menus, she discovered a timeworn, wrinkled sheet of pale blue paper covered in the obvious handwriting of a young child. "What's this?" She peered at it with curiosity, picking it up.

"Oh, that's just—uh . . ." Lincoln cast his gaze downward, fidgeting with the wine cork, suddenly overcome with shyness. "It's . . ."

Clara noticed that his cheeks had flushed.

"I—I went through some old stuff right before I left for Argentina. I must not have put it all—"

"*Link*," she interrupted. "This is from your time capsule. It's *your* list!" Clara stared at the old relic with wonder, unable to believe that she was actually holding it in her hands. "But, you—you said that you didn't keep it . . ."

Inhaling a deep breath, Lincoln remained silent, his brown eyes twinkling as he watched Clara read his official record of childhood dreams. He appeared to be waiting for something.

And then a slow, radiant smile stretched room-wide across Clara's face.

For there, at the bottom of the decades-old page, Lincoln had written in thick, blue crayon: *"Marry Clara Black."*

The Beginning

ACKNOWLEDGMENTS

I extend my sincere, heartfelt gratitude to the following amazing people, all of whom made this book possible, and most of whom I drove totally nuts during the process:

Mimsy and Big G, for supporting me.

Sister, for guiding me.

Gregory Shaver, for loving me.

Eleanore Bella, for sharing her two cents with me.

Amanda Bergeron, for editing me.

Holly Root, for everything. And then some.

ABOUT THE AUTHOR

ROBIN GOLD is the author of *The Perfectly True Tales of a Perfect Size 12*. She resides near Chicago with her husband Greg, who was well worth the wait, their baby Archie, eleven bicycles, and a bunch of boxes in the basement that will probably never get unpacked. Odds are high that she has a Cheerio stuck somewhere on her body and doesn't know it.